GIRLS CAN'T MAKE GUN NOISES

This edition published by Man Overboard Publishing
1
www.manoverboardpublishing.com

Author's website: www.paulsurridge.co.uk

Paul Surridge has asserted his right to be identified as the author of this
work in accordance with the Copyright, Designs and Patents Act 1988.

All rights reserved. No part of this publication may be reproduced,
stored in a retrieval system, or transmitted in any form or by any means,
electronic, mechanical, photocopying, recording or otherwise, without the
prior permission of the copyright owner.

This book is presented as fiction but are based on the experiences and
recollections of the author. In some cases names of people or dates of
events have been changed solely to protect the privacy of others.

Set in New Baskerville.
Printed and Bound in Great Britain by
TJ International Ltd, Padstow, Cornwall.

ISBN 978-0-9573123-0-2

MIX
Paper from
responsible sources
FSC
www.fsc.org
FSC® C013056

GIRLS CAN'T MAKE GUN NOISES

ONE BOY'S ADVENTURE IN 1970s SOUTH WALES

PaulSurridge

MAN OVERBOARD
EST. 2012

The
PUBLISHING
PEOPLE

Dedicated to the memory of
Clifford Sidney Surridge. Thanks Dad.

Contents

Part Three 1977

Part Four 1978

Part Five 1979

Part One
1975

Chapter 1

Book 'Em, Danno!

'I don't remember eating peanuts?' said Dad after he'd been to the toilet.

Mam told him off and said she didn't want to hear about his dirty business, she was trying to watch Mr & Mrs. Dad laughed and went to kitchen. Dad always goes to the kitchen when Mam watches Mr & Mrs.

'You'd have thought she'd have worn a better dress being on the telly,' said Mam, stuffing a Wagon Wheel in her gob. 'And that's a wig she's wearing, I'll tell you that for nothing.'

Mam loves Mr & Mrs. She likes the men and ladies being asked questions about each other, like what's their favourite colour or what flowers they like. Mam says Dad never buys her flowers. Not even for her birthday or if she's not very well. Dad says it's a waste of bloody money – 'If she wants some bloody flowers, she can pick some from the garden or pinch 'em from the roundabout in Abercarn.'

I was doin' my Lego, a massive spaceship with loads of pieces, all different colours so it looked brilliant. I'd been making it since the Six Million Dollar Man was on, but I'd run out of red bricks. I like using red bricks. The Six Million Dollar Man is smashing, but Mam tells me off for being too close to the telly. For my birthday I want more Lego, but I'd like a crossbow best – crossbows are brilliant. Mam says I shouldn't be so picky cos 'Beggars can't be servants.' There was a man on the telly with a crossbow, he shot it at another bloke and the arrow went straight through his body. I think he was dead cos there was lots of blood and stuff. Mam said he was just pretending, and it wasn't real blood, just red sauce. If we had a coloured telly it would've looked ace.

The man on the telly with the crossbow was a black man. I saw a black man on the bus once. Mam told me off cos I was staring. I'd never seen a black man before. He winked at me and laughed. I asked Mam why the man was black, she said cos he didn't eat his greens.

It's ages 'til my birthday, I'll be seven. Dad says I'm growing too fast and costing him a bloody arm and a leg in clothes and shoes. He said it's Mam's fault for giving me too much Ready Brek.

Mam says playing too close to the telly will give me bard eyes, like Mr Meredith. Mr Meredith's eyes are so bard he's gorra big magnifying glass, so he can see stuff. The Six Million Dollar Man has gorra bionic eye – so he can see the baddies being naughty from far away. Mr Meredith can't see when a big bus is coming. Dad says one day he'll get run over. I wish I was bionic. I'd run to the sweet shop really fast before they ran out of Warlord comics and Black Jacks. I like Black Jacks – they make my mouth go all black, like a monster.

'Well, fancy not knowing the colour of her dressing gown, he sees it every night. Then again, yuh bloody father wouldn't know the colour of my bloomin' dressing gown,' said Mam after the man on the telly got a question wrong.

Mr & Mrs is Mam's third best programme, but she likes Coronation Street and Crossroads the best. Mam loves

Crossroads, she watches it every day.

'Ooh, I'd love to go on Mr & Mrs, but yuh father would only embarrass me,' said Mam, looking at her knitting pattern.

Dad hates Mr & Mrs cos he doesn't like Derek Batey. He's the man who asks the men and ladies the questions. Dad says he's an up-hill gardener. Dad likes gardening, I don't know why he doesn't like Derek Batey. Dad likes Percy Thrower, he's always on the telly doing stuff in the garden.

Even though Mr Batey likes gardening up a hill, he's on Dad's slipper list. Anyone that Dad doesn't like is on his slipper list. That's when Dad throws his slipper at the telly. Mam wants a coloured telly but Dad won't have Derek Batey in colour under his roof. Mam told him it's the council's roof and we live in a ground floor flat. When Dad sees Derek Batey on the telly he shouts rude words. Dad has to go in the kitchen when Mr and Mrs is on.

'BLOODY BUGGER!' he shouts, even if he's gorra mouthful of scotch egg. Dad likes scotch egg.

There's lots of people on Dad's slipper list – Dick Emery, Bruce Forsyth, Prince Charles, the robots from the Smash advert, Elton John, Huey Green, Shirley Bassey, and Dad's most hated, getting both slippers thrown at 'em, Bert and Ernie from Sesame Street. They really get Dad's goat. I don't think Dad's ever had a goat, but a lot of people are trying to take it away from him.

Bert and Ernie make Dad really angry. Says it's bloody awful a couple of dinner-mashers should be on kids' telly. I asked Mam what a dinner-masher was, she said it was a man who didn't have a girlfriend. But I can't say dinner-mashers, I have to say fairies or poofs, cos it's more polite. I asked Mam if Uncle Malcolm and Uncle Graham were dinner-mashers, cos they don't have any girlfriends. Mam said not to be so stupid cos Uncle Graham was in the Navy – you're not allowed any girlfriends in the Navy – and Uncle Malcolm was just too drunk and stupid, and no woman in her right mind would touch him with a bloody bargepole. A bargepole is a big stick that's really heavy.

'Cliff! Hawaii Five-0 will be on now in a minute!' shouted Mam, 'Gwyn, don't pick yuh nose.'

I like Hawaii Five-0 and I like picking my nose. Hawaii Five-0 is smashing. Much better than Mr & Mrs. There's lots of fighting and blokes shooting guns. But the music is the best. I don't even play with my Lego when Hawaii Five-0 is on. When the music starts I like to sing along and pretend to paddle a boat – like the one they have at the end of the programme. Dad said it's called a canoe.

'The adverts are on now. You'll miss the beginning,' shouted Mam, getting her knitting stuff ready – Mam likes to do her knitting when Hawaii Five-0 is on.

Dad shouted something about holding her horses. I could hear him having a wee, Dad always leaves the door open. If I don't shut the door when I do a wee, Mam calls me a dirty Arab. Dad whistles when he does his wee and 'en does a big fart. It's horrible. Mam thinks so too.

'See Gwyn, that's why we can't go on Mr & Mrs. Yuh father would only embarrass me,' said Mam, 'I bet Derek Batey doesn't break wind and pee with the door open. Ooh, I bet he lives in a lovely posh bungalow, does Derek Batey.'

The adverts were on for ages. There was one about cigars, then another with some people in a balloon, I think that was about bread. Then there was advert for driving safe on the motorway and not falling asleep, but as Dad sat down with his cup of tea, the Smash robots came on.

'BLOODY BUGGERS!'

Mam hid Dad's slippers under the settee so he couldn't find 'em to throw at the telly.

'Bullo! Where's my bloody slippers?'

'Ooh, I dunno Cliff, wherever you left 'em.'

Sometimes, Dad calls Mam, Bullo. I dunno know why, Mam hates being called Bullo. If we're in the Co-op and Dad can't find Mam, he shouts 'Bullo' really loud. Mam gets really angry and her face goes all red like a radish.

The HTV Wales lady said it was time for Hawaii Five-0. The music started and I jumped on the arm of the settee. I paddled with my plastic cricket bat and sang along with the Hawaii Five-0 song, 'Da, da da, duh, duh, daaa, da da da duh duh...'. I like singing. But sometimes Mam and Dad tell me off. Like when we was up Pontllanfraith swimming baths, Mam made me take my pants off so I could put my trunks on. I grabbed my willie and sang 'Who Wants To Play With My Ding-a-ling'. Everyone was looking and Mam smacked my bum.

'C'mon and sit down nice and tidy,' said Dad, looking round the living room for his slippers, 'Or I'll smack yuh arse, yuh silly sausage!'

The beginning of Hawaii Five-0 is brilliant. There's a big wave in the sea and 'en some big buildings called skyscrapers. It zooms in really fast on Steve McGarrett's face and he does a little smile. Steve McGarrett's brilliant – he's the boss of the policemen. Then there's a pretty lady in a swimming costume and another lady that shakes her bum. Dad likes the lady shaking her bum – he blows a whistle – Mam tells him off. There's a flashing police light and then Danno. Danno is Steve McGarrett's butty, he does all the running around so Steve McGarrett can spend more time combing his hair. Danno's gorra butty called Kono. He does lots of fighting and doesn't have much time to comb his hair. Kono is really big like the wrestlers on World Of Sport, but not like Big Daddy or Giant Haystacks.

Mam started doing her knitting, she's making a cardie for Dad to wear in the garden – it's purple. He's gorra 'nother cardie Mam made that's orange. It's got one arm longer than the other. Dad says it makes him look like an orangutan. That's a big monkey that lives in the zoo and Africa.

'Ooh, I'm running out of purple. I'll have to go up Pam's wool shop on Monday morning, get some more.'

I've been bard, Doctor Davies said it's called the measles. I was much better, but Mam said I'd have to stay away from the other boys and girls for bit longer. If Mam has to go up Pam's, then I have to go as well. She said I still might have some germs. Germs are really small monsters that only Doctor Davies can see. He gave me some yucky medicine that the germs don't like so they go away.

When Mam was a little girl, she had something wrong with her, called the polio. Her arm doesn't work proper and she's got a limpy leg. It takes Mam ages to walk anywhere, but she's always up Pam's wool shop. Dad says she's always up there chopsing. Chopsing is when Mam talks rubbish and sticks her nose into other people's business. Mam's always chopsing.

The Hawaii Five-0 adventure was smashing. It was about a crazy doctor who wanted to kill everyone with some special germs. Steve McGarrett and Danno had to try and find him. The crazy doctor caught Kono and gave him drugs that made him go dizzy and sick. I asked Dad if Doctor Davies had any special germs in his medicine cabinet. Dad said Doctor Davies only has nice medicine. The medicine he made me drink tasted like poo.

When the adverts came on Dad went to the kitchen to make some supper. Mam went to my bedroom and turned on my electric blanket, so it would be nice and warm. Dad brought in some bread, cheese and onions on a tray he borrowed from the pub, it says 'Courage Beer'. Dad's always borrowing things from the pub – we've got lots of beer glasses.

Mam's on a diet so she didn't have any onion, but lots of cheese and another Wagon Wheel. Mam's always on a diet, she goes up the scout hut to do exercises with other big ladies. Dad calls it keep fat. Sometimes, I have to go with Mam, with a lady called Lorraine. Lorraine looks after me when Mam and Dad go up the Jubilee club to drink beer. Dad says Lorraine's arse is so big it needs planning permission to sit down. The ladies eat lots of chocolate biscuits and sometimes pop and crisps as well. I like going to Mam's keep fat club. I'm not allowed to tell Dad that they eat chocolate and crisps, but talk about salad and do star-jumps. I don't think Dad believes me, Mam can't do a star-jump cos of her bard arm and limpy leg.

'Right 'en, time for bed young man.'

Hawaii Five-0 finished and we have to wait till next week to see what happens. It ended with Kono looking really sick and tied to a chair. I hope Kono doesn't die. I like Kono.

I asked if I could stay up for ten more minutes, Dad said if I didn't get to bed he'd make me wish I wasn't born. He said he saw a copper down the pub and he'd get him to come and arrest me if I didn't do as I was bloody well told.

'Get to bed before I go un' get him,' said Dad, scratching his bum – Dad's always scratching his bum, like an orangutan.

Dad sees lots of people down the pub. He's always coming

home with things he's bought from the blokes down The Exchange. He got Mam a new fridge, he said it fell off the back of a lorry. It didn't look dented, it must have landed on some soft grass.

Mam told me to clean my teeth and get to bed and she'd tell me a story. Mam never reads stories from a book, she makes 'em up. They're a bit silly but sometimes really good. Like the one about the tramp who turned into a hedgehog, and the boy with the magic football boots who scored the winning goal for Newport County against Brazil. Mam knows nothing about football.

I cleaned my teeth and went straight to bed. I could hear Dad winding the alarm clock in the living room and Mam putting her knitting away in her Lipton's bag.

'I'll need some money so I can get some more wool for yuh jumper, Cliff.'

'I bloody give you five quid the other day!'

'Yeah, and I bought shopping for the cupboards. You don't know how dear things are in the shops. Alphabet Soup and Weetabix are not cheap, Cliff.'

Mam buys lots of Alphabet Soup, she says it'll help me read better.

'Where the bloody 'ell yuh buying it from, Harrods?'

'Don't be so daft, Cliff, I go up Lipton's. I'll be able to go up Leo's if I get a car from Mobility.'

'Gorra pass yuh bloody test first Bullo, can't just gerrin' a car and drive off soon as you get it.'

'I'm not as daft as I look, I wasn't born under a raspberry bush.'

Mam and Dad are always rowing. When we go shopping down the Co-op, Dad takes a pencil and paper and adds up the stuff Mam puts in the trolley. When Mam puts something in, Dad takes it straight out again – then they have a big row.

'How much will bloody wool cost?'

'I dunno, I'll need at least four balls. About a pound?'

'A quid? This bloody jumper's gonna send me to the bloody poorhouse!'

'Don't be so cowing tight, Cliff! You'll be glad of it when it's finished, yuh've wore yuh orange one out nearly.'

'It's only for the bloody garden, woman. Patch it up, it'll be fine. Don't know why you think I want to wear a bloody purple cardie, orange is bard enough.'

'Nothing wrong with purple, Cliff. It's all the rage. Val Doonican had a lovely purple cardie on the telly the other night. It looked wonderful on Linda's colour telly upstairs.'

'All the rage? Sending me in a bloody rage! Val Doonican? He's a bloody dinner-masher if I've ever seen one.'

'Cliff! Gwyn can hear you! I want you to look nice and tidy for when Maria and her new boyfriend come to stay. You don't wanna look like bloody Albert Steptoe. Anyway, I'm gonna tell Gwyn a story, have a Horlicks and watch the telly.'

Mam came into my bedroom, turned off my electric blanket and sat on my bed. Mam had her dressing gown with dragons on it. Aunty Maria bought it, she lives in Japan. Japan is far, far away, further than London, but not as far as the moon. Dad says it's full of Japs that are taking all our bloody jobs away. Aunty Maria comes home every year and brings loads of fab presents for everyone. Nana Balding and Aunty Maureen got big dolls in a big plastic case. They also have some chopsticks wrapped in a red ribbon that's got Japanese writing on it. Chopsticks are what the Japs eat their dinner with, Mam says the Japs are a bit backward. Nana Balding has her chopsticks on the wall behind the biscuit barrel, next to the cutting from the newspaper about Gransher going to jail for stealing washing machines.

'Right 'en, you tucked in all nice and tidy?'

'Mam, how will you drive a car when you get one? You don't have a good arm and you've got a limpy leg?'

'It's a special car for disabled people, like me, luv.'

'Is it bionic 'en?'

'Nor, don't be so silly. It's got special controls so I can drive it. That's all.'

'Will Dad drive it?'

'Nor luv, just me, now, do you wanna story or not?'

Mam's story was rubbish. It was about a boy who was good at knitting. He even knitted a cardie for the Queen. Mam said it was the best cardie in the world, made from wool from the Queen's private sheep.

'Why did he learn to knit?'

'Well, cos his Mam taught him.'

'Girls do knitting. Boys play football and conkers.'

'This boy wasn't into all that rubbish. He liked knitting.'

'Why did he like knitting? Knitting is stupid and girly.'

'Knitting's not stupid and girly. Yuh Uncle Graham can knit, he's not girly, he's in the Navy!'

'I don't wanna to learn to knit. Not even if the Queen wants another cardie. The boy in the story is a big girlo.'

'The boy in the story is a very good boy!' said Mam, who was getting a bit cross.

'I think the boy's a dinner-masher.'

'I DUNNO WHY I BOTHER SOMETIMES, YUH JUST LIKE YUH BLOODY FATHER!'

Mam got off my bed and turned the light off. She went to

the living room and I heard her talking to Dad.

'I just told Gwyn a lovely story and he said the little boy in it was a dinner-masher... it's not funny, Cliff!'

Chapter 2.

Pam's Wool Shop

I don't like going to Pam's wool shop. Mam and Pam do lots of talking and Mam doesn't let me take a comic. She says it's rude to read in the shop and it's a waste of money. Warlord only costs 5p, Mam spends loads of money on stupid wool. I have to read the carpet sample book or look through the patterns. I've looked through the carpet sample book loads of times. There's never any new ones to look at and the pattern book is rubbish – stupid pictures of blokes in jumpers smoking pipes and ladies in cardies with tennis rackets.

Mam wanted more wool to make Dad's new jumper. We walked through the park but Mam wouldn't let me have a go on the swings. She said we didn't have time and it was too cold and Pam might sell out of purple. Mam saw Val Doonican on the telly, she said he had a lovely purple cardie. Mam thought the other ladies would want to knit one now they've seen Val Doonican wearing his.

'Can I have a play on the swings, Mam?'

'I've told you, no! We've got to get a move on. Maybe on the way back if you behave yourself.'

'I'll be good, Mam, honest,' I said, checking my pockets for Black Jacks. Sometimes I find sweets in my coat pocket,

I wipe the fluff off and put 'em in my mouth before Mam sees me and tells me off.

Pam's shop is the only shop in the street. You can't see through the window cos it's got wood panels with bits and bobs stuck to it – knitting needles, pattern books and bits of carpet. Pam's door has gorra bell that rings when it opens. I like opening the door to make the bell ring. The bell lets Pam know there's someone in the shop. When I open and close it, Mam and Pam tell me off. Dad always says if I have to make a noise, I should make it quiet. If I'm naughty I have to sit on the off-cuts pile. It's a heap of old carpet bits piled up next to the door. There's a sign next to the off-cuts pile –

RUG AND CARPET OFF-CUTS 50 PENCE
MAKE A LOVELY GIFT
NO REFUNDS!

Pam came out from the back of the shop through a door of long strips of coloured plastic – all different colours, like my Lego. I asked Mam what was in the back of the shop and was it like in Mr Benn – lots of fun stuff like astronaut suits and divers helmets. Mam says I shouldn't be so bloody nosey and Curiosity killed the cat. Curiosity sounds nasty if they killed a cat.

'Hiya, Beryl, how are you luv?' asked Pam, doing up her buttons on her pinny – Pam always wears a pinny in the shop.

'Nor so bard, Pam. Got this little monkey with me still. The Doctor says he's to stay off school for another week. Reckons the other kids could still catch it from him,' said Mam, sitting down on a stool next to the counter. Mam's bum's so big it goes over the sides like a massive jelly.

'He's got his colour back though, Beryl.'

'Aye, he's a bloody pain in the arse as well. Should have seen him acting the goat during Hawaii Five-0 the other night. He's like a bottle of pop, Pam, he's got more energy than Rogerstone Power Station.'

'Well he's at that age. What can I get you, luv?'

'Need some more purple for Cliff's jumper.'

'Ooh, how's it going?'

'Dunna sleeve now, might make a start on one of the pockets later while Crossroads is on. Gwyn, what have I told you about picking yuh nose?'

Crossroads is rubbish. Lots of grown-ups being really grumpy. One of 'em's called Sandy – he's the most grumpy and lives in a wheelchair. He doesn't really live in a wheelchair cos I saw him on This Is Your Life and he was walking proper. Dad doesn't like Crossroads, but it's not on his slipper list. He just goes into the garden or fixes one of his broken clocks in the kitchen. He's got loads of broken clocks to fix. There's a big box full of parts under the kitchen table. I'm not allowed to play with 'em or mix 'em up. If anyone's got a broken clock, Dad takes it away and tries to make it work again. But I've never seen Dad fix a clock, they stay in the clock box being all broken.

'How much purple do yuh want, Beryl?'

'Ooh, dunno, just give me a couple of balls. Don't want too much, gives me an excuse to come out and get some more,' chuckled Mam.

'Well, Beryl, I have loads of it in stock. Got another two boxes round the back.'

'Thought you'd have sold loads since Val Doonican was on the telly in his purple cardie. Gwyn, I won't tell you again!'

16

'Not many people gorra coloured telly round 'ere, Beryl. Mrs Gould mentioned it, but thought purple would clash with Mr Gould's burgundy complexion.'

'Yeah, I know what she means. Got a very beetroot face has Mr Gould. What wool did she buy instead 'en, Pam?'

'Mustard.'

'Ooh, sounds posh. What's she knitting?'

'Think she said bed socks.'

'Woollen bed socks? Well, no wonder he's bloody beetroot.'

'Her Shirley's baby is due soon as well, thought she'd be knitting some baby clothes instead of bed socks,' said Pam.

'Has she decided what she's gonna call the baby yet?'

'Well, if it's a girl, Karen. But If it's a boy they're gonna call it Mark.'

'Mark? Every Tom Dick and Harry's called that,' said Mam, as she blew her nose in her hanky.

Dad says Mam can talk the hind legs off a donkey. But Dad can go into the garden, play with his broken clocks or go down the pub. I can't even read my Warlord comic. I got bored so I made up a game to play. I tried to stand on one leg like a flamingo I saw on the telly. I couldn't do it very long and I fell over and crashed into a rack of patterns.

'GWYN! What the bloody 'ell are you doin'? I thought you said you were going to be good?' shouted Mam. 'Sorry, Pam, he did this last time we were in, it's like Déjà vu, all over again.'

Mam smacked me round my head – it really stung.

'It's alright, Beryl. No 'arm done.'

I said sorry, but I didn't mean it. I wanted to go home.

'Be nice and quiet now. Look at the sample book and behave yuhself!'

I hate the carpet book. We've never even bought a carpet from

Pam's shop. She only sells the off-cuts from the off-cuts pile.

'Any news on the new car, Beryl?'

'Ooh, yeah, it's looking good. They said I'll gerra new Mini.'

'Ooh, that's lovely, Beryl, how about driving lessons 'en?'

'Well, my father said he'll take me out, and my friend's husband from Pontypool said he'd give me a few lessons as well.'

Mam told Pam about her new car – she's been telling everyone. She told the bus conductor when we went up the shops, the lady in the chip shop, and the lollipop man. Dad said she should put an advert in the Argus, then everyone will bloody know.

It's always cold in Pam's shop, even when it's sunny outside. She's gorra paraffin heater but it's behind the counter, just for Pam to keep warm. I was really cold and I wanted to have a wee.

'I had to hide Cliff's slippers again the other night.'

'Why's that 'en Beryl?'

'It's that bloody Smash advert, every time they're on the box, he throws 'em at the telly. I tell you Pam, he's going doo-bloody-lally! Hope he doesn't show me up when me sister comes to stay with her new Japanese fella. It'll be like treading on egg boxes.'

When Mam's not been telling people about her new car, she's telling everyone about Aunty Maria coming to stay. And she always tells them she's coming from Japan. Dad says he's fed up of hearing about it, 'It's like the royal bloody visit.' he said.

'When they coming over 'en Beryl?'

'Not til May or June she said in her last letter, possibly July.'

'Gor, that's ages away yet Beryl, we're only just in February.'

'Yeah I know Pam, but I want Cliff to wallpaper Gwyn's bedroom. They'll be sleeping in there see. Don't want this Jap feller thinking we're a bunch of gypos do I?'

'I've got some wallpaper left over from when I used to sell it. Should be plenty there for a bedroom. Tell you what, if you like the colour you can have some for half price.'

'Thanks Pam, but we might be moving house yet.'

'Moving! Where to?'

'Well, there's an old couple down in Risca. The woman's bed ridden and they wanna move to a flat. The council said we can just do a straight swap.'

'Well, I hope you still come and get yuh wool from me Beryl. Not from The Knit Nurse down Risca. Very pricey is The Knit Nurse you know Beryl. And you can't beat my prices,' said Pam, nodding her head and closing her eyes – like Mrs Vandenburg at school when she tells us not to talk in class or look up girls' skirts.

Mam and Pam did more chopsing and I really wanted a wee. If I ask Mam anything when she's chopsing, she tells me off. I was shivering cos I was cold, I thought I was gonna wee myself.

'Do you wanna cup of tea, Beryl?'

'Ooh, yeah, that'll be nice.'

'I got some biscuits in the back, I'll put some out on a plate.'

'Why not, you only live once. Anyway, the diet can take a break for today.'

'How's the diet going, Beryl?'

'Not so bard Pam. Lost a few pounds the other week, put on a few since though.'

Mam's always on the weighing scales. She says they don't work proper cos they make her too heavy, Dad says it's her big fat arse.

'It's good you keep sticking with it though, luv.'

'Well, I try to be strict.'

'Do you want sugar, Beryl?'

'Three please, and don't forget the biscuits.'

Pam went to the back of the shop to make the tea. She said I could have some squash but I didn't want any. I just wanted a wee, and 'en go to the park and have a play on the swings.

'Mam. I need to go to the toilet.'

'Gwyn! Why didn't you go before we left?'

'I didn't need to go 'en, Mam.'

'Oh, bloody 'ell. I'll ask Pam when she comes back, but she won't be happy about it!'

I could hear Pam her making noises with the water, running the taps and filling the kettle. It made me wanna wee even more.

I nearly wee'd myself on the bus once. Me and Dad were going up Nana Sugden's. When I told Dad I needed a wee, he told me to hold it in. I tried really hard but the bus kept stopping to let more people on and off. It got so bard I started to cry. If I cry, Dad says he'll give me something to cry about. Dad got a carrier bag from his duffel bag and told me to wee in it, then he'd throw it out the window. But the carrier bag had holes in it, my wee was squirting everywhere. Dad said rude words cos some wee got on his trousers. He opened a window on the bus and threw out the bag. The bus stopped at some traffic lights and there was a man on a motorbike, next to the bus. Dad didn't see him, and the bag of wee landed on motorbike man's head.

'Oh, shit,' said Dad. I'm not allowed to say shit.

But the bloke on the motorbike didn't follow us. Dad said it was a good job, he didn't wanna fight a bloke that stunk of piss. I'm not allowed to say piss.

'Here yuh go. Nice cup of tea and some biccies.' said Pam when she came back from behind the coloured plastic.

'Sorry to ask Pam, but Gwyn needs to go to the toilet. Don't suppose he can use yuh loo, can he?'

Pam doesn't let anyone use her loo. Not even Mr Pam can use Pam's loo. Dad says she's one sandwich short of a picnic.

'Well, Beryl, you know I have a strict rule on the shop toilet, employees only. But if the little monkey needs to go, he needs to go. I've gorra bucket at the back, one of the builders left it when I had the roof done. He can do his tinkle in that. I'll pour it down the drain when he's done,' said Pam, putting down the tea tray.

'Thanks Pam, luv. Sorry about this.'

Pam lifted the hatch of the counter to let me through. Even though I needed a big wee I was excited about going through the coloured plastic. I thought it might be full of stuffed animals, mummies and train sets – like on Mr Benn on the telly. But there was just more boxes of wool, knitting patterns and carpet samples.

Pam took me to the backyard. There was a dripping tap, a drain and even more carpet samples. Pam grabbed a yellow bucket that had bits of old concrete stuck to it.

'Right 'en young man, do yuh tinkle in this and when you've finished, wash yuh hands under the tap and come back in,' said Pam looking really cross, her face all screwed up like Nana Balding when she eats lemon sherbets.

The backyard was really cold so I did my business as quick as I could. I washed my hands and went back into the shop, Mam and Pam were talking about wool and Crossroads.

'All done 'en? Washed yuh hands like a good boy?'

Mam stuffed a biscuit into her mouth. I told her the water was cold and I had to dry my hands on my trousers. She said to stop complaining, but cos I washed my hands I could have a biscuit. I didn't want a biscuit, they were rubbish Rich Teas – I like chocolate biscuits the best.

'He doesn't want much does he Pam? Thinks he's at the bloody Ritz!'

I pretended to read the pattern books, but I wanted to get out of the shop and play on the swings – maybe go on the roundabout if Mam was in a good mood.

'Do yuh wanna bag for the wool, Beryl?'

'Yes please, Pam.'

'I'll have to go out the back and get some more. Won't be a sec.'

'Don't wanna cause a fuss, Pam.'

'It's no fuss, Beryl, won't be long.'

Pam went behind the coloured plastic. I could hear her looking through cupboards and going through boxes. I really, really didn't want her to look in the bucket.

'Mam, can I play on the swings on the way home?'

'Go on 'en, but not too long mind. I've gorra get yuh Dad's dinner ready.'

There was a loud scream from the back of the shop. Louder than when Pam thought she saw a rat, but it was only some brown wool. But I knew why Pam was screaming this time. Pam came back into the shop, her face was all red and her eyes were bulging like the man who got strangled on Hawaii Five-0.

'What's wrong, Pam?' asked Mam, 'Not another rat is it?'

'It's Gwyn, he's gone un' done a solid in the bucket! And he's wiped his arse on one of my carpet samples!' shouted

22

Pam, her face more purple than Mr Gould's.

I couldn't help it. After I'd finished my wee, my belly did a big rumble and I did a big fart. My tummy started to feel funny and I needed to do a number two. I tried to hold it in, but I needed to go really bard. Dad says, if you gorra go, you gorra go. I pulled down my pants and trousers and made a big horrible splash. There was nothing to wipe my bum with, just carpet samples. It was yellow with a stupid pattern on it – it was really brown when I finished.

On the way home Mam was really angry and we didn't stop to go on the swings. Mam said she'd never been so embarrassed, and it would be ages before she could show her face in Pam's wool shop again. Good, I hate Pam's wool shop.

Chapter 3.

Does He Wanna Penguin?

'Yuh all going to hell,' shouted the crazy man across the road, waving a bible in his hand.

'No we're not, we're off to Blackwood,' shouted Dad.

We were waiting on the bus stop, we were going to see Nana Sugden. She lives in a place called The Penllwyn, it's on a big hill. We catch the bus to Blackwood and walk all the way to the top. There's another bus that goes up the hill, but Dad says he'll be buggered if he's gonna pay for two journeys. 'I'm not bloody Rockafella,' he says.

Lipton's is by the bus stop. If we're early, Dad buys a bag of sweets. Dad likes butterscotch, I like Mojos and Black Jacks the best. Dad can't eat Mojos or Black Jacks cos they stick to his false teeth. Dad buys bacca, fag papers and matches. He gets Golden Virginia bacca, Rizla fag papers and Swan matches. He's always smoking his rollies – they're horrible and smelly.

If it's a double decker I like to go upstairs, and go to the front so I can pretend to be the driver. Dad tells me off, 'C'mon on now, enough's enough lad,' he says. And if I don't keep still, I have to sit on my hands.

Dad doesn't let me read my Warlord comic on the bus, cos it makes me feel sick. Once, I puked all over my new trousers and the bus seat. It was all pink and gooey – I'd had Angel Delight for tea. The sick ran down the aisle and another boy who was with his Mam, was sick as well. His was all yellowy, he must have had bananas for his tea. My pink sick and the boy's yellowy sick joined together and dripped down the stairs. Everyone had to change bus cos it smelt so horrible. So Dad doesn't let me read a comic on the bus anymore.

Mam had all her knitting stuff all over the living room, loads of purple wool. Dad said it was driving him up the wall.

'Come on,' he said, 'Let's go up to see yuh Nana Sugden.'

It was really cold, Mam made me wear my Parka. It's got fur round the collar. I like to zip it up so you can't see my face, I pretend to be a monster. Dad says I don't need to bloody pretend.

Dad said we'd have our tea up Nana Sugden's house. I like Nana's teas. Dad made some sandwiches before we caught the bus. Mam's on a diet so she only had two sausage sandwiches, a bag of crisps, a Kit-Kat and some Angel Delight.

'Think I've lost some weight, Cliff,' said Mam, before she put a Tuc biscuit in her mouth.

Dad says it's a good job we don't have a dog, cos Mam would eat his dinner too. I bet dog food tastes horrible. Dad's butty, Snoz, has gorra dog, his breath smells all pooey.

The crazy man with the bible walked off up the street. He was shouting at some birds and they flew away. I was playing a game of counting cars. I counted nine before Dad told me to shut up and count in my head. It was only me and Dad on the bus stop, then Mr Parry came. Dad said he's know Mr Parry for donkey's years, ever since everything was in black and white.

'Howbe, Cliff?' said Mr Parry.

'Nor so bard, Walter, nor so bard.'

'Un how are you young man?' asked Mr Parry, he ruffled my hair and pretended to steal my nose – Mr Parry's always stealing my nose and he never gives it back.

'I'm okay Mr Parry. Do yuh wanna a Black Jack?'

'I'm alright Gwyn, just had my dinner.'

'Where you off to, Walter? Up the Jubilee is it?' asked Dad, looking in his bacca tin to see if he had enough rollies for the bus ride.

'Aye Cliff. A couple of Double Diamonds and a game of cards with the boys. Ain't seen you up the Jubilee for a while. The missus got you trained at last has she?'

'Like bloody 'ell. I'm out and about more than Alan Whicker. Nor, I gor down The Exchange, play cribbage with some of the boys.'

Dad loves The Exchange. Mam says he spends more time down the pub than at home. 'He'd bloody sleep down there if he could.' Dad said if they had a spare bed, he would.

'Who's the landlord down there now 'en, Cliff?'

'Bernard Cox. You'll know him if see him. Small fella, always looks like he's standing further away than he actually is.'

'Oh aye, I know him, used to be up The Riflemans Arms. Didn't he get done for selling 'em stolen fags?'

'Aye, that's him.'

Dad and Mr Parry talked about the price of beer. A man called Denis Healey was making it too pricy. Mr Parry said it would be a lot worse if Maggie Thatcher gets to be Prime Minister.

'A woman Prime Minister? Not on yuh bloody life, I don't think the country would stand for it! She'll have us boiling our piss for drinking water!' shouted Dad.

Dad doesn't like Maggie Thatcher. Mam says she has lovely handbags. Mr Parry nodded his head and said the country was going to the dogs. I wish we had a dog.

Down the road I could see the bus was coming. It wasn't a double decker and the crazy mam shook his fist at it.

'Can we sit at the back, Dad?'

'Nor, we bloody well can't.'

Dad never sits at the back. He says it's too far to walk to, and too far to walk back off again. Dad likes to sit at the front, but he lets me sit by the window. I like to look out and pull faces at the people outside. If Dad sees me, he gives me a clip round the head. Mr Parry sat at the back, he said he was gonna read his paper.

'See yuh soon, Cliff.'

'Aye, see you once before Christmas, Walter.'

The bus drove off and Dad lit up one of his rollies. We stopped outside Pam's wool shop and there was a new sign in the window.

TOILET NOT FOR CUSTOMER USE
NO EXCEPTIONS!

Mam told Dad about me doing a poo in Pam's bucket. Dad said it was her own fault for not letting me use her royal throne. Said she thinks she's the Queen of bloody Sheba. I don't know who the Queen of Sheba is, but I bet she doesn't make people poo in a bucket.

A lady got on the bus and she sat behind us.

'Do yuh wanna Black Jack?' I asked the lady.

'No thanks luv, they stick to my dentures.'

The windows on the bus got all steamed up. I drew some patterns with my finger, Dad reached over and wiped it all clean.

'Stop larking about,' he said.

I zipped up my Parka and looked at my reflection in the window. I turned around to the lady behind and growled.

'It's alright luv. He thinks he's a bloody monster,' said Dad.

'Ooh, that's nice. Does he wanna Penguin?'

I made a noise like a monster I saw on Doctor Who, one that was made out of worms and nearly killed Tom Baker. Tom Baker is the man who is Doctor Who. Dad thinks he's a dinner-masher. I think he's ace. Mam thinks he's dishy.

'Don't growl at the lady, yuh daft apeth. Answer nicely or you'll get a thick ear.'

'Yes please.' I said, cos I didn't wanna thick ear.

The lady looked in her handbag and gave me a Penguin.

'Thanks missus.'

'That's okay. A monster must eat,' laughed the lady as she closed her handbag.

'Don't worry luv. This little bugger eats more Penguins than you can shake a stick at. He'll be looking like a bloody Penguin one day,' said Dad, blowing smoke out of his nose like a dragon.

Dad says I'll look like lots of things. He said I'll get square eyes cos I watch too much telly, and I'll turn into a fish finger or a Findus Crispy Pancake. But that's all Mam cooks. Mam says it's cos I'm a fussy eater, and the only greens I eat are carrots. I like carrots.

More people got on the bus and soon it was full up. I like singing on the bus, but Dad says it drives him up the bloody wall. Mam says Dad's just a grumpy sod and if I want to sing, I should sing. I like the songs we sing at Sunday school. I like the one about fighting with the devil, it's got actions to go with it. You have to pretend to fight – you punch like a boxer when we sing, 'When you're fighting with the devil and you don't know what to do'. Carl Goobie did it too hard and hit Lisa Griffin in her face. She had a big nose bleed, Mr Jones took her away and she didn't come back. Carl said she might have gone to heaven. I think she just went home.

But my best ever favourite song is called Sambo. Dad sings it when he comes home from the pub. Mam said Dad shouldn't teach me songs like that, cos I'll only sing 'em on the bus. Dad laughs when I sing Sambo, I don't know why, I sing it really good.

'Sambo had an aunty, an aunty very fat,
One day she said to Sambo, I'll give you seven and six,
Sambo feeling thirsty, he went into a shop,
Ten lemonades, ten ginger beers,
Then he went off pop, bang!
Another little job for the undertaker,
Another little job for the tombstone maker
All alone in the cemetery,
Sambo? That's me!'

When I finished my song some people on the bus clapped. A lady said I was very good at singing and I should go on Opportunity Knocks. I don't wanna go on Opportunity Knocks, Dad throws his slipper at Huey Green when he's on the telly. He's the man in charge of the show. I'd be worried talking to Huey Green. Dad might be in the audience and throw his slipper at him.

The bus stopped and a man gave me some money when he got off. Dad said he'd look after it for me. I wanted to buy more Black Jacks. Dad said I'd had enough Black Jacks and I'll be looking like a bloody Black Jack. I don't wanna look like a Black Jack. I don't want square eyes and don't wanna look like a Findus Crispy Pancake.

We got off the bus at the bottom of The Penllwyn and we walked up the big hill. Dad stopped half-way for a breather. A breather is when Dad sits on a wall to smoke a rollie. We got to Nana Sugden's house and stopped outside to say hello to Mrs Thomas – she's one of Nana's neighbours. Steven Whitby from next door was playing on his bike and singing the Banana Splits song – he's only five.

'Hiya, Gwyn,' said Steven Whitby, then he blew a big bubble with his bubble gum and it popped all over his face. He ran off crying.

We said goodbye to Mrs Thomas and went inside. Nana Sugden was reading a book, she's always reading books. She likes books about people being murdered the best. I could smell our tea and it made me hungry. Nana Sugden makes the best teas in the whole world. Her chips are better than Crosskeys Chip Shop and we never have Findus Crispy Pancakes. She's always got fizzy pop in the pantry and when she makes sandwiches she cuts 'em into triangles – Mam just cuts 'em in half.

Dad told Nana about Mam's special new car, me doing a poo in Pam's bucket, and Aunty Maria coming to stay from Japan.

'And this little bugger made some money on the bus again, singing his songs all the way up from Abercarn,' said Dad.

Nana laughed, but said I should give Dad some peace and quiet on the way home. Dad said I told a woman on the bus that he made toilet rolls and light bulbs – that's what Dad brings home from work. There's a big box of light bulbs in the cupboard with 'Property Of British Steel' written on it in big red letters. Nana said I was a little monkey.

I like Nana Sugden, she's better than Nana Balding. Nana Balding shouts all the time and chases my Uncle Malcolm with the boiler stick. Gransher Balding hides in his shed, Dad says it's the only place he gets left alone. Dad's always making fun of Nana Balding, he says she's a witch and rides a broom – I've never seen Nana Balding on a broom. Nana Sugden said Dad tells fibs and I wouldn't turn into a Findus Crispy Pancake or a Black Jack. But I might get square eyes if I watch too much telly.

Nana Sugden knows everything.

Chapter 4.

Dad's On Nights

Kim lives upstairs with her mam and dad, Mr and Mrs Davies. If I wanna watch Sesame Street I have to watch it on their telly. Dad hates Sesame Street. He hates Big Bird, the man who always drops the pies, Oscar the Grouch, the Cookie Monster and most of all, Bert and Ernie. Dad gets really angry when Sesame Street is on. He throws his slipper at the telly and shouts rude words, words I'm not allowed to say – my favourite is shithead.

Mr and Mrs Davies have gorra coloured telly, ours is only black and white. Aunty Maureen and Uncle Eric have gorra coloured telly. Mam says Uncle Eric is a lazy workshy slob. I wish Dad was a lazy workshy slob, then we might gerra coloured telly as well.

Mam calls Mrs Davies, Linda. I can't call her Linda, I have to call her Mrs Davies, she's nice. When I'm watching Sesame Street upstairs, I have fizzy pop. Mam never buys fizzy pop, only squash with water from the tap – Dad calls it council pop. Me and Kim gerra biccie as well, Mrs Davies keeps 'em in a big tin. Some are wrapped in coloured foil. I like the green ones best.

Mam says Kim's a proper little madam, she's older than me, she's eight and goes to the big school. There's no other boys to play with in Waunfawr Gardens, so I play with Kim, and sometimes Kim's friend, Jayne. Jayne pulls my hair and calls me curly wurly. I don't like Jayne very much. Kim and Jayne pretend to be nurses, I have to pretend to be not very well. They put bandages round my head and try to make me drink medicine. Jayne makes it from flowers and nettles from the garden, but I never drink any. I like it better when Jayne's not playing with us. I always have to be a doctor, a dead person, or a daddy. When I'm a dad, they make me a dinner from mud and worms. If Mam gave Dad mud and worms for his dinner, Dad would go bananas and go up the chip shop. Dad likes the chip shop.

I like it better when it's just me and Kim playing. Kim makes up the game we play but I don't mind cos Kim's games are fun. We played Hawaii Five-0 once, I was Danno. Kim was a lady I had to save from some baddies. My favourite game is Cowboys and Indians. For Christmas I gorra wigwam and cowboy outfit. Mam said she was fed up of me taking her bed sheets, so she asked Father Christmas to get me a wigwam. I also gorra golf set, a Spiderman t-shirt and a Bionic Man book. Dad got lots of socks.

I nearly saw Father Christmas once. He was having a row with Mam. He sounded just like Dad, but Mam said Dad was up the pub singing carols. Andrea Thomas at school said Father Christmas drank her Dad's whisky, then he was sick in the toilet.

Outside it was raining. Me and Kim like playing with my wigwam. But I'm not allowed to play with my wigwam outside when it's raining. You have to put pegs in the ground to make it stay up. When Dad's on nights we have to play upstairs. Mr Davies likes to watch the telly, he doesn't like us making any noise. Not like Mrs Davies, she's nice, she doesn't mind us playing upstairs.

Mam was up the shops, I had to stay and play with Kim. Mr Davies said he'd keep an eye on me. He was watching World Of Sport, Big Daddy was fighting Giant Haystacks. Mr Davies told us off for making too much noise. We were only singing the Sesame Street song, '*10, 9, 8, 7, 6, 5, 4, 3, 2, 1*'.

Mam likes watching the wrestling, Big Daddy's her favourite. I don't like Big Daddy's fat belly, he wears a big stupid leotard with a big letter D on it. Dad said Big Daddy was a fat poof with a small lady-pleaser. Mam shouted at Dad and told him to shut up and eat his pickled egg. When the girls at school do gymnastics, they wear leotards. Giant Haystacks doesn't wear a leotard. He's gorra big suit made from animal fur. I like Giant Haystacks, he's my favourite. But he's not butties with Big Daddy, they're always beating each other up. The crowd on the telly like Big Daddy, and if Big Daddy wins, he claps his hands in the air and shouts '*Easy! Easy!*' and everyone joins in. Giant Haystacks growls at 'em like a big bear – Giant Haystacks is brilliant.

'Will you two little buggers just be quiet,' shouted Mr Davies. We were only playing Snap, but Kim shouted 'Snap!' really loud. Mr Davies told us to play outside. It had stopped raining and he said not to come back in 'til the wrestling had finished.

Kim wanted to play Cowboys and Indians, but we couldn't put my wigwam up cos the grass was all wet. We couldn't go and play in my bedroom cos Dad was on nights and sleeping. Kim said if we were really quiet, we could creep into my bedroom and play a game. I wasn't sure. Last time I woke Dad up when he was on nights, he gave me a thick ear. Dad doesn't like being woken up – I don't like having a thick ear.

We played bounce against the coal house door with Kim's tennis ball. We can't play inside the coal house anymore, Dad put a big lock on the door. I got stuck inside playing Scooby Doo with Kim and Jayne – Scooby Doo is Jayne's favourite game. Jayne always pretends to be Daphne, Kim is Velma and I have to be Shaggy – I don't like being Shaggy. I like to be Captain Caveman, but Jayne says I can't be Captain Caveman cos he's not in Scooby Doo. I got stuck in the shed, pretending to be hiding from a ghost. Kim and Jayne closed the door and I couldn't get out. It was really dark and scary, I banged and kicked the door, but Kim and Jayne ran away. Brenda from next door heard me when she was putting her washing on the line. She got Mr Davies from upstairs to let me out. He was really angry cos he was watching World Of Sport and missed Big Daddy beating up Mick McManus and Big Daddy shouting '*Easy! Easy!*' Dad said the lock will stop little monkeys getting into mischief.

It was really cold outside and we were bored of playing bounce. Kim said if we were really quiet we could sneak in and play in my bedroom. We went through the kitchen and crawled along the passage, past Mam and Dad's bedroom. Dad was snoring, he always snores when he's sleeping. He's so loud, sometimes Mr and Mrs Davies can hear him upstairs. Mrs Davies said she heard Dad snoring when she was watching This Is Your Life. Mam says Dad's even louder when he's full of beer. We crept into my bedroom and I closed the door, I was careful not to slam it.

'Let's play Cowboys and Indians,' whispered Kim.

'But we can't use my wigwam. We can't play Cowboys and Indians without a wigwam.'

'We don't need the wigwam, we can play hunting cows. They hunt cows, the Indians do. There was a film on the telly and the Cowboys were fighting the Indians cos they were stealing all the cows.'

'But you'll have to do your Indian noises with yuh finger. That's really loud and you'd wake up my Dad.'

When we play Cowboys and Indians, Kim puts her finger in her mouth and rolls it round to make an 'Ooh' noise. She says it's what they do in the films and on Bonanza.

'We can play camp instead,' said Kim.

'What's that?'

I'd never heard of camp. I thought it might have something to do with coffee. Nana Sugden likes a coffee called Camp. Perhaps the Cowboys drank it as well?

'Camp is when the Cowboys have finished beating up the Indians and eat beans and spit in the camp fire.'

'How do we play it?'

'We'll have to make a camp site, we can make one underneath your window,' said Kim.

We sneaked into the kitchen to get some baked beans, but we couldn't find any. There was only some bacon, a black pudding and some stew in the fridge – we took the stew. Kim said we'd need a saucepan to cook the stew in. The Cowboys eat their dinner from a saucepan over the fire. We found one in a bottom cupboard, so I didn't have to climb up. Mam tells me off for climbing on the cupboards. That's where Mam keeps the Penguins and the Wagon Wheels, in a big tin. We were really quiet so Dad wouldn't wake up, he was still snoring. We got all the stuff we needed for our game and went back to my bedroom.

'We'll have to have a camp fire so we can cook our stew and

spit,' said Kim.

'How do we make a camp fire?'

'With some paper and matches.'

Dad keeps his matches by the side of his armchair. It's also where he keeps his bacca tin and ashtray. We went to the living room and looked everywhere but we couldn't find 'em.

'Where are they?' asked Kim.

'They must be in the bedroom, with Dad.'

Dad smokes his rollies in bed. Mam hates it when Dad smokes in bed. She says it makes the bed clothes smell like the bloody pub.

'You'll have to go and get 'em,' said Kim

'But I might wake Dad up, he'll go doolally.'

'He won't wake up. He's snoring. Don't be a scaredy-cat.'

'I'm norra scaredy-cat!'

I didn't want Kim thinking I was a scaredy-cat. Kim always calls me a scaredy-cat when she wants me to do something I might get a smack from Dad for. Once she dared me to draw a willy on the front of Dad's long johns when they were on the washing line. Dad was really angry and said I drew the willy too small.

I opened the bedroom door to Mam and Dad's bedroom, I was very quiet and tried not to make the door squeak. Dad was fast asleep, snoring like a monster. The matches were on the table next to Dad's ashtray and bacca tin. I crept over and picked 'em up. I was scared Dad would wake up and see me. I crept out again closing the door, making sure it didn't slam.

'Did you get 'em?'

'Yeah, told you I'm norra scaredy-cat.'

'Let's play camp before I have to go for my tea.'

Kim got some of Mam's knitting patterns and screwed 'em

up in a ball. She said it would make a really good camp fire to cook the stew. Kim said on Bonanza they have a camp fire, and sometimes the Indians jump out from the dark and have a fight with the Cowboys.

I was excited about having a camp fire, but hoped it wouldn't be too big. Kim said she knew how to do it – she saw her dad make one when they were on holiday. Kim took one of the matches and struck it against the match box – just like when Dad does it. Kim set fire to the knitting patterns, they went up in big flames and smoke got in our eyes. I wasn't excited anymore, I was scared. The wallpaper next to the window went brown and then caught fire.

'Kim – put it out – put it out!'

'I can't, I dunno how to.'

'Let's blow on it,' I shouted, but not too loud, cos I didn't wanna wake Dad.

We blew really hard – like the big bad wolf in my Ladybird book. But the fire didn't get smaller, it got bigger – loads bigger!

'Gwyn, you'll have to pee on it.'

'But I don't need to do a pee?'

'You'll have to try, you gorra!'

I got my willy out and tried to pee on the fire. The flames were getting bigger and were nearly by the curtains. But I couldn't pee.

'I can't go,' I said, 'We'll have to get some water from the kitchen to throw on it.'

Kim ran out of my bedroom, I thought she was gonna get some water from the kitchen. But I heard the back door slam and she ran away – the big stupid scaredy-cat. I was scared too and I didn't know what to do. I wanted to run away like Kim.

The flames kept getting bigger and bigger and my bedroom was full of smoke. I went to the passage and shouted really loud.

'DAD, DAD! MY BEDROOM'S ON FIRE! DAD, DAD!'

Dad stopped snoring and woke up. He came running out of his bedroom. He was wearing his long johns with the willy drawn on the front. Mam couldn't get it off and they have a big yellow stain as well.

'WHAT THE BLOODY 'ELL'S GOING ON?'

'My bedroom's on fire. Kim made me Dad, honest. She said it would be just like Bonanza.'

Dad started shouting swear words. He grabbed a blanket off my bed and threw it on the fire.

'BLOODY 'ELL YUH BLOODY BUGGER!'

Dad ran to the kitchen and filled a bucket with water. He carried it to my bedroom and threw it on the blanket. It made a funny swoosh noise and Dad stomped on the blanket, even though he didn't have any shoes or socks on. Dad lifted up the blanket to see if all the flames had gone out. There was lots of soggy black ashes and a bit of smoke, the wallpaper had a big black mark all the way up the window. It didn't look very good, I thought about hiding behind the settee, but Dad always finds me when I hide. Like the time I dropped Mam's purse in the wallpaper paste – I was in the airing cupboard.

Dad grabbed my ear and pulled it really hard. It hurt loads, but I didn't cry – but I wanted to.

'You stupid bloody bugger, what the bloody 'ell you playing at?'

'Sorry Dad. We were playing Bonanza.'

'I'LL BLOODY BONANZA YOU, YUH BLOODY LITTLE BUGGER!'

When Mam came home from the shops Dad told her about the fire. Mam didn't shout at me though, I thought she was gonna go mad.

'Well, that settles it, Cliff. You'll definitely have to decorate Gwyn's bedroom now,' said Mam.

Cos I was naughty, Dad said I couldn't watch the Six Million Dollar Man or Hawaii Five-0 for a week. But it wasn't my fault. It was Kim's game, she said it would be fun. Mam went upstairs and told Mr and Mrs Davies about the fire. I heard Kim crying, I think Mr Davies smacked her bum.

Dad went back to bed and later Mam made tea, but she said I didn't deserve any.

I had beans – just like the Cowboys on Bonanza.

Chapter 5.

Up The Exchange.

Dad says The Exchange is the only place he can go to get some peace and quiet. Dad's butties go there and play darts and a game called cribbage. I don't know how to play cribbage. It's not like snakes and ladders or Buckaroo. Sometimes, on Saturday afternoon, I go with Dad up The Exchange. Mam goes to Risca shopping cos she doesn't want me under her feet. Boys and girls are not allowed in the pub, but Bernard Cox lets me. Bernard Cox is the boss of the pub. He gives the men the beer and doesn't smile very much. Dad says if a policeman catches me in the pub, they'll have Dad's guts for garters. I have to sit by the fruit machine, out of the way and be nice and quiet.

I like going to The Exchange, it's much better than Pam's wool shop. Dad buys me a bottle of Coke and if I'm good I gerra bag of Oxo crisps – I like Oxo crisps. Dad drinks a beer called slops. Slops is the beer that Bernard Cox pours from a bucket. Dad says it's all the beer that Bernard spills and is too tight to throw away. If there's not any slops in the bucket Dad drinks a beer called Tartan. The beers come out of a special pump, with a sign so you know what beer it is. Tartan beer has an old man wearing a kilt, Double Diamond has a big box that lights up with two big letter Ds. Dad doesn't like Double

Diamond, he says it's cat's piss. I don't think anyone would want to drink cat's piss – it must taste horrible.

Dad said he had to show his face in The Exchange and would need to check his pools coupon. There's a big telly on the wall. It's a coloured one that only shows horse racing and the football scores. I don't like horse racing, it's rubbish – Dad doesn't like it either. Bernard Cox likes it, Dad says he's gorra passion for the gee-gees and the bookies like taking his money.

'Afternoon, Cliff. Pint of slops is it, butt?' asked Bernard, wiping a glass with a tea towel, watching the telly.

'Aye, please, Bernard. Give us a pickled egg, a glass of pop, and some Oxo crisps for the boy.'

Bernard poured Dad's slops and got a pickled egg from a big jar with a spoon. Bernard didn't look at what he was doing and was still watching the horse racing. He poured the beer into the glass, all the way to the top without spilling a drop.

'You left early the other night, Cliff. On a promise were you?'

'I should be so bloody lucky, the Pope gets more than me.'

Dad's always saying to his butties he's never on a promise. One time I promised to tidy my bedroom to cheer Dad up. But I think Dad wants a better promise, like winning the pools or his feet to stop smelling.

'Four bob, two pence. Yuh wanna tray?'

'Aye, please, butt.'

Dad gave Bernard a pound note and asked for some change for cribbage and the fruit machine. Bernard put our drinks and snacks on a tray that had 'Courage Beer' written on it – just like the one Dad's borrowed.

'You gorra horse in this race, Bernard?'

'Aye. Flash Lightning, seven to one. Not looking good though, way back in sixth, it's a bloody donkey.'

'What yuh got him, to win or each way?'

'Went for him on the nose. Never mind, got another one up after this.'

The pub was empty apart from Snoz who was snoozing in the corner. He's called Snoz cos he's gorra big nose. He wears a suit and tie and is always blowing his nose in a big red hanky.

'Afternoon Snoz.'

'Uh! What? Oh, afternoon Cliff. Just resting me eyes for a bit. Got up early this morning, took the dog for a walk. Bloody thing. It's the wife's really, but muggins 'ere has to look after the bloody flea bag.'

Sometimes Snoz brings the dog to the pub. He's a good dog, but he's a bit scruffy. He's got grey fur, is blind in one eye, and only has one ear. His back legs don't work proper either, and he smells a bit pooey. Dad says his name should be Lucky. It's not though – it's Rex. Rex drinks beer from a bowl and Bernard says it's no wonder he can't see or walk proper.

'Gonna play cribbage later with the boys, Snoz?'

'Might do, Cliff. Who'll be in?'

'Midge and Yanto should be 'ere soon, and I would imagine Paxo will show his face.'

'Don't think Paxo'll be in, Cliff, he had a right skin-full in 'ere last night. Went home with Tina Thomas,' chuckled Snoz.

I asked Dad why they call Paxo, Paxo, and Dad laughed. But I heard Bernard say it's cos he's always stuffing birds. Paxo gets really drunk and sometimes the other men have to carry him outside to a taxi. Mam says that's why he's never been married.

'How are you, Gwyn?' asked Snoz.

'I'm okay, where's Rex?' I asked, eating a big handful of crisps. Dad told me off for putting too many in my mouth at the same time.

'He's at home in front of the fire. He's got the life of Riley that dog has, I tell you,' said Snoz, as Dad sipped his beer and got out one of his rollies from his bacca tin – Snoz looked up at the telly and watched the horse racing.

'Bloody mug's game, Cliff. A bloody mug's game, I tell you.'

'Aye, yuh not wrong there, Snoz. Waste of good beer money if you ask me.'

'Look at Bernard. He hasn't taken his eyes off that bloody telly since the racing started. Hasn't had a winner yet either. He'll be in one of his moods this evening if one don't come in soon,' said Snoz, shaking his head.

Bernard started shouting at the telly. The horse he wanted to win was running really fast, but the other horses were running faster.

'COME ON YUH LAZY BASTARD!'

Bernard's always saying naughty words. Words I'm not allowed to say – or tell Mam. If Mam goes to the pub, Bernard doesn't swear. He does a really funny smile, like he's pooed himself. Adrian Jenkins pooed himself at school once. Adrian's mam had to come and take him home. Bernard's horse didn't win and he made a funny grunting noise. He poured himself some slops, then farted.

'There'll be no chance of a lock-in tonight 'en,' said Dad.

'Oh, I dunno Cliffy, he'll wanna try and get some of his money back.'

'Well, suppose he'll have to drown his sorrows,' chuckled Dad.

'Aye, but his sorrows have learnt to swim by now, Cliff.'

Sometimes Dad and his butties have a lock-in. That's when Dad comes home really late and drunk. Mam says it's naughty for Bernard to have a lock-in. She said if the coppers found out, they'd close the pub and throw everyone in the clink. The clink is what Mam calls prison. Gransher went to the clink for selling washing machines some robbers gave him.

After a couple of races and lots more swearing from Bernard, Yanto and Midge came in the pub. They work with Dad down the steelworks. Midge and Yanto are fab. Midge drives a car like from the olden days. He's always got a bag of humbugs and Yanto gives me money for the fruit machine. Dad has to press the buttons, cos I can't reach.

'Hello Cliffy boy!' shouted Midge from the bar.

'Hiya Midge, howbe Yanto.'

'Howbe Cliff?' said Yanto, looking at his pools coupon.

'Hello Gwyn, stuck with yuh old man are you, butt?' asked Midge.

'Aye, I've got the bloody little rascal, Beryl's up Risca spending my bloody money,' said Dad.

Bernard gave Midge and Yanto their beer. Yanto made a joke about Bernard having no luck with the gee-gees. Dad says Bernard's had a sense of humour removal operation and Yanto was skating on thin ice. I think Yanto's mean to make fun of Bernard if he's had an operation. Mam's always having to go hospital for operations – she takes ages to get better. Yanto should give Bernard some grapes or Lucozade if he's not been very well. Midge told Yanto to stop pulling Bernard's leg, they picked up their drinks and came and sat down.

'Howbe Snoz?' asked Midge.

'Alright butt, can't complain. More than can be said for laughing chops over there.'

Snoz calls Bernard Cox laughing chops. Everyone makes fun of Bernard. Dad says he looks like he's found a penny but lost a pound. Midge says he looks like a cat drinking vinegar.

'Game of cribbage 'en boys? No Paxo this 'arvo? Unlike him to miss a Saturday,' said Yanto.

'Duw duw, that bugger got steamed last night and went home with that Tina Thomas. I was just telling Cliff, before you came in,' said Snoz.

'What, Tina the screamer? They'll be burying her in a Y-shaped coffin, she's a big girl as well,' said Midge.

'Love comes in all shapes and sizes Midge,' said Snoz.

'Aye, and Paxo has come in most of 'em,' laughed Yanto.

'Not in front of the lad, boys. We playing cribbage or wha'?' shouted Dad.

Dad got the cribbage board and playing cards from under the telly. Another horse race was starting and Bernard was muttering about his horse. Said it had better be better than the others, cos they were only fit for the glue factory.

'So, what's Beryl spending yuh beer money on Cliff?' asked Midge.

'She's having a look at some bloody wallpaper. It's this little bugger's fault, isn't it yuh rascal? Gonna cost me an arm and a leg.'

'What you been up to 'en, Gwyn?' said Yanto, as he took one of my crisps and popped it in his mouth.

'It wasn't my fault. It was Kim. We were only playing Bonanza, like on the telly. We were playing camp.'

'I'll Bonanza you one of these bloody days. Him and the girl from the upstairs flat, nearly set his bloody bedroom on fire. The little bugger crept into my bedroom while I was asleep, took my matches and tried to make a fire. And they nicked my bloody stew from the fridge. That was gonna be my bloody tea, had to have jam sarnies. Can't do a night shift on jam bloody sarnies!'

Everyone in the pub was laughing. Even Bernard.

'So Beryl wants to decorate the whole bedroom. I said we can just patch the bit of wallpaper that got caught. Luckily, I woke up in time to put it out before it spread. But no, Beryl's sister, Maria's coming to stay later in the year and Beryl wants it looking like Buckingham bloody Palace.'

Yanto laughed so much he got hiccups. He always gets hiccups when he laughs.

'It's not bloody funny. Not only have I gorra fork out good money for wallpaper and paste, I gorra spend my day off next week pissing about up a bloody ladder. I don't know what's the bloody rush. Anyway, we might be moving down Risca soon.'

'Moving to Risca? When did all this happen 'en, Cliffy?' asked Yanto – then he did a big burp.

'Beryl wants a bigger place and this old couple wanna flat. The council said we can just do a swap. No problem they said. I'll get a bigger garden though.'

'Maria? Isn't that the sister who lives in Japan, who's a bit tasty?' asked Midge.

'Aye, that's the one. Little gold digger if you ask me. Out of your price range.'

'Yeah, I remember her, a couple of years ago, she came in with you and Beryl. Little cracker. Even Bernard went upstairs and came back down with a tie on,' said Midge.

'The last time I saw Bernard with a tie on was when he went to court for selling 'em stolen fags. How long ago was that 'en Bernard?' said Yanto, winking at Dad and Midge and drinking half his beer in one big gulp.

'Trust you to remember that. That was bloody years ago. March, nineteen sixty three. And you bloody well know it. You sold me the buggers, should have turned you in.'

'You wouldn't do tha', you love me too much.'

'Get out of it, yuh bloody poof. Let me watch me race in bloody peace or I'll set the wife on you.'

'Ooh, he's so butch isn't he lads? Give us a kiss Bernard.'

Yanto blew Bernard a kiss, Bernard flicked the V-sign at him and carried on watching the telly. Dad and his butties started playing cribbage. Snoz is the best at cribbage. He doesn't lose much, and when he does, Dad says he does it on purpose to give the others a chance.

'So, Cliff, who's this new bloke that Beryl's sister's bringing over 'en? Rich is he?' asked Midge.

'It's a Jap fella. Some high-flier she's picked up over there. That's why Beryl's all up for tarting up the flat,' said Dad, looking at his cards.

'He won't notice what your place looks like, Cliff. They have bad eyesight those Japs you know? They've very narrow eyes. It's why they kept crashing their planes in the war. They couldn't see the side of the ships,' said Yanto.

'Yuh daft bugger, just concentrate on the game,' said Dad.

More men came into the pub and Dad told me to sit by the fruit machine, in case a copper came in. I've never seen a copper in the pub. Dad's butty, Jack, is a security guard and sometimes comes in with his uniform on. It looks like a copper's uniform, but he has a flat cap – like the milkman's. I want to be a milkman when I grow up, but Dad says I'd have to get up early to milk the cows.

After I drank my pop, I needed a wee. Dad said it was okay to go to the toilet but not to go in the ladies again. I went in there once and scared Mrs Rees.

'And don't forget to wash yuh hands,' said Dad, not looking up playing his game. He wasn't winning cos Snoz had the most two pence pieces. I'm not allowed to tell Mam that Dad plays for money. He says it's the only bloody pleasure he gets.

'Hey Gwyn, if you pee on yuh shoes it might bring yuh Dad some good luck. He bloody well needs it,' shouted Yanto, as I skipped down the corridor.

It's lucky if you wee on yuh shoes. Dad says that might be so, but I was not to do it on purpose. He says if I wee on my new daps, he'll beat me black and blue.

I finished my wee and washed my hands – just like Dad told me. Next to the sink was a new machine. It was a machine like they have at the railway station that's got chocolate in. But there wasn't any pictures of any chocolate bars. There was a man and a lady holding hands walking through a field. They were all smiley and looked silly, like on Mam's knitting patterns. I thought it might be bubble gum. There's a bubble gum machine in Blackwood bus station, it's yellow and says Juicy Fruit on it. Dad never lets me have any though, says it's a waste of money and it will only get stuck in my belly and stop me pooing proper. The machine in the toilet was called Durex. I'd never heard of bubble gum called Durex. I dried my hands on my trousers and went back into the bar.

'Dad, what's Durex? Is it bubble gum?'

The men in the pub started laughing, even some men that were'nt Dad's butties.

'Nor, it's not bloody bubble gum. Sit down now, nice and tidy and keep quiet.'

'Is it chocolate 'en, Dad?'

Yanto was laughing so much he got hiccups again.

'Go on Cliff, tell him what it is. He wants to know, mun,' laughed Midge.

'It's not for kids. It's for grown-ups. It's not sweets, bubble gum, or bloody chocolate. So never mind,' said Dad, who was not laughing.

'Mam says you never buy her anything nice, why don't you get her something from the machine as a present?'

Everyone in the pub, except Dad, laughed even more. Dad was looking at his cards, I don't think he was doing very well. Perhaps that's why he wasn't laughing. But I don't know why they thought it was funny buying Mam a present. Perhaps it's cos they think Dad is mean – like Mam says he is.

'Look. It's the sort of present that yuh mother doesn't want. It's tights. Your Mam's got plenty of tights and she doesn't need any more.'

'Why do they sell tights in the toilets, Dad?'

'Cos if yuh late coming home from the pub, the shops are shut. Sometimes ladies need a pair of tights for the morning. Now, no more bloody questions,' said Dad.

'You'll understand when you're older, lad,' said Snoz, looking up from his cards, winking.

Dad bought me some more pop and crisps and made me promise not to ask any more questions. I sat by the fruit machine and Dad and his butties carried on with their game. Snoz won and bought Dad, Midge and Yanto a pint of slops. I got some more Oxo crisps and a glass of pop.

After some more horse racing had finished, and Bernard stopped shouting at the telly, the football scores came on. I always look for Newport County, they're our local team but they don't win much. They lost 4-0 to a team called Crewe Alexandra. Dad only likes it when the teams are 1-1 or 2-2 –

and only the ones that he's put a cross next to on his coupon. Dad didn't have many crosses on his coupon and he moaned that the pools was a big con. Dad finished drinking his slops and said that it was time to go home. On the way out, Bernard Cox shouted after Dad.

'Aye, Cliff! Not buying Beryl any tights 'en from the bubble gum machine?'

Dad called Bernard a rude word and I had to promise not to ever say it, or tell Mam. I wonder what a clunt is?

Chapter 6.

My Nana. A Witch. And A Wardrobe.

Dad never comes to see Nana Balding and Gransher with me and Mam. Dad says Nana Balding might put a spell on him. He likes to stay at home, do stuff in the garden or sleep in his chair.

Gransher picks us up in his car – it's called a Woolsey. It's big and shiny and it's got leather seats that make you slide when the car goes round a corner. Uncle Malcolm also lives with Nana and Gransher. Mam says Uncle Malcolm's always drunk or high as a kite. He's got lots of comics under his bed with pictures of ladies with no clothes on. Uncle Graham sometimes lives with Nana and Gransher, but only when he's not away on his ship in the Navy.

Nana Balding's really little and always wears a pinny. She smokes horrible fags called Woodbines. Even though Nana is little, she's very loud. She shouts at everyone, even if they've done nothing wrong. Dad says he feels sorry for Gransher, says it must be like living with an angry parrot in curlers. I think she looks like Hilda Ogden from Coronation Street – Dad thinks she looks the monkeys on the PG Tips advert.

Mam said Dad had to work some extra shifts to pay for decorating stuff. Mam got some cheap wallpaper from Pam's wool shop – it was orange. Dad said it would give me nightmares and wouldn't blame me if I set fire to the bedroom again. Mam had to take it back and swap it. She brought back more purple wool instead, Dad went doolally.

'C'mon on Gwyn, put yuh toys away. Gransher will be 'ere now in a minute.'

I was playing with my Tonka truck. My Tonka truck is brilliant and it's yellow. I wanted to take it up Nana and Gransher's, but Mam said no. I put my toys away in the bedroom and Mam made me put my coat on, cos it was cold. I stuck the hood over my head – like Batman. Mam told me to put it on proper. I like being Batman.

Mam sat by the window waiting for Gransher. Mam's always sitting by the window watching what people do. Mam says she just likes to see what's going on. Dad says she's just a nosey bugger. Gransher's Woolsey came round the corner. He beeped the horn and we went outside and got in the car.

'Hiya Gwyn lad, you been a good boy for yuh Mam?' said Gransher, sat behind the big wooden steering wheel.

I told him I'd been good and I'd put all my toys away. I didn't tell him I'd thrown 'em under my bed. I always throw my toys under my bed when I have to tidy up. Mam never looks cos of her bard leg. Dad never looks cos he says it's too far to travel for no bloody good reason.

'Good lad, 'ere, have a sweet.'

Gransher's always got sweets. He has 'em in a tin that's in the dashboard – Mam had two. Mam told Gransher about me and Kim making a fire in my bedroom. Gransher thought it was funny and his shoulders shook when he laughed.

'It's not funny, Dad, t'was a good job Cliff was there to put it out. The whole flat could have gone up in flames.' said Mam, sucking on her sweet.

Gransher stopped to get some petrol. I like the petrol station, it's got old cars piled up on top of each other. The man in the garage said they're cars that have been in accidents and couldn't be fixed. One of 'em was an old bread van, it had a sign on the side saying 'Evans Mobile Bread Shop'. Gransher says they couldn't buy another van cos they couldn't raise the dough. Gransher thinks his jokes are funny. Gransher's jokes are rubbish – just like Dad's. Mam bought me a Bazooka Joe from the garage shop, and said she hoped it would keep me quiet.

'Any news on the new car, Beryl?' asked Gransher, as we drove from the garage.

'We had a letter last week saying it's all been approved. They're sending a bloke round next week. Gorra gerra provisional driving licence now.'

'All sounds good. Won't be long before you can drive yourself up to visit. We'll have to sort some lessons out.'

Gransher told Mam about a wardrobe that Nana didn't want. Mam said we'd need a new one if we move to Risca. I stuck some Warlord stickers on my wardrobe, Dad couldn't get 'em off. I thought my Warlord stickers looked brilliant, Mam didn't.

When we got to Nana's house, she was outside in the front garden. Nana was picking weeds from round the yucca tree. Nana Balding's got two yucca trees in the front garden. Uncle Graham brought 'em back from one of his Navy trips. Gransher said that they were just little when he planted 'em.

'Hello Bach, looks like rain by the looks of yuh curls.'

Nana Balding says when my hair goes really curly, it it's gonna rain. She says eating the crusts of my jam butties makes my hair curlier as well. I never eat the crusts of my jam butties.

I hate my curly hair and I don't want it getting any curlier. Some of the boys at school make fun of me – Nigel Lewis calls me Shirley Temple. I don't like Nigel Lewis, he makes fun of everyone. Even though he can't read very well and smells like gone-off milk.

'Hello Beryl, where's Cliff, down the pub is he?'

'No, he's bloody well not, Mam, he's working afternoons, getting some extra shifts in to pay for decorating Gwyn's bedroom.'

'Decorating? What for? You'll be moving down Risca soon.'

'Yeah, well, Gwyn set fire to the wallpaper in the bedroom. The old lady that's moving in is bedridden. Can't have her staring at a burnt wall all day.'

Mam's been telling everyone about me and Kim's camp fire. She told the milkman, the insurance man, and a lady in the Co-op. Mam didn't even know the lady in the Co-op.

'Duw, he's uh boy an' half. Aren't you, yuh little bugger?' shouted Nana as she clenched her fist.

'Leave the lad alone Mary, boys will be boys,' said Gransher, checking the leaves on the yucca tree.

I followed Gransher round the back of the house, up the gwli, and to his shed. Gransher likes his shed and is always pulling things out and looking at them. Nana Balding doesn't go in the shed, Gransher told her a rat lives behind the tool box. I asked him how big was the rat, he winked and said it was big enough to stop Nana from bothering him. Gransher doesn't do much in his shed. He just sits on an old chair by the door and reads his paper. Sometimes he cleans the lawn mower or sharpens some knives.

'I've got something 'ere for you lad. I found it the other day in the long grass.'

Gransher opened the shed door and turned on the light. The shed is full of junk, old tools, bits of engines and even an old traffic light. He reached for a big wooden crate and pulled out a red football.

'This must have been yuh cousin Kevin's. I remember him playing with it when he was about your age. Right, 'ere yuh go. Don't break any windows, or you'll have yuh Nana chasing both of us with the boiler stick.'

'Wow, thanks Gransher!'

The ball was ace. It was really heavy and bright red. Gransher told me to only play with it round the side of the house – not to play in the road, or near his Woolsey. Gransher loves his Woolsey, he's always cleaning it. I played bounce against the wall. Mam came round to see what I was doing. I told her Gransher found the ball in the long grass.

'As if you haven't got enough toys that make a noise.'

Mam made me go inside and wash my hands. Nana made some Welsh cakes and put some on a plate with a glass of squash. I wanted to bring my ball inside but Mam said I had to leave it by the back door. Gransher was sitting in his chair reading his newspaper. Nana nagged him about giving me the ball, she said that I was gonna break a window. Gransher told Nana I'd be careful and asked for a cup of tea and some peace and quiet.

I ate my Welsh cake and drank my squash. Nana Balding's Welsh cakes are dry and not very nice. The squash didn't have much squash in it and was all cloudy. Dad says Nana thinks there's still a bloody war on. He says when she makes a pot of tea, it's for a midget who's not very thirsty.

'So 'en Beryl, when you gerrin' this new car?'

'They're sending a bloke round next week to do the forms.'

'I don't see why you need a car, you've managed all these years without one. Why doesn't Cliff learn to drive if you wanna car?' said Nana, spitting out bits of Welsh cake.

'Oh Mam, the world's getting faster. I'll need a car now Gwyn's growing up. Cliff hasn't got time to learn to drive.'

'He's got plenty of time to go up the pub though.'

'Mary, leave it out. Cliff works hard all week, he deserves a pint with the lads after a shift,' said Gransher while reading his newspaper.

'All I'm saying is, Beryl's only got one good arm. Don't think she should be taking too much on. Gwyn's a bloody handful as it is. He almost burnt down the flat the other week, the little bugger.'

Gransher shook his head and muttered something about God giving him strength. Nana Balding drank her tea and told Mam about the next door neighbour. Mrs Lomez came home drunk from bingo cos she'd won thirty pounds. She spent some of the money on a new garden gnome that looked like Jimmy Saville. Nana was going to write a letter to the council to get it removed. Nana Balding doesn't like Jimmy Saville.

'Here comes Malcolm. He looks half cut, don't know how he can drink so much during the day,' said Mam, grabbing another Welsh cake and stuffing it in her mouth.

'He came home the other week with only one shoe. I said to him, yuh drunken fool, you've lost yuh shoe. But he said he hadn't, he'd found one. Daft bugger.'

Uncle Malcolm walked up the front garden and past the yucca trees. He was wearing a leather jacket with the sleeves rolled up and he was holding a carrier bag. Uncle Malcolm looked through the front window and waved. His face was all red and he was laughing.

'What does he bloody look like? Like Alvin Stardust dragged through a bush,' laughed Mam.

Uncle Malcolm walked round the back of the house and came in through the kitchen.

'Here comes the bus conductor, let's see everyone's tickets,' shouted Uncle Malcolm, laughing.

'See look, I told you. He's as drunk as a navvy on payday,' said Mam, shaking her head.

'Yuh dinner's under the grill, probably all dried up by now. Should have been home at dinner time, like the rest of us. I expect you've been down the bloomin' Greyhound all afternoon, haven't you?' shouted Nana Balding, so loud some birds in the garden flew away.

'Only had a few beers, Mary. Only a few with the lads.'

'Don't you Mary me, yuh cheeky bugger. Yuh not too big to get the boiler stick across yuh arse.'

Uncle Malcolm laughed. He saw me sat down by the sideboard looking at the pictures in the Radio Times.

'Look Gwyn, yuh Nana wants to beat me up, go and gerra policeman, quick,' he chuckled.

'That's enough now, Malcolm, go and heat up yuh dinner and stop teasing yuh mother,' said Gransher.

Gransher doesn't talk much, but when he does, everyone listens – even Nana. Malcolm was still laughing as he went to the kitchen. He took his dinner, wrapped in foil, and put it in the oven. Malcolm got a piece of bread from the bread bin, put red sauce all over it, and stuffed it in his mouth. He did a big fart that sounded like he'd ripped his pants. I thought it was really funny.

'Yuh dirty Arab,' groaned Nana.

'It's only natural, better out than in, ain't that right Gwyn?'

'Don't give Gwyn yuh bad habits, he's a bloody handful already, without you teaching him more mischief.'

Malcolm put his carrier bag on the table and pulled out some cans and bottles of beer.

'Ere yuh go mother, nice bottle of Guinness for you. See, I'm a good son that comes bearing gifts.'

'Don't think you can get round me with a bottle of Guinness, Bach. I ain't that cheap. Stick it in the pantry, I'll have it later when I'm watching Sale Of The Century.'

Nana Balding loves Sale Of The Century, she watches it every week. I think it's stupid. Nana went into the kitchen to make another pot of tea. Gransher put down his newspaper and went outside to look in his shed. He said he wanted to sort out some wires. Uncle Malcolm sat down and started to doze off to sleep. Nana came back with a teapot and asked me to bring the biscuit barrel to the table.

Nana's biscuit barrel's always full of broken biscuits. There's never any nice ones like Mrs Davies upstairs has. Never any chocolate ones, but sometimes there are some with icing on.

'Look, Malcolm's falling asleep. His dinner's still in the oven. It'll be all ruined and only fit for the birds to eat,' said Mam.

'Oh, the bugger. OI, MALCOLM, WAKE UP!' shouted Nana.

Uncle Malcolm opened his eyes and he looked like Dad when Mam wakes him up after he's been down the pub.

'Where's the fire 'en?'

'I'll fire you, yuh drunk skunk. Yuh dinner's in the oven, and I'll be buggered if I'm gonna sort it out for you.'

Malcolm got his dinner from the oven. We could hear him complaining his Yorkshire pudding was all dried up and the gravy had turned to cement.

'If you want yuh dinner all nice and tidy, come home and eat it when it's ready, instead of staying out boozing. Don't know why I put up with your nonsense. You were less bother when you were a baby.'

Uncle Malcolm put his dinner on the table and started to eat it. He didn't look like he was enjoying it very much and pulled funny faces as he chewed. The roast potatoes looked rubbish, and the peas were all shriveled up and wrinkled, like my fingers when I've been in the bath too long.

Gransher came back in from the shed and washed his hands in the sink. He watched Malcolm eat his dinner, shaking his head as Malcolm made loud noises and got peas all over the table. Nana said it was like watching an animal.

'When yuh ready, Beryl, I'll run you back home, luv.'

'Okay, we'll go now in a minute.'

Mam finished her cup of tea and popped a broken biscuit in her mouth.

'You eating for two 'en Beryl? You've nearly eaten half the barrel.' said Nana.

'Don't be so daft, Mam, I've only had a couple. Anyway, I only had a small dinner with Cliff being at work.'

Mam was telling fibs. She had loads to eat for dinner. She had lots of roast potatoes, three Yorkshire puddings, two chickens legs, some boiled potatoes, carrots, runner beans and a big dollop of stuffing. For afters she had a can of fruit cocktail with syrup and cream.

Mam told me to put my coat on and Nana put some Welsh cakes in a bag for us to take home. When we bring Welsh cakes back from Nana Balding's, Mam eats 'em all before we get home.

'Right 'en Arthur, get yuh hands in yuh pocket and give

Gwyn some tuck money. Come on, dig in deep, don't be mean,' said Nana.

Nana Balding always makes Gransher give me some money for sweets. If Uncle Graham is home from the Navy, he gives me some too. Gransher gave me a bunch of change from his pocket and did some pretend boxing. Gransher used to be a boxer in the olden days. Dad told me he was very good.

'Thanks Gransher,' I said, counting the coins in my hand. I had nearly seventy three pence. That's enough to buy a Corgi car or even a water pistol. Mam doesn't like it when I buy toys that make a noise or fire things out. If I had a water pistol, I could fire it at next doors cat. Dad doesn't like next door's cat, it digs up the garden and wees over the cabbages.

I got my new red ball from the back door, and said goodbye to Nana and Uncle Malcolm. We got into the Woolsey and Gransher gave me another sweet from his tin – Mam had two. We drove a different way back so I could look at the water mill. I like the water mill. Mam said she used to play around there when she was a little girl – before she got a bard leg and bard arm.

'Our Malcolm needs to cut back on the booze, find himself a nice girlfriend and stop acting the goat,' said Gransher.

'Who the 'ell would wanna go out with Malcolm? It would be easier running a farm.'

'If he got his hair cut, smartened himself up a bit, you never know.'

'Well, she'd have to be desperate, that's all I'm saying.'

Gransher dropped us off at home and it was nearly night-time. Gransher didn't come in for a cup of tea, said he'd better get back before Nana strangled Malcolm. We waved goodbye to Gransher and watched him drive away til we couldn't see

the red lights on the back of the Woolsey. We went inside and
Mam made a cup of tea. We didn't have a Welsh cake though
– cos Mam had eaten 'em all.

Chapter 7.

Pins And Needles.

John Sibby said Mrs Vandenburg was a Nazi in the war. In Warlord the Nazis are really nasty – just like Mrs Vandenburg. Mam said John Sibby's talking rubbish cos Mrs Vandenburg comes from Cardiff.

Mrs Edwards is our headmistress, she's really old and smells like wet dogs – just like Snoz's dog, Rex, when he's been fetching sticks from the river. At playtime, she walks round the yard making sure no one's being naughty. We're not allowed to bring toys to school. If we do, the teachers lock 'em in a cupboard. I've got some plastic soldiers and a yo-yo in Mrs Edwards' cupboard.

One day I was playing with Lisa Jenkins and I fell over and cut my hand. There was lots of blood and it made me feel sick. Mrs Edwards came over to see what was going on. Some of the girls where shouting 'Urgh!' when they saw the blood. Mrs Edwards looked at my cut hand and hit me round my head. She said that I'd not been careful and I was very stupid. The school nurse washed my cut and put a big plaster on it. Then I had to sit on a bench outside Mrs Edwards' office for being naughty. Nobody at Waunfawr School likes Mrs Edwards.

Every morning we have assembly. We go in the hall and sit on the floor with our legs crossed. Sometimes when I sit down too long I get pins and needles. It's really hard to walk back to class cos my leg goes all numb and wobbly.

Mrs Edwards does the assembly and starts by telling us off. Like for running in the corridor or bringing sweets to school. We're not allowed to bring sweets to school. She even makes some boys and girls stand up if she's talking about 'em. It can be about something good but she'll still make 'em stand up in front of the whole school. Emma Joseph had to stand up cos her Mam had a new baby. Emma started to cry and Mrs Edwards made her stand in the corner of the hall with her hands on her head. We could hear her crying all the way through All Things Bright And Beautiful.

Before we go to assembly, Mrs Vandenburg reads out the register. If any boys or girls don't answer, she reads their name out again – but really loud. John Sibby said that when I was away bard with the measles, she still called my name out every day. Even though Mam gave her a letter from the doctor and told her I'd be at home for ages.

'William Cowell?'

'Yes, Miss.'

'Phillip Davies?'

'Yes, Miss.'

One time, Andrea Thomas didn't answer cos she felt sick. When Mrs Vandenburg made her say 'Yes miss', Andrea puked all over the desk – it went everywhere. Over her Ladybird book, down the side of her leg, even in the ink well.

'Karl Harris?'

'Yes, Miss.'

'Adrian Jenkins?'

'Yes, Miss.'

After Andrea Thomas was sick, Mr Salmon, the janitor, had

to clean it all up. Andrea Thomas had to go and see the nurse. When she was feeling better, Mrs Edwards told her off and made her cry. She said if she was gonna be sick, she should've been sick before she got to school.

'Nigel Lewis?'

'Yes, Miss.'

'Andrew Rees?'

'Yes, Miss.'

Susan Weeks pee'd herself once – it was horrible. Her wee went everywhere, just like Andrea Thomas' sick. Tracy Vass jumped up on a chair and screamed. She had new pair of Clarks on, and didn't wanna get Susan's pee on 'em. Girls are silly.

'John Sibby?

'Yes, Miss.'

'Gwyn Sugden?'

'Yes, Miss.'

'Who's talking in the back of the class? Is that you Nigel Lewis?' shouted Mrs Vandenburg, looking over her glasses to see who was making the noise.

'No Miss, sorry Miss,' said Nigel, who was showing Karl Harris a big bruise on his leg. He said he'd done it playing Germans with Robert Perry from Class Two.

Mrs Vandenburg told Nigel off and finished doing the register. She told us to sit still and be quiet while she got ready for assembly. The bell rang and Mrs Vandenburg made us stand at our desks ready to go to the hall.

'Right, Class Three, I want a nice quiet line please. Front row first, come on, quickly does it,' she said, waving her arms about like Magnus Pike, off the telly.

Mrs Edwards does assembly, and she makes sure we're all

quiet, then we have to say the Lord's prayer:

Our father, in charge of heaven,

Alan be thy name...

Then Mrs Edwards makes us sit down.

'Good morning, boys and girls.'

'Good morning, Mrs Edwards,' everybody says, even the teachers.

'Now then, before we sing our first hymn there's something I want to tell you.'

We looked around to see who she was gonna pick on.

'Everyone here at Waunfawr school is very lucky. You can all run, jump, skip and play. But not everyone is so fortunate,' she said, looking around the hall, making sure everyone was listening.

Mrs Edwards talked about handicapped people. She told us about boys and girls that can't walk proper and have to be in a wheelchair. There was a girl in school who had a bard foot. She had a special shoe that was massive and had bits of metal stuck to it. We called her Herman.

'Stand up, Gwyn Sugden.'

I felt my face go red. I hadn't been naughty and I didn't wanna stand up. I wanted Mrs Edwards to leave me alone. All the other boys and girls were looking at me – some were whispering, wondering what I'd done wrong.

'Settle down now children. Come on, Gwyn Sugden, stand up,' said Mrs Edwards, sounding a bit angry cos I didn't stand up straight away.

I stood up and looked down at my daps. I could feel my face getting redder and my belly went all funny and I needed to do a wee.

'Gwyn's mother is a very special lady. She can't walk or run like most people, and she can only use one hand. But she's going to get a new, very special car. Mrs Sugden will be one of the first people in Wales to have one.'

I knew Mam was gonna gerra car, and I knew it was a special one. But I didn't think it would be so special that Mrs Edwards would make me stand up. I didn't wanna look up cos I knew everyone was staring at me. I really needed a wee and the longer I stood up, the more I needed to go. More than in Pam's wool shop.

'So, boys and girls, Gwyn Sugden's mother will be driving a car just like a normal person. Isn't that fantastic, boys and girls?' she asked, and everyone said 'Yes Mrs Edwards'. I could feel 'em staring at me.

I wanted to shout at Mrs Edwards cos Mam's normal like everybody else. She's not strange like Cousin It or The Thing on The Addams Family. And Mam can knit faster than anyone else, she knitted me a bobble hat once, really fast. But it didn't fit proper and made me look like Benny from Crossroads.

'Also, Gwyn will be leaving us soon and going to a new school. Isn't that right Gwyn Sugden?'

'Yes Miss,' I said, but my throat was really dry and Mrs Edwards told me off for not speaking up. I'm glad I won't have to go to Waunfawr School anymore. Mam said my new school will be really nice. But Mam sometimes tells fibs. She told me that the injection that Doctor Davies gave me wouldn't hurt. But it did. It hurt loads, but I didn't cry. Dad tells me off if I cry and calls me a big baby. He says the Bionic Man doesn't cry when he gets an injection, but that's cos he's bionic. Mrs Edwards told me to sit back down. I didn't wanna do a wee anymore.

Mrs Edwards read some stories from The Bible. They

weren't good stories like Union Jack Jackson or Drake of Malta from Warlord. They were boring about a man who built a wall cos God told him to. My Uncle Ronnie built a wall in the back of his garden. He painted it white and made plant pots out of old tyres. After The Bible story we sang 'Morning Has Broken' – but I can never remember the words. I hate 'Morning Has Broken', it's stupid. When we finished singing, Mrs Edwards told us to go back to our classrooms. We sat down at our desks and waited for Mrs Vandenburg.

'Is your Mam's car a supercar, like Batman's?' asked John Sibby, picking his nose and wiping it on his jumper. John Sibby is always picking his nose. Sometimes he eats it as well.

'We haven't got it yet, but Mam said it will be just like a normal car, but with a special steering wheel.'

'Does your Mam have a wooden leg like a pirate?' asked Nigel Lewis, who had a big silly smile on his face.

'No, she doesn't, stupid face.'

'You're stupid, you curly wurly head.'

Mrs Vandenburg came into the classroom and told us to be quiet. Nigel pulled a face at me, he went cross-eyed. Mam says if you pull too many faces, one day the wind will change and you'll stay like it. I wished the wind would change, then Nigel Lewis would look like a silly bum face forever.

'NIGEL LEWIS, WHAT ON EARTH ARE YOU DOING, BOY?' shouted Mrs Vandenburg.

'Nothing Miss, sorry Miss.'

'Don't lie to me Nigel Lewis, I just saw you pulling a face. I've got eyes in the back of my head, boy.'

Mrs Vandenburg was really angry. She's always telling us that she's got eyes in the back of her head. John Sibby said he saw a monster on Doctor Who that had loads of eyes on his head. He said it was so scary he hid behind the settee 'til The Basil Brush Show came on.

'Stand up, Nigel Lewis.'

Nigel stood up and his face was really red.

'Do you think it makes you clever pulling faces in my classroom?' asked Mrs Vandenburg.

'No Miss.'

'That's right, you're not clever, are you Nigel Lewis?'

'No Miss,' whispered Nigel.

'If I catch you pulling faces or misbehaving in my class again, I'll send you down to Mrs Edwards and you can pull faces at her. Would you like to do that, Nigel Lewis? Well, would you, boy?' shouted Mrs Vandenburg, pointing at him with a stick of chalk.

'No Miss, sorry Miss. I won't do it again Miss.'

Mrs Vandenburg told Nigel Lewis to sit down. His face was still really red and I thought he was gonna cry. But Nigel Lewis never cries. Not even when Karl Harris made fun of him cos his Dad had died and gone to heaven. Mrs Vandenburg made us get our books out and do some sums. We had to read out the three times table. We got to five times three is fifteen, when I smelt a smelly fart. I think it was John Sibby cos it smelt like Spangles, he eats loads of Spangles does John Sibby.

At playtime, some of the boys asked me about Mam's car. I told some fibs and said that Mam's car would be like the ones in Wacky Races. I said it might be like Peter Perfect's Turbo Terrific, or Dick Dastardly and Mutley's Mean Machine. I didn't tell 'em she was getting a Mini.

John Sibby said he was sorry I was moving cos he would have to find somebody else to play with. Linda Jenkins told me that she knew about us moving house, she said she heard her

Mam telling her Dad. My Mam knows Linda Jenkins's Mam cos she goes up Pam's wool shop. Linda said her cousin goes to my new school and they can take toys with 'em to play with. I'm looking forward to my new school. I don't like Waunfawr school. I don't like Mrs Vandenburg or Mrs Edwards.

Linda Jenkins used to be my girlfriend. She made me hold her hand. She wanted me to kiss her on the cheek but I said no. She said that's what boyfriends and girlfriends do. She stopped being my girlfriend and asked Andrew Rees to be her boyfriend instead. Andrew Rees had a new purple coat and Linda Jenkins liked it better than mine. Mam says purple is very popular. Dad's new jumper is purple, but Dad won't wear it. Mam said she'll buy me a new coat, just like Andrew Rees's to go to my new school. But I'm not gonna wear the jumper she's knitting me. It looks stupid and has one arm longer than the other.

Chapter 8.

A Big Lorry To Risca.

A big lorry pulled up outside our flat. It was so big a man had to guide it past all the parked cars in the road. It was the biggest lorry I'd ever seen. Bigger than the bus that goes to Nana Sugden's. It was to take our things to our new house in Risca, Mam had been putting stuff in boxes for ages. Every time Dad wanted something, Mam would have put it away in a box. She put Dad's slippers in a box last week. Dad said she'd put us in a bloody box if we sat still long enough.

'Ooh, look Gwyn, the big removal lorry's 'ere. Exciting, isn't it!' said Mam, wrapping one of her ornaments in a page from the South Wales Argus.

Dad says Mam's been like a bottle of pop ever since the council told us we could move. Uncle John from Pontypool came to help as well. He's not my real uncle, he's Betty's husband. Betty is one of Mam's friends and Uncle John is teaching Mam to drive. When she goes in her new car, she has to have someone with her who can drive proper. Mam's been having loads of lessons, but she's still not very good. She hit a shopping trolley and got told off by a policeman for parking on a zebra crossing.

When Mam got her new car, a man from the newspaper came to take her photo. She was in the paper, smiling and giving a thumbs-up. Mam bought loads of papers and gave 'em to lots of people, she even gave one to the milkman. Cos Mam's got a limp and her arm doesn't work proper, she's got a special sticker that's stuck to the car window. It's orange and it's got a drawing of a man in a wheelchair. Mam says it's to let other drivers know she's disabled, and she can park outside the Co-op. Dad said it's to let everyone know to get out of the bloody way.

The removal men were Dad's butties from The Exchange. They had brown overalls and drank lots of tea. Yanto and Midge were gonna come and help, but Dad said they had too much beer and made 'em sick. Mam said they're a pair of boozers.

'Bullo, where's my bloody hat?' shouted Dad, looking through some boxes.

'I dunno Cliff, wherever you left it,' said Mam, as she wrote 'Kitchen Stuff' on a big brown box with Dad's bits of clocks in it.

'It was on the coat hanger in the passage. You haven't bloody put it in a bloody box, have you?' Dad shouted, looking in the bread bin.

Dad always wears a hat when he's outside, even when it's hot and sunny. Mam says she's gonna bloody bury him in it. Dad says it's to keep his head warm cos he's not got much hair. He says he's not bald, he's growing his forehead. He puts loads of stuff called Vaseline on his bits of hair and it makes his head go all shiny. Mam says he looks like Bobby Charlton.

All morning, Dad, Uncle John, and the other men lifted all our furniture into the big lorry. Mam wrote on the boxes what room they had to go into in the new house. Brenda from next door brought some tea and biscuits. After the removal men finished drinking more tea, we got ready to go. Cos I'd been good and hadn't got in the way, Dad said I could ride in the front of the lorry. I was really excited, I'd never been in a lorry before.

Dad made sure we'd packed everything and all the doors and windows were locked proper. Mam got in her new car with Uncle John. Me and Dad went in the lorry. It was really big and had two rows of seats. In the back I could see some magazines, just like the ones Uncle Malcolm has under his bed.

'Look Dad, it's the same comics that Uncle Malcolm has with the naked ladies in,' I said, pointing to the pile behind our seat. 'Can I read one?'

The blokes in the lorry laughed. Dad said I wasn't to look at those sorts of comics cos they were not for children.

'Do they get a free gift in 'em? Like in Warlord? You get free army stickers in Warlord,' I said – army stickers are great. I put some on the fridge. But Mam said she didn't want a Luftwaffe badge on the fridge door. I thought it made the fridge look ace.

'No, you don't get bloody free gifts. Now sit there nice and tidy and shut your row up,' shouted Dad, as he lit his rollie and put his cap on. He found it in a box with the kettle that had Bedroom written on it.

The lorry driver was really fat. So fat he only just fitted in his seat. He's one of Dad's butties from the pub. He's called Tiny. He's bigger than Giant Haystacks and he smells like sweat and rollies. Tiny smoked lots of rollies, more than Dad. Tiny only stopped smoking to drink his tea.

Brenda and Bill waved us goodbye. Mr and Mrs Davies and Kim said goodbye in the morning while we were still packing. They'd gone away in their car to visit Kim's Nana in hospital. Kim said her Nana was getting ready to be with Jesus. Mam said her Nana would be fine, and was only having an ingrowing toenail removed.

We followed Mam's car down to Risca in the big lorry. Mam's car was full of blankets, pillows and loads of coats. I could see my red football against the back window by the disabled sticker. As we drove away I waved to Bill and Brenda. I waved at our old flat and when we reached the end of the road, I waved goodbye to Waunfawr Gardens and the conker tree.

'Dad, will there be Warlords and Black Jacks in Risca?' I asked, cos I wanted to find out if Union Jack Jackson had escaped from the Japanese ambush. Dad said there would be and not to ask any more silly questions cos we were only moving up the road, not to Timbuk-bloody-tu. I don't know where Timbuk-bloody-tu is, I think it's in Scotland.

It didn't take long to get to Risca. Risca is lots bigger than Crosskeys and has lots more shops. We passed The Knit Nurse and I wondered if Mam would buy her wool there instead of Pam's. I hope she does, cos the shop next door is a sweet shop.

We got to our new street and the lorry parked outside our new house. I was looking forward to living in a house. It was gonna be fun having stairs. As we arrived, the old couple who were moving out, were getting into their removal van. The old lady was being lifted into the back of the van in a wheelchair. Her legs were all puffy and blotchy – like sausages Dad cooks for supper before they burst and the fat spurts out. The old lady was crying and saying she didn't wanna move.

'It's a bit bloody late for that, the crazy old bat,' said Dad to Tiny.

The crazy old bat told Mam she'd been living in Springfield Road since 1937. That's ages ago. Mam said that she wasn't even born 'en, but Dad was, and in 1937 they didn't have any telly. How did they watch Hawaii Five-0 or the Six Million Dollar Man? It must've been rubbish in 1937.

Our new next door neighbour came out to say hello. Her name is Mrs Morgan. She said Mr Morgan was away at work but would come and say hello when he got home. Another lady came to say hello as well, she's called Mrs Knight. She's really nice and brought us some cake. Dad said she looked like she'd eaten enough cakes herself, and Mam should ask her where the Risca keep fat club was.

After the old couple drove away in their van, we started to put our stuff in our new house. Mam and Dad had a row, while Tiny and the other blokes got the kettle from the box marked 'Bedroom' and made some tea. It was ages before they got the big stuff into the house. Tiny said this moving lark was going to give him a bloody hernia. Tiny was getting really sweaty and smelt worse than a hundred of Dads socks and pants.

It took ages, but all our furniture and boxes were in our new house. My new bedroom had all my toys in it and a new wardrobe. We got it from Nana and Gransher Balding – I'm not allowed to put any Warlord stickers on it.

Our new house is much bigger than our flat. We've got a garden in the front and one at the back – all to ourselves. There's three bedrooms and an attic. An attic is a room in the roof. Dad said it's where naughty boys go and where the bogeyman lives. Mam said Dad was talking rubbish and it's just full of creepy crawlies and big spiders.

Uncle John got a lift with Tiny in the big lorry. Dad said he was gagging for a pint and had a throat like an Arab's dap.

I didn't know Arabs had daps, I thought they wore sandals. Mam told him to wait 'til all the boxes were unpacked before he could go up the pub. Dad said something about Rome not being built in a day.

Our new house is ace, but Mam said it needs decorating and some new curtains. Dad told Mam to bugger off and went up the pub. When he came back, just before bedtime, he was singing 'On The Good Ship Lollipop'. He had some fish and chips, and Dad said cos I'd been good, I could have a chip buttie. Mam found some plates in a box that had 'Stuff for the shed' written on it.

We now live at 74 Springfield Road, Risca.

Chapter 9.

Shit, Fuck, Bollocks!

Wayne Ashby and Martyn Summers are my new butties. They're in my new class – in my new school. I like my new school. It's loads better than Waunfawr and the teachers are really nice and don't shout very much. They shout at Wayne Ashby though, that's cos he's always mucking about. He gets told off all the time. He drew a picture of a willy on Tracy Taylor's Ladybird book. Miss Gally made him stand in the corner of the classroom. He kept looking around, pulling faces, trying to make us laugh.

At playtime we play football or tag. Tag is when you have to touch someone and then run away – like they've got the mange. Then they have to touch someone else. Wayne Ashby's really good at tag. He can run really fast and no one can catch him.

It's been really sunny, but the girls still wore their tartan scarves, just like the Bay City Rollers. Wayne likes to nick their scarves and run away. Judith Goole loves The Bay City Rollers, all her clothes have bits of tartan on 'em. She says she's gonna marry Eric Faulkner when she grows up. Eric Faulkner plays guitar in The Bay City Rollers and all the girls fancy him. At playtime, they sing the Bay City Rollers song, marching around the playground:

B-A-Y, B-A-Y, B-A-Y, C-I-T-Y,
With an R-O-double-L, E-R-S,
Bay City Rollers are the best!

They sing it over and over, until Wayne Ashby sneaks up and takes one of their scarves and runs away. They try to catch him but he's too fast and climbs up a tree. I've got some Bay City Rollers socks but I haven't told Wayne Ashby. He'll make fun of me cos he says The Bay City Rollers are shit. I didn't even want the socks, Mam bought 'em for my birthday – I was seven. I also got a Hawaii Five-0 scrapbook and a Matchbox Superfast track set. Nana Sugden got me a Postal Order. Dad said he'd look after it for me.

Wayne Ashby's always teasing the girls. He told me girls wee and poo through the same hole. He said their fannies and bums are joined together. He said it starts from the front, where a willy should be, and then finishes at the back, by their bum. Wayne Ashby said that when girls grow up, that's where the babies come out from. They fall out when they unzip their fannies. Wayne Ashby knows loads of stuff. He's got two sisters, so he knows lots about girls.

Mam likes Martyn Summers the best out of my new butties. She says he's nice and polite. Mam says that Wayne Ashby is naughty. She doesn't like it when he comes home to play football or watch Hong Kong Phooey. Mam says he's a cheeky devil and he's gonna be a right trouble maker when he's older.

Mam doesn't come and walk me home from school anymore – not like Waunfawr. Ty-Isaf school is only up the road from our new house. I walk home with Martyn Summers. Sometimes we go to the shop, next to school and buy Black Jacks. If Wayne is with us, he nicks some sweets. I'm scared he might get caught and Mrs Shilling, who runs the shop, might think we steal sweets as well. But Wayne Ashby's really good at nicking sweets and never gets caught. He stole a Curly Wurly once, he hid it down his trousers. When we got to the park, the Curly Wurly was melted. Me and Martyn didn't want any.

On the last week of school, we went to the shop to get some sweets. Martyn had some new plastic planes for his birthday and he said we could play with 'em after school. Dad had loads of sand to make some concrete – he's gonna make a path in the back garden. Dad said we could play with Martyn's planes on the sand pile. We pretended it was a big Nazi mountain and we had to bomb it.

We walked through the park eating our sweets. Wayne Ashby had his pockets full of gobstoppers. He grabbed a load when Mrs Shilling had her back to us measuring Crazy Crocodiles and Dracula Fangs.

'Do yuh know what bollocks are?' said Wayne, chomping on a gobstopper.

'Bollocks? Dunno, don't think it's something very nice. My Dad caught his hand in the door and shouted bollocks. Mam told him off,' I said.

'I know what bollocks are. It's a cock and balls,' slurped Wayne.

'Is it a naughty word 'en?' I asked.

'Yeah, really naughty. If you get caught saying it you'll get a smack, I reckon,' said Wayne, sucking a gobstopper that made his mouth go all blue.

'It's not worse than saying piss!' said Martyn, his mouth all red from his Dracula Fangs.

'It is! Loads worse! Do yuh know what other word is really bard? And if you say it and get caught, you'd get sent to Borstal!' shouted Wayne.

I knew piss, shit and bollocks, but I didn't know there was a really naughty word that could get you sent to Borstal! I knew bastard, but that didn't count cos it's in The Bible, but I'm still not allowed to say it.

'FUCK!' shouted Wayne, in the middle of the football pitch.

'What does it mean?' I asked, Martyn stared at me with his mouth open. I could see his mashed up Dracula Fangs in his gob.

'It's when a man does a piss over a ladies fanny,' said Wayne, smiling. 'It's where babies come from.'

Martyn went all quiet, staring at me and Wayne. I wondered why you'd wanna piss on a fanny. Is that what Mams and Dads do? Martyn looked like he was gonna be sick but he'd eaten five Dracula Fangs and two Crazy Crocodiles.

'That's horrible!' said Martyn. 'I hope my Dad doesn't piss on my Mam's fanny!'

'FUCK! FUCK! FUCK!' I shouted.

Martyn and Wayne burst out laughing. It was ace having new swear words. We could say 'em in the summer holidays in the park. Then the bigger boys might let us play football with 'em.

'FUCK! BOLLOCKS! FUCK! BOLLOCKS! PISS! SHIT! FUCK! BOLLOCKS! FUCK!' we shouted, running with our hands and pockets full of gobstoppers, Dracula Fangs, Crazy Crocodiles and Dip Dabs. We were by the park gates shouting and laughing. We were laughing so much we didn't see Mr Shepherd walking his dog.

'Oi! You boys! Stop that filthy language at once! My ears are not a public convenience!' he shouted, shaking his walking stick around, while his stupid little dog barked at us.

We didn't say anything and I could feel my face going red.

Mr Shepherd lives across the road. He's really old and grumpy. Dad said he killed loads of Germans in the First World War and then killed loads more in the next one. Dad was worried about Aunty Maria bringing home a Jap fella. He said Mr Shepherd still thinks there's a bloody war on. But Aunty Maria isn't coming to stay anymore. Mam got a letter saying that they'll be coming to stay next year instead. Mam was in a really bard mood for ages. Dad was really happy cos he didn't have to decorate the spare bedroom or buy a new bed.

'There's no need for language like that. I saw men wounded by the Nazis that didn't use that sort of language. I'll be having a word with your fathers!' shouted Mr Shepherd, his face really purple and a bit of spit was at the side of his mouth. 'We'll see what you have to say for yourselves then!'

Martyn Summers said he was really sorry and asked Mr Shepherd not to tell his Dad. He said he would get into trouble and would gerra smacked arse. Martyn didn't wanna smacked arse. I didn't either, I didn't wanna smacked anything – Wayne didn't care. He stood there smiling, making Mr Shepherd even more angry.

'Why are you just standing there smirking, boy? Don't you have any respect for your betters and elders?'

Wayne shrugged his shoulders. Martyn was sobbing, looking down at the ground. He was holding his bag of Dracula Fangs and kept saying sorry. Mr Shepherd told us to get out of his sight and he never wanted to hear us swearing in the park again. We ran to my house faster than Tommy Rhys on sports day – without stopping.

'My Dad's gonna kill me!' sobbed Martyn.

'I don't think the stupid old fart will tell yuh Dad,' said Wayne.

'I hope not, he'll go mental, if he does.'

We played in Dad's sand pile with Martyn's plastic aeroplanes. It was a good game. I was the Japs and Wayne was the Germans. Martyn would only let us play if he was the RAF. Dad said it was okay to play in the sand, but said to make the most of it. He was gonna be using it for cement soon. He said if we were good, we could write our names in it when it was still wet. Wayne said we should write 'Fuck'. I don't think Dad would like the word fuck written in his new path.

After we finished playing war with Martyn's planes, Dad said we could watch Hong Kong Phooey in the living room. We sat on the settee and Dad gave us a glass of squash. I love Hong Kong Phooey. It's much better than Scooby Doo and Captain Caveman. Dad likes it as well. Mam came back from the shops and she wasn't very happy cos we were sitting on the settee. Mam said after the cartoons had finished we'd have to clear off, cos she wanted to watch Crossroads. Mam went the kitchen to put her shopping away.

There was a knock at the door and Mam shouted at Dad for him to go and see who it was. Dad said he didn't get any peace and bloody quiet. I could hear a bloke at the door, Dad was talking to him for ages.

'Gwyn, get yuh bloody arse 'ere!' shouted Dad.

'Shit, I reckon that's Mr Shepherd,' whispered Martyn.

'GWYN! I SAID GET YUH ARSE 'ERE, NOW!'

Martyn was right, it was Mr Shepherd, his face was still all purple and he still looked really angry.

'Now, what's this about you and the other stooges running through the park, swearing like a bunch of thugs?' said Dad.

'Dunno Dad.'

'What yuh mean, yuh dunno?'

I didn't say anything, I wanted Mr Shepherd to go away and leave me alone.

'Say sorry to Mr Shepherd, yuh foul-mouthed little bugger!'

I said sorry, but didn't mean it. Mr Shepherd said it was okay and didn't wanna hear me or my mates swearing again. I went back in the living room, Martyn was looking really scared. Wayne was watching telly, drinking his squash, laughing at Hong Kong Phooey getting tied up in a carpet. Dad closed the front door and came into the living room.

'Right 'en, yuh buggers, it's time you went home for yuh teas,' said Dad, pointing at Martyn and Wayne.

They jumped up from the settee and left the house as fast as they could. So fast, Wayne tripped on the front door step and nearly fell over. Mam wanted to know what was going on, and what all the shouting was about. Dad told Mam what about Mr Shepherd and about us swearing in the park.

'It's that bloody Wayne Ashby, Cliff, he's a little bugger, I tell you!' shouted Mam.

After my tea I had to go straight to bed. It was still really sunny outside. Even with my curtains closed, it was still bright and sunny, I couldn't get to sleep. I wanted to be in the front garden, kicking my football about. Or throwing stones at Mrs Haines' fat ginger cat. Later, I heard Dad outside in the shed. He was putting some tools away, and he must have dropped one on his foot.

'FUCK!-SHIT!-BOLLOCKS!'

'Cliff! Mind yuh bloody language!'

Chapter 10.

Weebles Wobble But They Don't Fall Down.

In the summer holidays I had to stay with Nana Sugden. Mam wasn't very well and had to go to hospital. She had something wrong with her leg and had an operation. Mam's had loads of operations, just like Steve Austin in The Six Million Dollar Man. But Mam can't see through walls or chase a fast train.

At Nana's, I played with Steven Whitby and sometimes my cousin, Rachel. She lives down the road from Nana – she's only five. Me and Steven made her eat a mud pie, she spat it out and was sick. Dad came to visit every Sunday and brought some toys and sweets. I got an Airfix kit and a new Tonka truck. Dad said it was for not being naughty for Nana Sugden – he didn't know about the mud pie.

When Mam got out of hospital, I went back home. Dad said I'd have to be good cos Mam still wasn't very well. She spends lots of time on the settee eating Jaffa Cakes and watching telly – just like before her operation.

My new school is called Danygraig. It's lots bigger than Ty-Isaf and has lots more boys and girls. Wayne Ashby is in my new class, but Martyn Summers is in a different one. Miss Davis is my teacher. She told us she was new at school as well and we were her first class. There are other boys and girls in my class that were not in Ty-Isaf, like Paul Button. He keeps dropping things cos he's really clumsy. We call him Coco.

We don't play football in the big yard cos the older boys in Years Three and Four play there. We go by the side of the school, on a small bit of yard, next to some bins – we play a game called spot. Spot is taking it in turns kicking the ball against the wall. You have to kick it back from wherever it lands from the last boy who kicked it. Coco likes to play spot with us, but he's not very good. He toe punts the ball and it goes all over the place. One time, he hit Mrs Combes, the dinner lady, in the side of the head. He knocked her false teeth out and they fell on the yard. She went mental. We had to go to the headmaster, Mr Powers, so he could tell us off. Coco told him about Mrs Combes' false teeth. Mr Powers laughed and told us to be more careful in the future. He told Coco he should play a different game, but he didn't call him Coco, just Paul.

Another boy in my class is called Lloyd Branson, but everyone calls him Pickles. Pickles isn't very good at football either but sometimes plays spot with us. Pickles likes drawing but he's rubbish at that too. He drew a picture of King Kong and Miss Davis thought it was a poodle. I thought it looked like one of Mam's balls of wool with some eyes on it.

In my class there's some older boys and girls. They're not very good at reading or writing so they have to do lessons with us. One girl is called Claire Pearson. Pickles likes Claire Pearson and he wants to be her boyfriend. I think having a girlfriend is stupid. They're rubbish at football and they can't throw stones very far. They don't like Doctor Who and are rubbish at playing war. If they play with us when we play war, they have to be nurses cos girls can't make gun noises.

Claire Pearson likes David Essex and went to see him in a concert. Pickles says he likes David Essex but he doesn't have any David Essex records. Wayne Ashby said he saw Pickles and Claire Pearson holding hands. We asked Pickles and he went all red and said they were just playing tag. Wayne called him a liar.

'I'm not a liar!' shouted Pickles.

'Yes you are, I saw you holding hands. You big girlo. You LOVE Claire Pearson you do! You wanna pick flowers and look at her knickers!' laughed Wayne, doing a little dance and blowing little kisses.

Pickles ran away, I think he was crying. Wayne ran after him singing 'Pickles is a girlo'. I went and played spot with David Pryce and Martyn Summers. They said they saw Wayne chasing Pickles, I told 'em Wayne reckoned he saw him holding hands with Claire Pearson. David Pryce laughed and said Pickles was a bummer.

'What's a bummer?'

'That's when you rub your bum with another boy's bum.'

'Why would you wanna rub yuh bum with another boy's bum?' asked Martyn.

'Dunno, my brother said it's what they do in Borstal,' said David, kicking the football really hard, sending it smashing against a drainpipe – SMACK!

After dinner time we did art. We had to make pictures with leaves, Miss Davis said we were making autumn collages. Pickles was helping Claire Pearson with her picture. Wayne Ashby went over to have a look, but lifted Claire Pearson's skirt so we could all see her knickers. They were yellow. I thought Claire was gonna scream, she didn't, she just punched Wayne in the belly. He fell on the floor holding his guts, he was groaning and said he couldn't breathe. Miss Davis went over to see what was happening.

'What's going on?' she asked, looking down at Wayne, who was curled up in a ball and rolling around.

Claire didn't say anything and carried on doing her picture. Pickles was holding a leaf, pretending Wayne wasn't on the floor. Tanya Burns told Miss Davis what happened.

'Is this true, Claire?'

'Yes Miss,' said Claire, still doing her autumn collage.

Pickles was all red and was still holding his leaf. Wayne said he was dying and had a broken belly.

'Oh, get up Wayne, stop being such a drama queen,' said Miss Davis, 'And get on with your picture.'

She told Claire off for hitting Wayne but said he was very naughty for lifting up Claire's skirt. Wayne got better very quickly and went back to his picture. Mark Slaters, one of the older thick boys, made fun of Wayne. He said he was a bummer for being hit by a girl. Wayne said it didn't hurt and he was only pretending. Mark Slaters called him a liar. We finished our pictures and Miss Davis put the best ones on the wall. She didn't put mine up. Miss Davies thought the Bionic Man wasn't very autumny. I thought it looked ace, and I did use lots of brown like she told us to.

The bell went for afternoon playtime and we all ran out into the yard. Mrs Davies shouted after us not to run, cos we could fall over and be in a wheelchair – like Ironside on the telly. I told Martyn Summers what happened in class. He thought it was funny Wayne got beat-up by a girl. And I told him Claire Pearson had yellow knickers.

Me and Martyn saw Wayne making fun of Amanda Dibley. She can't walk proper and sways from side to side. Wayne's always making fun of Amanda Dibley. He was singing 'Weebles wobble but they don't fall down'. Mrs Marsh heard him and grabbed him by his ear and marched him off to see the headmaster. Martyn said Wayne Ashby was stupid. On the way back to classes we saw him waiting outside Mr Powers' office.

Wayne still hadn't come back when our lessons started. Miss Davis was reading us a story called 'Charlie and The Chocolate Factory', it's really good. Miss Davies reads it to us every day. We're nearly at the end – Charlie and his grandad are the only ones left on the tour of the factory. Miss Davis was reading out a bit about Willy Wonka showing Charlie some crazy sweets, when Mr Powers came in the class with Wayne. Mr Powers said sorry to Miss Davis and asked if he could have a word with the class. He told Wayne to sit down at his desk.

Mr Powers said Amanda Dibley has something called spider biffida. And it's really naughty and mean to call her names. He said we shouldn't treat her any different to anyone else in school but we mustn't pick on her. I never make fun of Amanda Dibley cos Mam can't walk proper either. I don't know why Wayne Ashby makes fun of Amanda Dibley – he doesn't make fun of my Mam. If he did, she'd tell him off and I wouldn't be allowed to play with him anymore. When Mr Powers was talking about Amanda Dibley, Wayne's face was really red. Mr Powers thanked Miss Davis and said she could carry on with our lesson.

'Right then class, settle down,' said Miss Davis, some of the boys were asking Wayne what he'd done. Tanya Burns asked Miss Davis if she could catch spider bifida from Amanda Dibley. She said she couldn't catch it and not to be so silly. Miss Davis told us to be quiet and carried on reading our story.

After school I walked home with Martyn and Wayne.

Martyn's mam came to walk him home, she'd been shopping up Risca and gave us a Club biscuit. Wayne told us Mr Powers was really angry and, if he gets caught making fun of Amanda Dibley again, he'll get the cane. Wayne lives a couple of streets before my house, just before Jacky Jones, the newsagent. He thanked Mrs Summers for his Club biscuit and ran up the road singing the Hong Kong Phooey song.

When we got to my street there was an ambulance parked outside my house. Mam was being lifted out of the front door by some ambulance men. I ran to see what was wrong. Mrs Morgan from next door said she was okay, but just had a little fall. She'd hurt her bard leg and had to go back to hospital. Before Mam went in the ambulance, she said I'd have to stay with Mrs Mogan 'til Dad came home from work. Mrs Morgan said she'd make me a lovely tea – I had fish fingers, peas and chips.

Mr and Mrs Morgan don't watch telly, they listen to the radio. I asked if their telly was broke, they laughed and said they didn't like watching telly much. We've always got the telly on in our house – even when there's nobody in the living room. Mam says having the telly on makes it more homely. But Dad has the sound down when Songs Of Praise is on. I'm glad I don't live with Mr and Mrs Morgan, it would be really boring. I was glad when Dad came home, he let me watch News At Ten, then a bit of the weather forecast before I went to bed.

Dad said Mam would have to spend some time in hospital. He wouldn't be able to look after me cos he had to go to work. He said I'd have to stay with Nana Sugden again. I like staying up Nana Sugden's, but Dad said I'd have to go to a different school for a while as well. I didn't wanna go to a different school. I like Danygraig school cos all my friends are there. I like playing spot with Martyn Summers and David Pryce. I like messing about with Wayne Ashby and teasing Pickles cos he holds hands with Claire Pearson. And I wanna find out what happens at the end of Charlie and the Chocolate Factory. But most of all, I want Mam to get better and come home.

Chapter 11.

Nana's Jazz Fags.

Mr Thomas drove me back to Nana Sugden's in his big car. I had to hold a plastic bag, just in case I was sick again. He said he didn't want any vomit over his clean seats. Nana wasn't very happy when Mr Thomas brought me home. She thought I'd been naughty, but Mr Thomas told her I'd been sick. She asked me if I'd eaten too many sweets on the way to school. I said I'd only had a couple – but I'd eaten loads.

On the way to school I bought some Black Jacks, a packet of Chewits and the new Warlord with a free gift – a crack-shot pistol. It's ace. The man in the shop said he'd sell out by the end of the day. Keith Barrow bought Warlord as well, he doesn't even like Warlord, he likes Whizzer and Chips. He said he was gonna chase Tina Lewis with his pistol. He put some worms in the hood of her coat last week, Keith's always being mean to Tina Lewis. Like the time she wanted a wee and he held her on the ground 'til she pissed her pants.

When I got to school I was feeling sick. I'd had all my Black Jacks and I only had a couple of Chewits left. I'd drank some of Keith Barrow's Top Deck as well – it was horrible, it had bits of crisps in it. I was in sick in the yard by some girls playing hopscotch. They screamed and ran away to get a teacher. My Black Jacks and Chewits were splattered over square 3.

Cos Mam's not been very well and staying in hospital, I've been at Nana Sugden's – even at Christmas. It was okay though, Uncle Roger and Aunty Nita came and Nana made Christmas dinner. We drove down to the hospital in Uncle Roger's new car to see Mam. I had loads of presents, the most ever. I got a Meccano set, some Hong Kong Phooey pyjamas, a book about football and a chemistry set. Uncle Roger said he'd show me how to make a stink bomb – Nana Sugden told him off and said I was only allowed to make nice things.

After Christmas, I went home and stayed with Dad for a bit. He said it was to give Nana Sugden a rest. I went out to play with Martyn Summers and Wayne Ashby. They said that Pickles spends all his time with Claire Pearson. We thought that was horrible. Being friends with a girl is stupid. They play silly games, like nurse and kiss-chase and want to go and pick daisies up the fields. I liked playing with Martyn and Wayne, I'd not seen them in ages. But after a couple of days, Dad said I had to go back and stay with Nana Sugden.

I'll be going home again soon though, cos Mam is nearly better. Then I can go back to my proper school. Penllwyn school is okay but I like Danygraig better. I made friends with Adrian Harris and Richard Temple. They live in the same street as Nana and we play football by the garages. I told 'em about the swear words Wayne Ashby taught me. Richard Temple told his sister, Lucy – she's only five. When Lucy was watching The Magic Roundabout, her mam told her to get ready for bed. Lucy told her to fuck off. I'm not allowed to play football with Richard Temple anymore.

Nana Sugden made me eat some bread and soup. She said it would settle my stomach cos I'd been sick. While I was eating my soup, Nana looked through my coat pockets for sweets. I knew she wouldn't find any cos I'd ate 'em all.

After my soup and bread I felt much better. I didn't tell Nana I was feeling better, just in case she made me go back to school. She let me watch the telly, Pipkins was on. Nana doesn't like Pipkins, she says it's a load of rubbish. I like Pipkins. I like Hartley Hare and Topov the monkey. But my favourite bit is when it's time for a story, they show lots and lots of clocks ticking and getting louder and louder. That's the bit Nana doesn't like and she says it's too noisy. When she doesn't like something on the telly, she goes outside to the garden.

Nana Sugden likes the garden. Dad does all the big digging cos Nana's too old. She looks after the greenhouse and all the little plants. She grows lots of things like tomatoes and cucumbers. Dad helps her grow the big stuff like potatoes and onions. I like potatoes, that's where chips come from.

Nana grows other plants as well in the greenhouse. Plants with special leaves that Nana uses when she does her cooking. Nana's favourite plant, one that she picks the most, she doesn't use for cooking at all. She puts the leaves under the grill and crunches 'em up. Then she mixes 'em up with her bacca. Nana does rollies like Dad, but she makes 'em in a little machine. She makes 'em all neat and tidy. Not like Dad's rollies that are all bent with bits of bacca sticking out the ends. Dad calls Nana's rollies, 'Jazz Fags', and they are good for her half-righteous. I don't know what half-righteous is, but Nana Sugden says it gives her gyp in her joints.

We had to write a story at school about what we did at Christmas. We could draw a picture as well. Sandra Howell wrote about using her make-up set on her dog, Holly. She drew a picture of Jesus roller-skating. I wrote about going to see Mam in hospital and about Nana making her rollies with her special leaves. I drew a picture of Hong Kong Phooey beating up a baddie.

Nana came in from the garden and said it was too cold. She put some of her special leaves under the grill and made a cup of tea, Nana gave me a glass of milk.

'You look better now, got some colour back in your cheeks,' said Nana, rolling one of her jazz fags.

Pipkins finished and The One O'Clock News came on with Leonard Parkin. Nana likes Leonard Parkin. He told us about an aeroplane called Concorde. Concorde is a new super aeroplane that can fly around the world really fast. One plane flew from London and another one flew from somewhere called Paris. Nana said Paris was in a country called France, where they don't speak proper like we do, but French.

Nana lit her jazz fag, sipped her tea and watched the news. Nana has her tea in a cup and saucer. Mam and Dad have big mugs – Dad never washes his mug. Mam says Nana Sugden is a proper lady, she doesn't talk like everyone else. Nana Sugden was born in London and Mam says that's why she's a bit posh. When Nana goes out somewhere, even if it's just down the shops, she dresses up all smart and tidy. She wears pretty dresses and has white lace gloves and a posh hat. Dad says she's always dressed all posh, even when he was a little boy and they were skint.

After Nana smoked her jazz fag, she went all quiet and had a little nap in her chair. While she was napping, I read my Warlord. Nana doesn't like me reading Warlord, she says it's a load of nonsense. Nana likes it better if I read one of my Ladybird books instead. In my comic, Union Jack Jackson was fighting the Japs with his American butty, Sean O'Bannion. But they ran out of ammo so they had to sneak up behind the

Japs and hit 'em over the head with some sticks. The Japs in Warlord are really nasty, so Union Jack Jackson beats 'em up or shoots 'em.

Aunty Maria is bringing home her Jap boyfriend soon. Aunty Maria wrote Mam a letter saying they'd be staying with us for a week. Dad wasn't very happy, he had to put up new wallpaper in the spare bedroom and buy a new bed. He said it was lucky his butty up the pub could get one on the cheap. It fell off the back of a lorry, just like our washing machine and fridge.

After the news finished and the weather man said it was gonna rain, Crown Court started. Nana Sugden likes Crown Court, she watches it everyday and thinks it's ace. It was about a lady who was found beaten up in a garden, a man in a funny wig said her husband did it. He was telling everyone in the court about how naughty he was, when there was a knock on Nana's back door. Nana turned off the telly and went to see who it was. I could hear a man talking and he said he was from something called Social Services. He sounded like a teacher from school and was a bit posh.

'What can I do for you?' asked Nana.

'Well, Mrs Sugden, it's a little awkward and I'm just here to check things out really,' said the man, 'It's nothing to be worried about.'

Nana told the man I was only staying while Mam was getting better in hospital. He said he knew that already but was visiting about a story I'd written at school. Nana asked the man to sit down and poured him a cup of tea from the pot. He was really nice and looked like Leonard Parkin off the telly.

'Gwyn's class was asked to write a story about what they did over the Christmas holidays. But Gwyn's teacher was a little alarmed, when Gwyn described in his story what seemed to be the preparing and smoking of cannabis.'

Nana's face went a funny colour and she put her hand over her mouth. Just like when I smashed one of her ornaments.

'Now, I'm not here to pass judgement, Mrs Sugden, but as you may or may not know, the cultivation and smoking of cannabis is a criminal offence. I have been asked in this instance to have a word without involving any of appropriate authorities,' he said, then drinking some tea.

Nana told the man about her half-righteous, and she only has a bit now and again to ease the pain. The man listened to Nana and was very nice. Nana looked very worried and I hoped she wouldn't have to go and have the cane or anything.

'Look, Mrs Sugden, I would advise you to be more careful in the future. I understand your need for pain relief but children say what they see, without understanding the consequences.'

The man told Nana he'd say, that in my story, I was getting all my facts mixed-up. He said everything would be okay and not to worry. Nana Sugden thanked the man and said she was very sorry.

When the man left, I thought Nana Sugden was gonna shout at me for getting her into trouble. But she said I was not to tell anyone about her special leaves ever again. She's not supposed to have any, and she was lucky not to be told off by the police. Nana let me watch some more telly and later I was allowed to play with Steven Whitby from next door when he got home from school.

Nana Sugden doesn't drink much booze, not like Dad, but before tea, she had a very big glass of whisky. She said I was a boy an' half and I gave her bad nerves.

Chapter 12.

Noodles And Chips.

Mam went down the railway station with Uncle Graham to pick up Aunty Maria and her Jap boyfriend. Mam still has to have someone with her when she's driving cos she still hasn't passed her test. She thought she was gonna pass but she did lots of things wrong. She hit a bollard, didn't stop at a zebra crossing and went through a red light. Mam said the driving examiner had it in for her. Dad said she's just a dangerous driver.

Dad took me up The Exchange for my dinner – I had a pie. He told his butties about me getting Nana Sugden into trouble cos of her jazz fags. Everybody laughed and Dad said I almost gave Nana a heart attack. When we got home, Dad made me have a wash, put on my new shirt and purple tank-top. Dad said he didn't know why we had to dress up like the bloody Queen was coming round for tea, but he said it would keep Mam happy.

I wanted to go out and play football with Martyn Sayers. Dad said I had to stay home 'til Mam got back with Aunty Maria. I went out to the front garden and waited for 'em to turn up. It was ages before Mam's blue mini came down the road, Uncle Graham was driving. Aunty Maria and Mam were in the back. Aunty Maria's Jap boyfriend was in the front, next to Graham.

In Warlord, Union Jack Jackson calls the Japs, Nips. Dad said I can't say Jap or Nip cos it's not very nice. Mam made me put my Warlord comics away in my bedroom. She said there's too much Jap-killing in it, and Maria's boyfriend might see it. I didn't want Maria's Jap boyfriend getting upset. There was a film on the telly called *Tora! Tora! Tora!* with lots of Japanese pilots bombing the Yanks. Dad said the Japs were evil little buggers.

I ran to the front gate, they got out of the car and Maria's boyfriend saw me and smiled. He looked nice and not like the baddies in the film. Aunty Maria told me to give her a kiss, and she said I'd grown lots since the last time she saw me.

'This is Junichi,' said Aunty Maria.

Junichi shook my hand and did a little bow. I nearly laughed, I'd never seen anyone bow before. Maria said that he didn't speak much English and not to ask him too many questions. Dad came out and shook Junichi's hand and said hello to Aunty Maria. Uncle Graham was taking two large suitcases off the roof-rack. He said they weighed a ton.

Mrs Morgan from next door was in her front garden watering her flowers. She watered the same flower for ages cos she was looking at Junichi. Dad took Aunty Maria and Junichi inside. Uncle Graham was trying to carry the suitcases, he said they must be full of stones. Mam saw Mrs Morgan and pointed to inside our house.

'He's Japanese,' said Mam.

'Ooh, that's unusual, Beryl,' said Mrs Morgan, trying to peek through our front window.

'Gorra go luv, gorra put the kettle on. Ooh, I hope he likes Mellow Birds, it's all I've got in,' said Mam, grabbing my arm and taking me inside.

Junichi was in the back garden with Dad. Dad shows everyone round his garden. Aunty Maria told Mam about Junichi and his family. She said they were very successful business people and Junichi wants to open a new night club in Tokyo. Tokyo is where Aunty Maria and Junichi live. Mam told me everyone in Japan lived in wooden houses and the walls were made of paper. Dad said Mam talks a load of old codswallop.

Uncle Graham took the big suitcases upstairs to the spare bedroom. When he came back down he was puffed out and had to sit down and have a rest. Uncle Graham's home from the Navy and was staying with Nana Balding and Gransher, so Aunty Maria and Junichi have to stay with us.

'How long you home for, Graham?' asked Aunty Maria, sipping her Mellow Birds from one of Mam's best mugs that had Weston-Super-Mare on it. She only gets the posh holiday mugs out when we've get visitors.

'I go back in two weeks, going to South America next, then the Caribbean,' said Graham, still puffed out.

Dad and Junichi came in, Junichi said Dad's garden was very nice and he called Dad, Mr Cliffson. Mam and Aunty Maria finished their coffee and got ready to go up to Nana Balding's. Dad was staying home cos later he had to go to work – he was on nights. Nana Balding and Aunty Maureen were doing a special surprise party for Junichi. Mam helped make some decorations and make a welcome sign. Dad said he couldn't imagine what on earth they've done, but it was bound to be a monstrosity. I like monsters.

We walked out to the car and Mrs Morgan was still in her garden. She still had her watering can but had Mrs Harris and Mrs Wakefield with her. They were chopsing and staring at

Junichi. Uncle Graham said we should sell tickets.

I sat in the back of the car with Mam and Aunty Maria. We drove through Risca and Mam pointed things out for Junichi. She showed him the chip shop, Mr Bryant's broken van, and the pub where Mam and Dad used to live in the olden days. Aunty Maria told Mam that Junichi didn't need to know what everything was. But Mam still told him all about Pam's wool shop, and and how how many different colours of wool Pam sold. She didn't tell him about me doing a poo in her bucket though.

'Ooh, I could knit Junichi a scarf, do you have scarves in Japan?' asked Mam.

'Yes, Beryl, of course we have scarves in Japan,' laughed Aunty Maria, 'We don't live on the moon.'

When we got to the old water mill, Junichi asked if we could stop so he could take a picture. We got out of the car and Uncle Graham took a photo in front of the water wheel. I pulled a face like a monster but Uncle Graham saw me and told me to stop acting the goat. We finished having our photo taken and drove up to Nana's. Junichi was looking at the smoke coming out off all the chimneys. Mam saw him looking at the smoke, he was smiling and said something in Japanese to Aunty Maria that made her laugh.

'What did Junichi say, Maria?' chuckled Mam.

'Oh, it's just a Japanese joke, Beryl, it doesn't make much sense in English.'

Mam doesn't like it if she doesn't know a secret, Dad says it drives her bananas. If someone knocks on a neighbour's door and they're not in, Mam goes out and asks if she can take a message.

Uncle Graham parked Mam's car outside Nana's house.

Nana Balding was looking out of the front window. She saw us and looked all excited, and then disappeared. Aunty Maureen came to the front door, waving her arms about like a mad loon. We got out of the car and Maureen started shouting.

'They're 'ere! They're 'ere!'

'I know they're bloody well 'ere, Maureen, I was the one that just bloody told you!' shouted Nana Balding from inside the house.

Aunty Maria didn't look very happy, she whispered something in Japanese to Junichi that made him chuckle. Aunty Maureen wouldn't let us through the front door, even though Mam said she needed a wee.

'Why ever not?' shouted Mam, trying to look round Aunty Maureen to see what was going on inside.

'We're not ready yet, hang on a minute,' said Aunty Maureen, still blocking the front door.

'We can't stand here all day, come on, I need a wee!' said Mam, 'I'm sorry about my sister, Junichi, she's bloody simple.'

Aunty Maria had her head in her hands saying 'Oh my God' over and over, 'What have they done?'

From inside the house, Nana yelled it was okay for us to come in. There were balloons all over the walls and Christmas tinsel hanging off Nana's pictures. Hanging over the table, at the back of the room, was a big sign:

Welcome To Wales From The Orient

Nana's living room was full of people, some of 'em I'd never seen before. Nana Balding was wearing a strange pointy hat and a dressing gown with dragons on it – just like Mam's. Uncle Malcolm was waving some chop-sticks, Uncle Ronnie had a pretend long moustache, like Ming the Merciless on Flash Gordan. Mam had a little flag of Wales and was waving it round her head. Nana shouted at Malcolm to play some music. On a chair, next to the telly, was Uncle Malcolm's record player from the front room. He put down his chopsticks and put on a record. It was 'Kung Foo Fighting' and when it came on, it was really loud.

Aunty Maria was stood in the middle of the room with her mouth wide open. Gransher was sat down with a bottle of beer. He didn't look like he was having much fun, neither did Junichi. Aunty Maria said something to Junichi in Japanese, Junichi shrugged his shoulders and smiled. Nana Balding grabbed Junichi's arm and said she would tell him who everyone was. She was talking really loud and was doing lots of pointing.

'That's Malcolm, that's Graham, that's Beryl...'

'He know's who I am, Mam. I picked him up from the bloody station!' said Mam.

Nana carried on telling Junichi who everyone was, even Mr Wallace, the bread man. Junichi said hello to everyone and shook their hands.

'I saw him looking at the smoke from the chimneys on the way up,' said Mam to Aunty Maureen as 'Kung Foo Fighting' finished for the third time.

'He probably hasn't seen our sort of houses before,' said Aunty Maureen, still dancing even though the music had stopped.

'Well, they do be living in caves out there don't they?' whispered Mam.

After Junichi had met everyone, Nana said it was time for the buffet. A couple of ladies and Aunty Maureen went to the kitchen and brought out lots of big bowls and plates with tin foil over 'em.

'Come on everyone, tuck in. There's loads of food 'ere,' shouted Nana, taking off her silly pointy hat. 'We even got some Japanese type of food, so Junichi wouldn't feel left out, Maria.'

'What do you mean, Japanese type of food? Oh Mother, what have you done?' asked Aunty Maria.

When the foil was peeled back from the bowls and plates, there were loads of chips and sausage rolls. In the biggest bowl, in the middle of the table, there was a big pile of noodles. Aunty Maureen said there were six packets of Vesta Chow Mein.

'You like Vesta Chow Mein, Junichi?' asked Maureen, munching on a mouthful of chips.

'Sorry, what Vesta Chow Mein?' asked Junichi, looking at the big bowl.

'Ooh! It's all the rage here now, very modern it is, it's what they eat in outer space, so they say,' said Aunty Maureen, spitting out bits of food.

Gransher took Junichi outside to show him his Woolsey. Aunty Maureen said Junichi wouldn't wanna see Gransher's old banger and should leave him alone to enjoy the party. Aunty Maria said Junichi likes old cars. Junichi came back in to get his camera. He told Aunty Maria he wanted to take some pictures of Gransher's Woolsey. Mam thought he was doo-lally taking pictures of the Woolsey. But Mam's always showing people a picture of her Mini, she carries one round in her purse.

Nana Balding saw Junichi taking pictures, she said it would be a good idea for everyone to have their photo taken.

Junichi was taking a picture of the front of the Woolsey when everyone went out to the front garden. Uncle Graham had an old camera that was loads bigger than Junichi's. It was big and grey, and you have to look down from the top to take a picture. Junichi's camera looks really ace, like the man's from the newspaper when Mam had her picture taken with her new car.

Nana made everyone stand in front of the yucca tree. Every time there's any photos taken at Nana's house, it's always by the yucca tree. Uncle Graham says that it's been in more pictures than the Statue Of Liberty – that's in America where the Cowboys and Indians live.

Aunty Maria wanted a picture of me, Gransher, Nana, Mam, Uncle Graham and Junichi. We bunched close together in front of the yucca tree. I climbed on Uncle Graham's shoulders and we all said 'Cheese' – I pulled a face like a monster. There were loads more photos taken, even Mr Wallace, the bread man, had one taken with Junichi. Aunty Maureen said we should go back inside cos it was getting cold.

When we got back in, Uncle Malcolm had a big pile of noodles and chips and drinking more beer. He looked a bit giddy and kept laughing. Gransher said he didn't want any noodles cos he had a bit of a bard belly. He said he wasn't feeling very well and had to sit down for a bit. Nana said he'd probably had too much beer. Gransher said he hadn't had many and thought he was coming down with a cold.

Mr Wallace, the bread man, and the other neigbours, said goodbye to Aunty Maria and Junichi and went home. Uncle Malcolm was sat down next to the big bowl of noodles. There were lots of empty beer bottles under his chair – I counted seven. He looked a bit funny and he wasn't laughing anymore.

All of a sudden Uncle Malcolm jumped up from his chair and ran out through the kitchen and into the back alley. He made a big horrible sound – like a big burp. Then, SPLASH! Uncle Malcolm was sick all over the outside wall and into the drain. Everyone was really quiet, even Nana Balding.

'Hah! Vesta Chow Mein!' laughed Junichi.

Chapter 13.

Hong Kong Phooey.

Dad makes the best bacon sandwiches in the world. Mam likes her bacon really crispy, but me and Dad like it juicy. Mam has red sauce on hers. I like brown sauce, lots, so it spills out the sides when I eat it. Junichi likes bacon sandwiches too – 'Very nice, Mr Cliffson,' he says.

Mam was worried that Junichi would only eat Japanese type food. Like the noodles Nana and Aunty Maureen got for the party. But Junichi likes proper food, like we eat. He loves chips, sausages, fried egg, Findus Crispy Pancakes and even black pudding. He likes beer as well – just like Dad.

Martyn Summers came over after school to see Junichi. He said he'd never seen a proper Jap before. The blokes up the Chinky didn't count – they're from somewhere called Vietnam. Wayne Ashby wanted to see Junichi as well, but Dad's still angry with him cos he wrote 'Pissflaps' in Dad's wet cement. Pissflaps is Wayne's new favourite word. He nicked a big marker pen from school and writes it everywhere. He wrote it on the bins by the old people's home. Mrs Tringle called the police but they don't know it was Wayne.

Before Junichi has his bacon sandwich in the morning, he gets up early and does slow kung fu. It's not like what Hong

Kong Phooey does from his book of 'The Hong Kong School of Kung Fu'. It's really slow, like in slow motion. Like when The Bionic Man does a big jump to catch a baddie.

Junichi's got a special kung fu suit. It's got baggy trousers and a baggy jacket. On the day Junichi and Aunty Maria had to go back to Japan, I got up extra early to do slow kung fu. I followed Junichi to the front garden, I wore my Hong Kong Phooey pajamas that I'd got for Christmas.

Junichi's slow kung fu is called tiecheese. Tiecheese is really hard. You have to stand still and do slow things with your arms and legs. Junichi did some big breathing really loud and pushed his arms out. He lifted his leg in the air and spun round really slowly. I tried to do the same, but I fell over and crushed some of Dad's flowers.

Mrs Bidder and Mrs Combstock, from down the road, were on their way to the shops. Mrs Combstock had a shopping bag with Harrods written on it. Mrs Bidder had her tartan trolly. They stopped by the front gate to see what we were doing. They were whispering to each other and, when Junichi did a special move – one I couldn't do proper and nearly fell into the daffodils – they both went 'Ooh!'.

'He's very professional, isn't he?' said Mrs Combstock to Mrs Bidder, clutching her Harrods shopping bag.

'Ooh, he's like that oriental fella off the telly, Elsie,' said Mrs Bidder.

Mark Slaters was peddling up the street on his Tomahawk. He'd just finished his paper round and was going back to Jacky Jones' to drop off his empty bag. He saw the old ladies by the gate and wanted to know what they were looking at. He pulled his bike up onto the pavement and watched us in the garden.

'Wha' they doin'?' Mark asked Mrs Bidder.

'Some sort of karate luv, like on the telly,' she said.

Mark Slaters and the old ladies watched us do our tiecheese. I was getting cold and my feet were wet from the soggy grass. Junichi did one last move and stood still, he did another big breath and put his hands together – like in Sunday school when we say the Lord's Prayer. Mrs Combstock and Mrs Bidder clapped their hands. Junichi opened his eyes and saw the two old ladies and Mark Slaters. He was so busy doing tiecheese he didn't know they'd been watching. He smiled and did a little bow. Mrs Bidder and Mrs Combstock walked up the street, I could hear them saying to each other how good Junichi was, and they'd never seen the like in Risca before.

'Oi, Sugden, who's the Chinky and why you wearing yuh pajamas?' shouted Mark Slaters, pulling the front of his bike in the air, pretending to do a wheely.

'He's norra Chinky, he's from Japan!'

'Same thing, aint it?' said Mark Slaters, getting on his bike and riding off up the street, flicking Vs.

'He your friend?' asked Junichi, as we walked back into the house.

'No, Mark Slaters is stupid.'

'Yes, not nice boy,' laughed Junichi, 'Velly rude is the Mark Slaters.'

Dad was in the kitchen cooking the bacon.

'You two black belts finished yuh hai karateing?'

I told Dad about Mrs Bidder and Mrs Combstock, and how good Junichi is at tiecheese. I didn't tell Dad I fell into his flowers though.

'Well, ready for yuh breakfast then?'

'Smell velly nice, Mr Cliffson,' said Junichi.

Aunty Maria was having a bath, Dad says she spends more time in the water than a bloody mermaid. She has lots of bubble bath, special soaps and creams. Mam say's she thinks she's a bloody film star. I think Aunty Maria is very pretty, and if I have a girlfriend when I grow up, I'd like her to be as pretty as Aunty Maria.

Dad gave us our bacon sandwiches and I put lots of brown sauce on mine. Dad made a pot of tea and Junichi had a cup of Mellow Birds. Mam had already eaten her sandwich while we were doing our tiecheese. She was in the back garden talking to Mrs Morgan from next door. I heard her say that she was going to drive Junichi and Aunty Maria down to the station with Uncle Graham. It made me sad, I didn't want Aunty Maria and Junichi to go back to Japan. I wished they could live with us, that would be ace. Dad gulped down his tea and did a big burp.

'Oops, better out than in,' said Dad, wiping off some brown sauce from his mouth with the back of his hand, then wiping it on his trousers.

Junichi laughed and took a big gulp of coffee. Dad and Junichi don't say much to each other, Dad can't speak any Japanese, and Junichi doesn't speak much English. But they did lots of things together while Junichi was staying with us. Dad took him for a walk up the mountain to he could see the view from the top. Sometimes you can see as far as Cardiff, and you can see the Severn Bridge. Dad even took Junichi up The Exchange for a beer. Dad said Bernard Cox's face was a picture when he walked in with him. Junichi bowed and said hello, and Bernard bowed back. Yanto and Midge didn't stop laughing for ages. They now call Bernard Cox, Grasshopper, like the man on the telly programme, Kung Fu.

After Aunty Maria had her bath, Junichi went and changed out of his tiecheese suit. Dad told me to put some clothes on and take off my Hong Kong Phooey pajamas. Uncle Graham arrived to take Aunty Maria and Junichi to the railway station with Mam. Dad helped Uncle Graham put the suitcases on the roof-rack and moaned they were heavy.

Aunty Maria gave me a hug and a kiss goodbye. Kissing and hugging is stupid but I don't mind hugging Aunty Maria. Dad said lots of blokes up the pub would like to hug and kiss her as well. Junichi did another little bow. I gave him a big hug cos I think he's ace and I'll miss him loads. I think Dad will as well, but he just shook Junichi's hand and said goodbye.

Junichi is nothing like the Japs in Warlord.

Chapter 14.

Save Your Kisses For Me.

Mam bought the new curry Findus Crispy Pancakes, they're really nice – much better than the ham and cheese ones. We had chips from the chippy to go with 'em. Lots of salt and vinegar, so my chips go soggy. I like to open up my crispy pancakes and dip my chips in the yummy filling. Mam does too.

We were having a special tea to have in front of the telly. Mam loves The Eurovision Song Contest, and singing for the United Kingdom was Brotherhood Of Man. Their song is called Save Your Kisses for Me. It's always on the radio and Mam really likes it, it's okay, but it's a bit girly. Dad had to go to work but he hates the Eurovision Song Contest. He hates programmes that have singing and dancing, but he likes Miss World – there's loads of singing and dancing on that.

Mam bought a big bag of sweets and some chocolate to eat after our tea. She said not to tell Dad, she hid 'em behind the settee when he was getting ready for his night shift. Mam's been looking forward to the Eurovision Song Contest for ages. She bought the Radio Times special, it had a chart with all the songs that were gonna be sung from all the different countries.

When Dad left to go to work, Mam got the sweets and

chocolate from behind the settee. She bought 'em from Jacky Jones' when she was getting bacca and Rizlas for Dad. Mam went up in the car, even though she's not supposed to cos she still hasn't passed her test. She failed her test again the other week. She scratched the car when she drove into the side of a bus stop. Mam said she should have passed cos she didn't hit anything else.

The show started and a lady talked in foreign and then in English. A man called Terry Wogan talked over the Eurovision programme saying what was going on. Mam likes Terry Wogan, she listens to him on the wireless in the morning. He's the only man on the wireless that's on Dad's slipper list. Terry Wogan said Brotherhood Of Man were gonna sing first. I was glad they were gonna sing first, cos I might fall asleep and miss 'em. I fell asleep during Miss World, Mam woke me up to watch a lady with a crown on her head. She was crying and there were lots of photographers taking her photo. Dad watched it too, and said the lady had a nice set of knockers.

Before the group sang their song there was a little film about Brotherhood Of Man. Then a man came on who conducts the orchestra. He waves a stick about in front of the men with the violins and trumpets. His stick looks like one of Mam's knitting needles. I asked Mam if I could have a knitting needle so I could pretend to be a conductor like the man on the telly. She said okay, but I was to be careful, and not act the goat.

The song started and Mam sang along. She didn't know the words proper and made some of 'em up. The bloke that does most of the singing looked like Dickie Davies from World Of Sport. Mam thought he looked like him too. Brotherhood Of Man finished their song and everyone in the audience clapped. Mam clapped as well, but she can't clap proper cos she's only got one good hand. When Mam claps she uses her good hand and claps it on her bard one.

'Ooh, I think they're gonna win this, I reckon,' said Mam.

The next group to sing was from a place called Switzerland. They were called Peter, Sue and Marc and they sang in English. They weren't as good as Brotherhood Of Man. The next singers and groups all sang in foreign – they were rubbish – from countries like Germany and a place called Luxembourg. I asked Mam where Luxembourg was and she said it's somewhere foreign – I don't think she knew.

After a bloke from Belgium sang, it was Ireland's turn to sing a song. Mam said Ireland always have a good song and they're really good singers. A bloke called Red Hurley sang for Ireland, Mam said she'd never heard of him. Terry Wogan said he was very famous in Ireland and had a very good voice. Mam thought Red Hurley sounded like Tom Jones, I thought he was shit. I looked at the Eurovision Song Contest chart in the Radio Times, it said that there was another ten acts to sing after Red Hurley – I counted them.

I was bored of pretending to be a conductor and gave Mam her knitting needle back. It was gonna be ages before the voting started, so I went upstairs and got my Meccano set. I made a sports car, just like the one James Hunt drives on the telly. James Hunt is the bestest racing driver, Mam thinks he's dishy. I asked Mam what dishy was and she said it's a fella that the ladies like. I asked if Dad was dishy and she started laughing until she went a funny colour and couldn't speak.

James Hunt's car is ace, it's the best car in the world. I wish Mam's car was like James Hunt's, but his car's only got one seat. I don't think it's got a boot either, so Mam wouldn't be able to put her shopping in the back. There aren't any windows in James Hunt's car so there'd be no room for Mam's disabled sticker.

Terry Wogan was making fun of the foreign singers, it made Mam laugh and she said he was a daft bugger. After every song, Mam said it was a pile of old rubbish. I was building my racing car when a group called Fredi & Friends came on to sing. Fredi was really fat. He was bigger than Uncle Griff and as big as Tiny, Dad's butty who helped us move from Waunfawr Gardens. The song was very good and had a brilliant bit that went 'Pump-Pump' and Fredi and two ladies shaked their bums together. I thought Fredi & Friends were the best group on the Eurovision. Mam thought they were silly and she said Fredi should lose some weight, as she got a sweet from her dressing gown pocket. All the groups and singers had done their songs and Terry Wogan said it was time for the voting.

'Well, I think Brotherhood Of Man should win this, I reckon,' said Mam, with her mouth full of sweets.

I wanted Fredi & Friends to win, cos the winner had to go back on stage and sing their song again. I wanted to see Fredi and his mates do their funny dance. Brotherhood Of Man were a bit rubbish and they didn't have a good dance – they just wiggled their feet.

The voting started and Mam was all excited. The United Kingdom voted first and gave twelve points to Switzerland – you can't vote for your own song. Brotherhood Of Man were doing really well, they were getting lots of top marks with twelve and ten points. Ireland only gave us three points and Terry Wogan said it was mean – 'Come on lads,' said Terry. Mam said Ireland were just jealous cos our song was better than Red Hurley's. After all the countries finished voting,

Brotherhood Of Man had 164 points and was the winner. The two ladies in the group jumped up and down and were crying. The two blokes just smiled and shook hands.

After the two ladies stopped crying, Brotherhood of Man went back on the stage to sing their song again. Mam tried to sing along, but she still didn't know the words. Mam sang and jiggled her foot, and I played with my racing car. I pretended to be James Hunt, beating Niki Lauda to win the World Championship. I used one of my Corgi cars to be Niki Lauda, cos I didn't have enough wheels in my Meccano set to make two cars.

Mam said it was time I got ready for bed. I put my Meccano away and Mam went to the kitchen to make me some Horlicks. Mam's not very good at making Horlicks, she always has bits floating in it. Mam brought in my Horlicks and told me to drink it, then go to bed – it was so hot it burnt my tongue. She went back out to the kitchen when the phone rang. She moaned it was late for the phone to be ringing, and it had better be important.

'Yes, this is Mrs Sugden,' she said, talking in her posh voice – Mam tries to be posh when she's on the phone.

'Ooh, I see, is he alright?' asked Mam, sounding worried.

Mam talked on the phone for a bit and then came in the living room.

'You'll never guess what's happened? Yuh father's gone and hurt his hand at work,' said Mam. 'They've sent him to the hosptial to get it x-rayed, they reckon he could have broken it. They're gonna send him home in a taxi.'

'Can I stay up and wait for him to come home to see his bandages?'

'No you bloody well can't, get to bed, you can see yuh

father's bandages tomorrow.'

I finished my Horlicks and went upstairs. I asked if Dad would get a bionic hand, like Steve Austin off the telly. Mam said to stop being so bloody stupid. She said she'd have to make Dad some supper, ready for when he got back from the hospital.

Before I fell asleep, I could smell Findus Crispy Pancakes and hear Mam singing Save Your Kisses For Me.

Chapter 15.

The Parkie.

Dad's been home from work with a bard hand. It's in a big bandage and it looks like a boxing glove. Dad said he'd never known a summer like it. He said the garden was a write-off cos he's not allowed to water it cos of the hose pipe ban.

A fight nearly started in our street. Mr Lovesy was washing his car, Mr Harris shouted at him that he shouldn't be cos of the water shortage. Mr Lovesy told him to fuck off. Mr Harris went crackers and they were in the middle of the road, shouting and swearing at each other – it was ace.

I went on the Sunday school parade, it was so hot I got sunburn on my arm. I didn't want to go, but Dad said if I didn't he'd give me a smack. We marched round Ty-Isaf, past my old school, up Channel View and back round to the end of our street. We had a big sign with the name of our chapel on it – Ty-Isaf Baptists. Loads of people watched the parade. Old people clapped when we marched past, some sang the hymns we were being made to sing. I saw Tanya Burns from my class, I hoped she didn't see me. I didn't want anyone from school knowing that I went to Sunday school. Martyn Summers goes to Sunday school, but he doesn't care if anyone knows. He likes Sunday school – he likes the singing.

It was so hot during the parade, Linda Moses fainted.

Mr Dolman picked her up and carried her on his back, still singing 'Oh Jesus I Have Promised' at the top of his voice. Dad thinks Mr Dolman's a nutter. When I got home my arm was bright red. It was so sore I had to have some cream on it. The next day the skin started peeling – I showed everyone. Mrs Shilling in the sweet shop said it was horrible. She told me off and said she didn't want flakes of skin getting mixed up with the Candy Necklaces.

The hot sun made the school field all hard and there were big cracks in it. On sports day, the janitor filled them in with sand. I ran a race and came second, I couldn't catch Tommy Rhys, he's the fastest runner in school. He can even run faster than the older boys. Mr Evans said he's so good at running, one day he might run for Britain. But Tommy Rhys doesn't wanna be a runner, he wants to be a zoo keeper, like Johnny Morris on Animal Magic.

After school we play cricket in the Welfare – that's the park in Ty-Isaf by our street. All the boys play from my road, Wayne Ashby plays as well. We play for ages 'til someone's mam comes over to say their tea is ready. It's normally Mrs Wakefield, Julian's mam. He has his tea at the same time everyday and it's always Birds Eye beefburgers, chips and peas.

There's lots of boys that play cricket, some I don't know. The older boys pick the teams and decide if we do overarm bowling. Overarm is really fast and it's hard to hit the ball. Tommy Rhys is really good at doing overarm bowling. Martyn Summers tried doing overarm once and it went backwards and up in the air. It hit Tony Hislop on the head, he was lucky we were only using a tennis ball. Cricket balls are really hard and it would have smashed Tony Hislop's skull in.

We play in the middle of the football pitch, sometimes the

parkie comes and chases us away. We hate the parkie – he looks after the Welfare and the Bowling Green, across the road, near the river. We're not allowed to go on the Bowling Green – that's where the old blokes play bowls. The Bowling Green's flat and smooth. It's so smooth and perfect, it looks like a carpet. If we go anywhere near it, the parkie or Slurp, comes running out of their hut and chases us away. Slurp is the parkie's mate – we're really scared of Slurp. The older boys said he went to prison for sucking boys' cocks. And if he catches you, he'll take you in his hut and mess about with yuh privates. Wayne Ashby said Slurp caught a boy from Tany-Bryn, and he's still in his hut tied up, with his pants pulled down.

When the football season is over the football pitch doesn't have any goal posts. Risca United play on the Welfare. The pitch never has much grass on it, the goal area has no grass at all. That's why we play cricket in the middle of the pitch. But cos of the hot sun, the grass was all yellow, like straw. Dad reckoned there'd be no grass at all by start of the new season. He said it would be like a bloody mud bath by October.

Wayne Ashby had a new cricket bat, we all wanted to have a go of it. His dad got it from the new sports shop in Risca. Mr Ashby said it was the same bat that Geoffrey Boycott uses. He also said Wayne's football boots were the same as Kevin Keegan's, and his snooker cue was used by Ray Reardon to win the World Championship. Martyn Summers' dad said Wayne Ashby's dad is full of shit.

'Geoffrey Boycott hit over two hundred runs against India with a bat like this,' boasted Wayne, hitting a long dandelion into the air.

'Yeah, but my old man says that Geoffrey Boycott doesn't

hit sixes, he just sits in front of the wicket hitting singles,' said David Pryce, spitting his chewing gum out and kicking it in the same direction as the dandelion.

I didn't know what they were talking about. I like playing cricket, but I don't know about the rules. When we play cricket in school, Mr Evans shouts at me for not knowing what to do. I just like hitting the ball as hard as I can. But I never get it in any of the back gardens around the park like Tommy Rhys does. If it goes in one of the gardens we take it in turns to sneak in and get it back. But if it goes into Mr Shepherd's, it's really hard to get the ball back. Mr Shepherd stands at the end of his garden watching us. He shouts if the ball goes anywhere near his fence. Dad says he's got sod all else to do and he's losing his marbles.

David Pryce's brother, Ian, and Michael Knight pick the sides. They take it in turns and everyone wants to be on the team that Tommy Rhys is on. He's the best bowler and the best batter.

Julian Wakefield came running over, eating a Curly Wurly. He said his tea would be ready soon and asked if he could bat first. Michael Knight said he could bat second if he gave him a bite of his Curly Wurly. Tommy Rhys was bowling and he kept hitting Michael Knights' legs. Ian Pryce said it was LBW – that means he should be out. But Michael said that the ball was going wide and he was still in.

'You cheating fucker!' shouted Ian Pryce, going up to Michael Knight's face, so close it looked like they were kissing.

We looked at each other waiting for a fight to start, but Adrian Hendon told 'em to get on with the game. Adrian Hendon is really big and everyone does what he says.

The next ball, Tommy Rhys bowled really fast. Michael

Knight hit it right up in the sky, and Tommy Rhys caught it as the ball fell back down.

'HOWZAT!' shouted Tommy.

Michael Knight wasn't very happy. He gave the bat to Julian Wakefield, who was worried that his mam would be in the park any minute calling him for his tea. Julian stood in front of the stumps, they weren't proper stumps, we used a bit of old gate we found.

'Come on then, Tommy,' shouted Julian.

Keith Taylor was behind the stumps being the wicket keeper. A wicket keeper stands behind the batter and tries to catch the ball if he doesn't hit it. Tommy Rhys did a long run and bowled the ball. It rushed past Julian's head, who took a big swing with the bat. He swung the bat so hard it flew out of his hands and smashed Keith Taylor in the face. Julian Wakefield ran off, out of the park as fast as he could. He didn't even pick up his Curly Wurly.

Blood was dripping from Keith's hands as he held his face, and he was making strange noises. We all stood there staring – we didn't know what to do. Michael Knight bent down to look at Keith's face. He pulled his hands away from his mouth so he could see how bard it was. It was horrible.

'Is it bard?' cried Keith, blood gushing from his face and onto his Bionic Man t-shirt.

'FUCKIN' HELL!' shouted Wayne Ashby, picking up his cricket bat from the grass, checking to see if there was any blood on it.

Keith's teeth looked like they'd been pushed back into his face. His top lip looked like a burst black pudding. Then Keith saw the blood on his Bionic Man t-shirt.

'Fuckin' bollocks! I only just got this t-shirt! My mam's

gonna fuckin' kill me!' cried Keith, holding out his shirt.

'Nothing gets blood out, our mam told me,' said Martyn Summers

'Think you'd better go home Keith, I reckon you'll need to go to the hospital,' said Tommy Rhys, who had picked up the ball and was throwing it up in air and catching it.

Keith slowly walked out of the park, clutching his face, groaning. Tommy Rhys walked with him, some other boys went with 'em as well. Martyn Summers said he wanted to go home and watch Rentaghost and have his tea – he was having fish fingers and beans. Me and Wayne walked out the other end of the park. Wayne swung his bat at flies that were hovering round some white dog poo – white dog poo comes from poodles. We were by the park gates when we heard a man shouting behind us. It was the parkie and he was running and shaking his fist.

'Bollocks! Lets run for it!' shouted Wayne, already sprinting out of the park.

The parkie's not a very good runner. He caught Tony Hislop once though. He was pissing down the slide and the parkie saw him. He was still trying to do his flies up and fell over. The parkie took him home to tell his dad what he'd done. Tony said his dad told the parkie to piss off.

Me and Wayne ran out of the park and hid in someone's front garden. We didn't run to my house cos then the parkie would know where I lived. We heard him panting as we crouched down behind a hedge. Mrs Bidder was coming down the street with her tartan shopping trolley.

'Excuse me, you haven't seen two boys running, 'ave you?' asked the parkie, still out of breath. 'One of 'em's got a cricket bat.'

Mrs Bidder could see us hiding and gave us a little wink, without the parkie seeing.

'You're a bit old to be chasing young boys about ain't you, luv?' laughed Mrs Bidder.

The parkie walked back to the park and we waited for him to disappear. We thanked Mrs Bidder for not giving us up and Wayne ran home for his tea. When I got to my house I saw Keith Taylor in the back of his dad's car. His mam was in the back with him, I think she was crying. Keith had a towel against his mouth and it was all red from blood. I waved but they didn't see me. I told Dad what happened in the park and about Keith's smashed face. I didn't tell him about the parkie chasing us though. But I did tell Dad about Slurp, and about the boy in his shed with his pants pulled down. Dad laughed and was still chuckling while we watched Rentaghost.

Chapter 16.

He Dribbles On His Plastic Banana.

The summer holidays were ace. It was really sunny and I played football and cricket everyday. The parkie chased us a couple of times, but he never caught us. Slurp doesn't run after us anymore. He just sleeps outside his hut. We saw inside and there was a pile of nudey magazines.

Mam failed her driving test again and she was grumpy for ages. Dad said if she fails any more she'll have to bribe the driving test man. A bribe is what you pay someone to do you a favour. On The Sweeney, there was a bent copper. A bent copper is a copper that takes a bribe. Regan hates bent coppers. He and Carter, beat 'em up in a pub or in a scrap yard. They beat up slags as well – slags are the robbers. The Sweeney is ace.

In the summer holidays, Mam was always up Nana Balding's. Gransher's not been very well. He had to see a special doctor in Bristol, we drove down in the Woolsey and on the way home we had a picnic. Gransher was really quiet and didn't say much – neither did Nana Balding. Mam said Gransher's not very well cos of the dust from working down the pit. Nana said he used to come home from work as black as the ace of spades. They didn't have a bathroom in the olden days. Gransher had to have a bath in an old metal tub in front of the fireplace. I hope Gransher gets better.

When I went back to school I was still in Miss Davis' class – but she's not called Miss Davis anymore. She said in the summer holidays she got married, her new name is Mrs Powell. There are some new boys and girls my class that are a year younger. The older ones from last year are now in a different one. Mark Slaters is in Mr Parker's class, he got the cane on the first day back. He did a piss in the sink cos he couldn't be bothered to go to the bogs.

On Saturday and Sunday I stay with Nana Sugden cos Mam is always up Nana Balding's. Dad comes and gets me on Sunday night and we go home on the bus after Nana makes our tea. Where Nana Sugden lives, they're building lots of new houses. The builders don't work on Saturday and Sunday, so me and Steven Whitby sneak round to have a look. We have to be careful, there's a guard who makes sure no one steals anything. We've only seen him once, he's an old fella who lives in a caravan on the building site. He saw us playing in some sand and he went crazy. He chased us away, waving a big stick. He's talks funny and we can't understand what he's saying. Nana said he's Irish and to stay away from him.

Dad's got a butty up The Exchange, he's called Paddy, he's Irish. He works for the council. He got so drunk he pissed himself in the pub once. He was fast asleep under the telly when there was a dripping noise. Bernard Cox shouted who'd spilt their pint, but coming from Paddy's trousers was loads of wee, dribbling down on to the floor. Bernard chucked him out and had to scrub the floor with Domestos.

Me and Steven Whitby went up the building site looking for treasure. There's long bits of plastic, screws and tins of paint. If the guard is in his caravan, we sneak round the back of the houses and look inside. We know when the guard's in his caravan – he has his wireless on really loud. Steven Whitby's dad says the guard is always down The Penllwyn Arms getting tanked up, or calling in on one of the widows with a bottle of stout. Mr Whitby says there's a lot of lonely old sods in the Penllwyn that just want a bit of company – even if it's an Irish pisshead covered in dried cement. I think he means the guard.

There's lots of empty beer cans outside the guard's caravan. They're all called Colt 45, he must really like it cos he drinks loads. We took a few empty cans once, and went up the Common to throw stones at them. The Common is behind the building site. There's an old car there that we play in, we pretend to be Regan and Carter from The Sweeney. But sometimes we have to hide behind the bushes if the older boys come. They drink beer and sit in our old car. I don't like it when they're there.

One of the big boys, I think he's called Jeno, had his girlfriend with him. We hid in the bushes cos last time he saw us he said he'd smash our faces in. We didn't want our faces smashed in. They were drinking beer and started kissing, then he unzipped his trousers and it looked like he was doing press-ups on top of her. His girlfriend was making funny noises and kept saying 'Oh God'. Later, I told Adrian Harris and he said they were shagging. Shagging is what grown-ups do when there's nothing on the telly.

We saw the guard go in his caravan with a bag full of beer cans and some chips. We thought he would be ages so we went into the building site and had a look around. One house had a new staircase, we crept in and went upstairs. Not many of the houses on the site have an upstairs yet – some don't even have a roof. Steven found a big bag of nails, I grabbed some and put 'em in my pocket. We looked for a hammer to hit our nails with. The builders' tools are locked in a shed but sometimes they leave stuff around. I found a screwdriver once and I gave it to Dad. He asked where I got it from, I told him I found in the street and it must have fallen off a back of a lorry.

'Gwyn, look what I've found,' shouted Steven.

He found a bag – a bag full of tools. This was the best treasure ever. It was too heavy to carry, even with both of us trying to lift it. There were too many big tools inside. There was loads of ace stuff – saws, measuring tapes, screwdrivers and hammers. I found a small hammer that fit into my pocket, we took out all the big heavy stuff so we could carry the bag and carried it out of the house.

We could still hear the wireless from the guard's caravan, we thought he must be still inside – drinking his beer and eating his chips. We carried the tool bag past the caravan and hid it behind a big hedge. We ran back into the building site and found some bits of wood. We got out some nails from our pockets and hit 'em in with the small hammer, taking it turns. Nana Sugden says it's good to share. We pretended to be builders, Stephen found some workmen's gloves. They were huge and looked really funny. We hit some nails into a door that was next to a wall. We were hitting 'em really hard – it was ace. BANG, BANG, BANG!

'YA FECKIN' LITTLE FECKERS, YA!'

The guard was runing at us. His face was all red and he was holding his trousers so they wouldn't fall down. He tried to grab me but I was too quick for him. I ran round him and out into the road. Steven Whitby went between his legs and into one of the houses on the building site.

'I'LL FECKIN' KILL THE PAIRS OF YA!' shouted the guard.

I ran up the road as fast as I could. I saw Steven coming out of a house and he hid behind a big steamroller. The guard was still shouting and swearing – I'd never heard anyone swear so much, not even up The Exchange. Steven Whitby ran out from behind the steamroller and was running behind me. The guard picked up a rock and threw it, I could hear bits of it smash as it hit the road.

'YA BASTARDS, I'LL FIND WHERE YA LIVE!' he shouted.

We knew he wouldn't be able to catch us – but we kept running up the road. The bus from Blackwood was next to the bus stop by Nana Sugden's house. We couldn't see the guard behind it so we didn't know if he was still chasing us.

'What shall we do?' asked Steven.

We were panting and puffed out from running so fast. Nana Sugden was down the shops, I'd have to wait 'til she got back to get in. We're not allowed to play in Steven's anymore cos we broke some glass in Mr Whitby's greenhouse.

'Let's go to Mrs Williams' house,' I said.

Mrs Williams lives across the road. She looks after Paul, he's older than us, Nana said he's sixteen. He can't talk proper and dribbles like a baby. He has to wear a nappy, Nana said he's got brain damage, so Mrs Williams has to look after him. We go and see him sometimes, Nana says it's good for him to see other boys. But we only go cos Mrs Williams has lots of pop and we always get a fig roll. I like fig rolls.

We ran up the front garden of Mrs Williams' house and up round the side of the house and knocked the back door. Steven kept a look out for the guard, making sure he wasn't coming down the road. Mrs Williams opened the door, she was wearing her pinny and a pair of washing up gloves, bright yellow with soap studs over 'em.

'Ooh, hello boys, nice to see you,' she said, with a big smile – Mrs Williams is always smiling.

'Hello Mrs Williams, we've come to see Paul,' I said, while Stephen kept looking up the road.

'Ooh, that's nice. He'll like that, come on in, I'm just finishing the washing up.'

Me and Steven nearly got stuck in the door as we tried to get in at the same time.

'Bloomin' 'eck! What's the rush, lads?' laughed Mrs Williams.

The kitchen smelled like biscuits. Mrs Williams is always making things. She brings Welsh cakes, biscuits and sponge cake round to Nana Sugden's all the time. Her Welsh cakes are much better than Nana Balding's.

Paul was sat on the settee making his baby noises. Mrs Williams told us to go and say hello. He was in his pajamas and dressing gown, even though it was the afternoon. If I stay in my Hong Kong Phooey pyjamas too long after I get up, Mam tells me off.

Steven Whitby's scared of Paul. He says he's frightened that he might bite him. Steven is younger than me and a bit of a scaredy-cat – he's only seven. At Danygraig I don't play with anyone younger than me, except Julian Wakefield, but only cos he lives down the road and he's got a rabbit.

We said hello to Paul, but he carried on playing with his baby toys. He has loads of 'em, some aren't even toys for babies – they're for dogs. Paul puts his toys in his mouth and sucks 'em. His favourite is a plastic banana. He's always putting that in his mouth, he dribbles all over it. Mrs Williams has to keep wiping his spit off. It's horrible.

'Do you boys wanna glass of pop and a fig roll?' asked Mrs Williams, from the kitchen.

Mrs Williams always has lots of coloured pop. She buys loads from the popman who comes once a week in a big lorry. Nana Sugden only gets a bottle of white, but Mrs Williams gets red, black, yellow, orange – even a blue one. I like red pop the best, Steven Whitby likes orange. Paul's not allowed any pop. It makes him burp and then he's sick. Paul drinks milk from a beaker, like a baby. Mrs Williams has to put it in his mouth and make sure he drinks it. If he doesn't want any, he screams really loud and sometimes growls like a dog. That's why Steven Whitby thinks he might bite him.

We drank our pop and scoffed our fig rolls. We had two each – they were yummy. Paul's not allowed any fig rolls, he eats baby food from a plastic bowl, Mrs Williams feeds him with a plastic spoon. Most of his food goes over his face. Dad gets his dinner all over his face as well. Once he got gravy behind his ear, Dad found it when he was having a scratch, watching Columbo.

We helped Mrs Williams tidy up Paul's toys that were on the floor. He likes to throw them across the room. Mrs Williams keeps Paul's toys in a box next to the settee. We put all the toys that he'd thrown, back in the box – we found some behind the telly and one in a plant pot.

'I reckon the guard would have stopped looking for us now,' said Steven, as he put a rubber monkey in the box.

'Yeah, my Nan should be back from the shops by now as well.'

We were just about to tell Mrs Williams that we were going, when there was a knock on the back door.

'Ooh, I wonder who that could be?' said Mrs Williams, checking her hair in the mirror.

Mrs Williams straightened her pinny. She checked her hair again and said she wasn't expecting anyone.

"Ooh, hello Mr Doyle, what a nice surprise. I'm getting a lot of visitors today, it's like Spaghetti Junction in this house,' laughed Mrs Williams.

She asked the man to come in. We couldn't see who he was, and when he was talking to Mrs Williams, he was very quiet. But I went cold and scared when I heard his voice – it was the guard.

'It's the bloke from the building site,' I whispered to Steven.

Steven Whitby said he wanted a poo. We looked round the room for somewhere to hide. There was behind the settee, but we would have to move Paul off, and pull it out to get behind it – and Paul would start screaming. I hoped the guard wouldn't come into the room and go away. Steven said he was gonna shit himself.

'You wanna say hello to Paul, Mr Doyle?' asked Mrs Williams, 'He has two young boys visiting from across the road, nice boys there are. They pop in all the time to see our Paul.'

I could feel my heart beating, and I could smell Steven's fart. I thought the guard was gonna kill us. I could smell poo.

'Say hello to Mr Doyle, boys,' said Mrs Williams, who'd brought in the guard into the room.

'Hello dere, lads,' said the guard.

He was smiling, but then his eyes went really wide and his face went purple, like the colour of Ribena. He had a blazer on and it was buttoned all the way up. His hair was combed flat and it looked greasy. Normally his hair is all crazy and standing up. He was holding a some flowers and bottle of beer. He looked stupid, but he looked angry.

'Well, say hello to Mr Doyle then, boys,' chuckled Mrs Williams, 'Cat got yuh tongues?'

We said hello to the guard, who was staring at us.

'Would you like a cup of tea, Mr Doyle?' asked Mrs Williams.

'Yes, please, three sugars, that would be grand,' said the guard, still staring.

We told Mrs Williams we had to go home for our tea. We brushed passed the guard really quickly, just in case he tried to grab us. We thanked Mrs Williams for the pop and fig rolls and opened the back door.

'Aye, boyos,' said the guard, just as we opened the back door, ready to run home, 'I'll be seeing ya round 'den, lads?' he said, winking.

I made sure Nana Sugden bolted the back door before I went to bed. She wanted to know why I wanted it locked, I said I heard there was a mad axeman on the loose. She told me not to be so stupid. I'm never gonna play on the building site again. And I'm not going to Mrs Williams' any more. Even though she does have lots of coloured pop and fig rolls.

Chapter 17.

All I Want For Christmas Is My Two Front Teeth.

Dad said if I was good I might get a new bike from Father Christmas. I'd been very good – Mam and Dad hadn't caught me doing anything naughty for ages. All the other boys at school have bikes, Robert Cummings has gorra racing bike, brand new, it wasn't even a Christmas present. He got it cos his mam and dad got divorced. That's when mams and dads don't live together anymore and they take you to the zoo and buy you stuff. I wished my Mam and Dad would get divorced so I can get ace presents and go to the zoo.

The bike I want for Christmas is called a Chopper. It's ace. It looks like a motorbike, like what the Hells Angels ride on the telly. It's gorra big seat and a big gear knob. The back wheel is massive, but the front one is small. A boy up the road has got one, he's gorra flag on the back tied to an aerial he nicked from an old car. He rides round the park on it with a radio strapped to the back seat. It looks cool. Martyn Summers has gorra bike, he had it for his birthday. His birthday's in July, I'm older by thirteen days. Martyn worked it out. Martyn is better at sums than me, even though he's younger. Martyn's bike looks just like a Chopper, but it's smaller and called a Tomahawk. Mark Slaters has got one as well, he does his paper round on it. When I get my new bike from Father Christmas, me and Martyn are gonna go on a bike ride up the canal.

I'd been awake for ages. My Doctor Who alarm clock said it was five o'clock when I first woke up. I wanted to go downstairs and open my presents. Dad goes mental if I get up early. I tried to go back to sleep, but all I could think about was my new bike and my Christmas presents. Mam likes to open all the presents together. But I don't care what Mam and Dad get for Christmas. Dad gets lots of socks, Mam has smelly perfume and tights but she does get some chocolates. I like to eat some when I'm opening my presents. Mam tells me not to eat too many, she says it'll spoil my Christmas dinner. Christmas dinner is horrible, we have sprouts and parsnips. I'd much rather have Toblerone or some Quality Street.

I heard Dad get up for a wee, my Dalek's laser gun said it was seven o'clock. I jumped out of bed and ran downstairs.

'Dad! Can it be Christmas now?' I shouted, as Dad pulled the flush, even though he was still doing a wee.

He said not to go in the living room til Mam got up. I shouted upstairs to wake her. She shouted back down telling me not to be so loud, said I'd wake Mrs Morgan, next door. I could see Mrs Morgan in the garden, feeding the birds. Mrs Morgan always gets up early and feeds the birds.

'It's okay Mam, she's in the garden.'

Mam says I've got a bloody answer for everything. Dad said if I went into the living room he'd give me a thick ear. I had to go in the kitchen, I didn't wanna go in the kitchen. There wasn't any presents in the kitchen, just a turkey and lots of things in Tupperware, ready for Dad to cook the dinner.

Mam got out of bed and I could hear her moving about upstairs.

'She's got the grace of a baby elephant, yuh mother has,'

said Dad, lighting a rollie and putting the kettle on for a pot of tea.

Every morning Dad makes a pot of tea to drink with his rollie. He makes it in a big teapot and uses loads of teabags. He uses the same cup, it's white on the outside but inside it's all brown. Mam thinks it's disgusting. She says that's what Dad's insides must look like. He says if you clean it, it will take away the flavour of the tea. He likes four sugars as well and proper milk. Mam bought slimming milk from the milkman, Dad went mental when she put some in his tea. 'Whatcha trying to do to me woman? Bloody poison me?' he shouted.

Mam came downstairs and she was wearing her Japanese dressing gown. Dad poured her a cup of tea and put in her slimming milk and three sugars. He made a face and grunted when he poured the slimming milk, 'Bloody white water, its that stuff is,' he said.

'Can we go and open the presents now Dad, look, Mam's up.'

'Hold yuh bloody horses, just give us five minutes. Go and clean yuh teeth 'en you can have a Quality Street,' said Dad, blowing out smoke that went all over the runner beans.

I cleaned my teeth, it didn't take long. Dad said I should always spend at least three minutes brushing. That's ages, that's nearly as long as a Tom and Jerry cartoon. Dad says if I don't clean my teeth proper they'll fall out. Dad doesn't have any teeth, he has false ones that he soaks in a coffee mug in the living room.

After I cleaned my teeth and Mam and Dad finished their tea, we went into the living room to open the presents. Mam made me close my eyes as I went through the door. In the middle of the room was a brand new, big red Chopper with a

136

load of tinsel on it. It was the bestest bike I'd ever seen.

'Can I take it outside for a ride?'

'Not 'til later, and not 'til you've got dressed. You can't ride round Ty-Isaf in yuh Y-fronts on Christmas morning,' said Mam, grabbing some Quality Street.

Under the Christmas tree there were lots more presents. I looked at the tags. I put Mam and Dad's all to the side and piled mine up ready to open in front of the telly. Dad made me move them to the settee so he could see what was on.

'Oh Cliff, for goodness sake, nothing will be on yet. It's still early,' said Mam, munching on a toffee.

I don't like the Quality Streets with yellow wrappers. They're always hard and chewy.

Mam and Dad got rubbish presents. Socks, perfume and tights. Mam gave Dad a new jumper, one she didn't knit herself. It looked the right shape – not like one Mam knitted, but it had a big reindeer on the front.

'Where the bloody 'ell to you think I'm gonna wear this to?' asked Dad.

'I thought you could wear it down the pub. It's nice and snazzy, Cliff, you'll be the talk of the pub!'

'Course I'll be the bloody talk of the pub! They'll be locking me up and throwing away the pissing key!'

'Cliff! No need to swear, it's Christmas bloody day!'

While Mam and Dad were rowing, I opened my other presents. I got a Warlord annual, a Shoot football annual, a Doctor Who writing set, two selection boxes, a chocolate orange, a toy gun, a new football – it was brown – and Nana and Gransher Balding got me a Jim'll Fix It soap-on-a-rope. Mam said I could have one chocolate from a selection box. I didn't want any chocolate, I wanted to go outside on my new Chopper.

'You like chocolate from the selection box, it's Christmas, Gwyn!' said Mam looking worried.

'You only want him to open his selection box so you can have a bloody bar of chocolate,' laughed Dad.

'No, I don't, Cliff. I've only had a couple of Quality Streets, I'm not greedy.'

'Couple? You've had half the bloody tin! You only opened it last night,' said Dad, rolling a load of rollies to smoke while he got Christmas dinner ready.

Mam made me go upstairs and put my clothes on. From my bedroom I could see Julian Wakefield playing outside with his new Evel Knievel toy. I got dressed really quickly, I wanted to show Julian my new bike. Dad helped me carry it outside and said not to go too fast. Julian was on the pavement with his Evel Knievel. I got on my new Chopper and rode it up the street. Dad stood by the gate making sure I was okay and looked up the road for any cars. I went up to the end of Springfield Road and back to where Julian was playing.

'Aye, Gwyn, is that a new bike?'

'Yeah, it's a Chopper.'

'It's massive!'

Julian showed me his Evel Knievel. You had to put Evel Knievel and his bike in a red machine. Then you turned a handle round and round and Evel Knievel shot off really fast. It was brilliant – I wish I had one. Julian asked if he could have a go on my Chopper.

'You can't, my Dad's watching, he'll go crackers,' I said, but I didn't want to give him a go anyway.

Some of the older boys in our street came out with their Christmas presents. Michael Knight had a Liverpool football kit – his legs were all purple from the cold. His brother showed us his Action Man helicopter and Amanda Harris had a doll and pram. Julian's sister got a big plastic doll's head that you put make-up on. Girls' toys are stupid.

Mam called me in and Dad put my Chopper in the back garden. He said he'd put a cover over it. He'd borrowed a padlock and chain from work to make sure no one could come round and nick it. Mam made me open a selection box when Dad wasn't looking and took a Topic bar to eat with her Snowball. Mam went into the kitchen to help Dad with the dinner. I read my Shoot annual – about Kevin Keegan and how he keeps fit training with Liverpool.

I was starting to feel a bit hungry, I went to the kitchen to see how long dinner was gonna be. Mam and Dad didn't see me, Dad had his hand on Mam's shoulder, she looked upset. 'Don't worry, luv, he's a tough bugger, yuh father,' said Dad.

'I know Cliff, I'm just really worried, that's all.'

Mam started crying and Dad gave her a cwtch. I didn't want Mam and Dad to see me, I went back in the living room and pretended to read my book. I could hear Mam crying in the kitchen and Dad was trying to get her to stop. He said it was Christmas and I might hear her being upset. I knew Mam was crying about Gransher and I hoped he wasn't in trouble. Dad told me that he went to prison once for selling washing machines that had fallen off the back of a lorry.

When we had our Christmas dinner, Mam wasn't crying anymore. She ate all her food and asked Dad for more turkey, roast potatoes and some stuffing. She even had three bowls of trifle and some Christmas pudding. We pulled lots of crackers but the jokes and presents were rubbish, Dad wouldn't put on his paper hat. He said it made him look stupid. Dad did the washing up. I went in the living room with Mam, we had some more chocolate from my selection box before Dad came in. I had a Mars Bar and Mam had a Caramac.

'Mam, what's wrong with Gransher, is he in trouble?'

'Look luv, he's not very well. It's all the years he spent down the pits, see,' said Mam.

She looked like she was gonna cry again, but she didn't, and I was glad. I didn't want Mam to cry. Mam took a big bite out of her Caramac and watched On The Buses.

I got a piece of paper from my Doctor Who writing set and wrote a letter to Jim'll Fix It:

Dear Jim'll,

Please could you fix it for me to make my Gransher better. He is not very well. I watch your show every week and I think it is smashing.
Gwyn Sugden.
Age 8 and a half.

PS. The lady next door to my Nana has got a gnome that looks like you.

Chapter 18.

Gransher's Bard In Bed.

Mam's not been very happy. Dad says that Gransher's not very well and it's making Mam very sad. He said I must be very good and not muck about otherwise he'd give me a bloody good hiding. Mam's been so upset she's stopped reading her Highway Code, she's learning it for another driving test. She's supposed to have someone with her when she's driving, but Mam's been going up the shops and Nana Balding's on her own. Dad says if the filth catch her they'll lock her up and throw away the bloody key. In The Sweeney the villains call the policemen the filth.

I wanted to go out on my Chopper with Martyn Summers and my new butty, Kevin Walsh. Walshy's in my class, he's gorra new bike as well, but it's not as good as my Chopper. He has to be careful on his bike, cos he has fits. We know when he's gonna have one, Walshy goes all funny and doesn't know who anyone is. He dribbles, just like Paul at Mrs Williams'. After a couple of minutes, Walshy's okay again, but he has to go home and have a tablet. We ride our bikes by the canal. We're not allowed to go too far, but one day we're gonna go to Asda. I'm not gonna tell Mam and Dad though – they'd go mental.

Martyn, Wayne Ashby and Walshy called for me and asked if

I was coming out on my bike. But Mam said I had to see Nana Balding and Gransher. I wanted to go out with my butties, but Dad said to do what I was told. Martyn said they were gonna muck about by the river, then they were gonna make a den. I wanted to muck about by the river and make a den as well. I told 'em that I had to go up and see my Nana and Gransher, Wayne called me a bummer.

I got in the car with Mam, we pulled out off Ty-Isaf and saw my butties racing up Fields Road on their bikes. Wayne was swerving from side to side and he almost hit a car. I wished I was going with 'em. Mam drove really slow past the police station, she said she didn't wanna be speeding just in case they came out after her. She gets really scared when she drives without anyone with her. She takes the L-plates off and puts 'em back on when we get home.

Mam stopped for some petrol in the garage where Mrs Davies works – she used to live upstairs in the top flat in Waunfawr Gardens. Mrs Davies said I'd grown and gave me a packet of crisps from the garage shop. Mam told her about Gransher not being very well.

When we got to Nana Balding's, Mam told me to behave myself and be nice and quiet. She told me to sit down and read my football book. Nana Balding was in the kitchen, she didn't look very well and didn't tell me off like she normally does. She asked if we wanted a cup of tea, Mam said she'd help make it. The telly was on but the sound was turned down. I watched the wrestling, it was funny seeing the big fat men swing each other round, hitting the floor without any sound. The crowd was shouting and waving their fists in the air. Mam came in to put her coat on the chair and told me off for having the telly on.

'It was already on Mam, honest,' I said, but I wanted to turn the sound up so I could hear the men shouting at each other. I wanted to see if Giant Haystacks was gonna be fighting – I like Giant Haystacks.

'Look, turn it off or there'll be trouble,' snapped Mam.

I turned the telly off and watched the little dot in the middle of the screen disappear. Nana came in from the kitchen and told me to take my coat off. She said I made the place look untidy.

'Ooh, why is the telly off, Beryl? I only just turned that on for the wrestling, I like the wrestling,' said Nana.

'Don't just stand there Gwyn, turn the telly on for yuh Nana.'

The kettle started whistling and Nana Balding went back to the kitchen. She came back with a tray with a teapot and cups. She said she had some stale Welsh cakes somewhere that needed to be eaten.

'I'll just take this upstairs for Arthur,' said Nana. Her hand was shaking as she poured the tea.

I asked if I could take it. I said I'd be careful and I wouldn't spill any. Nana said okay, but not to mess about and come back downstairs after I've said hello to Gransher.

Since Gransher's so bard he's been staying in bed. Mam says he has to get lots of rest, he gets really tired cos of the drugs that the doctors give him. I was really careful with Gransher's tea, just like I promised. I didn't want Mam and Nana shouting at me for spilling any.

The door to Gransher's bedroom was open, the curtains were closed and it was dark. Gransher was sat up in bed but he was having a nap. He looked different, he looked grey. He was wearing a cardigan and underneath he had a white vest on. Gransher likes to dress smart, even when he's just out in the garden or in his shed. I'd never seen Gransher in a vest before. Round his neck was his medallion, he won it doing boxing. Gransher used to be a boxer in the olden days. Mam said he used to be really good, he beat up loads of blokes and won lots of medals and cups. He used to fight in the circus and he had a special boxing name – Kid Balding. The medallion is gold and has a drawing of a boxer on it. Gransher lets me put it on sometimes. It's brill, even better than a Jim'll Fix It badge.

I wrote to Jimmy Savile and asked him to help Gransher get better. I posted it myself. He never wrote back, but Mam said he gets lots of letters from boys and girls. I didn't tell Mam that I asked Jimmy Savile to make Gransher better. I said I asked to be on The Sweeney.

'Aye, hello Gwyn, lad,' smiled Gransher, as I put his cup of tea down on the bedside table.

'I got you a cup of tea from Nana.'

There was lots of drugs and things on the table, pill pots, tablet packets and a box of tissues. I noticed Gransher's hair had gone and he looked like he was bald – like Dad. Gransher had lots of hair, big black curly hair sprouting out of his head like Captain Pugwash. It was too dark to see in the bedroom proper at first, but then my eyes got used to it. On the dressing table there was a black wig – it looked like Gransher's hair. I didn't know Gransher had a wig. I thought his big hair was his proper hair. It looked scary, like someone had chopped it off. I saw a film on the telly where some Indians cut off some cowboy's hair – they called it a scalp. I wondered if Gransher had been scalped by the doctor to make him better. But I could see the label inside the wig.

Gransher reached for his tea and took a sip. He only had a little bit and he started coughing. He put his tea down and wiped his mouth with a tissue. I went over to the dressing table and looked at his wig.

'Put it on if you want, lad,' he laughed, and he started coughing again.

I didn't know if I wanted to try on Gransher's wig. It looked like it was dead, like a cat I saw once on the side of the canal. I reached over and picked it up the wig. It was heavy and smelt funny, a bit like the pub. I put it on my head and turned round so Gransher could see me.

'Aye, lad, you look tidy – like Elvis Presley.'

He started laughing and then he was coughing loads – it made me feel sad. Stuff came out of his mouth and he wiped it away with a tissue. I took off the wig and put it back on the dressing table. When Gransher stopped coughing he told me to sit on the bed.

'So, yuh being a good boy at school and doing what your teachers tell you?'

'Yeah, Gransher, I'm being good.'

I didn't tell him about pulling Janet Sayle's knickers up when she was doing a handstand. She screamed loads and everyone could see her fanny – Wayne Ashby dared me. Girls' fannies are funny. Pickles says he thinks they look like a mouth on one of the Muppets.

'It's important that you learn from your teachers and you pay attention.'

'Yes Gransher, I try my best and I'm really good at drawing cars.'

'That's good, lad,' chuckled Gransher, 'You only get one chance when you are at school see, if you don't pay attention or get in with the wrong crowd, it'll be really hard to get back on track.'

I didn't know what Gransher was talking about. He never asks me about school and stuff. Just if I've been good for Mam or if I've been playing football.

'Don't make the same mistake as I did, study hard and don't hang around with idiots. You're a bright little lad and I know you can go and do something with yuh life.'

I think Gransher was telling me not to hang around with Wayne Ashby. Perhaps Mam had been telling him about us mucking about. I'm sure she doesn't know about us painting Fuck Off on the canal bridge, we found some paint in Dad's shed.

'Go and get me that picture frame from the dressing table, there's a good lad,' said Gransher, pushing himself up in bed. 'Quick before yuh bloody mother and Nana get up 'ere poking their nose in.'

I went over to the dressing table and grabbed the picture frame. It was of Gransher and Nana Balding with Mam, Aunty Maureen and Uncle Ronnie when they were little. Gransher had an army uniform on, just like the ones in Warlord. I gave the picture to Gransher, he told me to keep my ears open for Mam and Nana. He turned the frame over and took the back off. Inside was some money – paper money. Five, ten and even a twenty pound note. So much money I bet you could buy a bike, some football boots and have enough left for loads of sweets. Gransher took out five pounds and put the picture frame back together.

'Put this back on the dressing table before we get caught,' he said.

I put the picture on the dressing table and sat back on

Gransher's bed. It was ace that Gransher had a secret hiding place for his money – like a pirate.

'Right lad, take this money and don't tell yuh Mam or Nana. Keep it safe and don't spend it all on sweets.'

'Thanks Gransher, I've never had so much money!'

'That's alright lad, go downstairs now. I'm gonna have a little nap, and remember, don't tell yuh Nana or yuh Mam.'

Gransher did some pretend boxing. Gransher always pretends to box with me. He can move his hands really quick – like the boxers on the telly. Like Muhammad Ali and Henry Cooper. But this time he was really slow and could only do a couple of punches. I felt sad in my belly that Gransher couldn't do fast boxing. I wished Jimmy Savile had fixed it so Gransher would be better. Fixed it so he could be in the garden with his wig on, looking at the flowers, or reading his newspaper. Like before.

I went downstairs and the telly was still switched off. I could hear Mam in the kitchen with Nana. Nana was crying. I'd never heard Nana Balding cry before. Mam cries all the time, she even cried during the end of Crossroads once.

'I'm just so tired, Beryl, he's not getting any better and I'm bloody scared,' cried Nana.

'I know, Mam, I'm scared too, we all are.'

Chapter 19.

Touché Away!

Mrs Powell drew a picture on the blackboard. It was a flag and was red with four small yellow stars and one bigger one. Mrs Powell said it was the flag of China. There was gonna be a new boy in our class and China is where he's from. She said he didn't speak any English and was a lot older than us. I told Mrs Powell about my Uncle Junichi, and he doesn't speak much English. Dad took him down the pub and they came back drunk and best mates.

'Well, that's very nice Gwyn, but we can't take the new boy down the pub,' said Mrs Powell.

Wayne Ashby reckoned the Chinese boy will know how to do karate. He said if we made friends with him we could use him like a bodyguard – like Oddjob in Goldfinger. Goldfinger was on the telly at Christmas. I think Goldfinger is the best film in the world, but Wayne and Martyn like Jaws better. I've not seen Jaws, we queued to see it down the ABC in Newport, but a man came round to tell us the film was sold out. We saw The Return of the Pink Panther instead. It was rubbish.

When the new Chinese boy came to school, the headmaster brought him into class. The boy was really big and looked scared – I'd be scared too. Mrs Powell said his name was Kung Cheng and she wrote it on the blackboard. 'Hello Kung,' we all said, while he stood at the front of the class looking at the floor. Wayne Ashby whispered Kung Cheng's name sounded like King Kong.

Mrs Powell sat Kung Cheng next to me, and made Wayne Ashby sit next to Pickles. 'Oh, Miss, do I have to?' said Wayne. Mrs Powell said he did. I wondered if Mrs Powell put Kung Cheng next to me cos Uncle Junichi's from Japan. I told her that I didn't speak any Japanese and that Chinese is nothing like Japanese. And I told her the Japs and the Chinkies don't like each other and they're always fighting. But I didn't say Japs or Chinkies, I said Japanese and Chinamen.

Mrs Powell said we could do some drawing. She gave us some paper and we had to share the crayons. Me and Kung Cheng had five crayons, red, blue, yellow, green and a purple one. We could draw anything we liked. Kung Cheng knew what he had to do cos Mrs Powell did an impression of drawing – and Kung Cheng nodded. I drew a picture from The Sweeney, Regan and Carter beating up some slags. Mam told me to stop calling the baddies slags. I had to draw Regan's motor in blue cos I didn't have any brown. Janet Sayle had a brown crayon, but she wouldn't let me borrow it cos I pulled her knickers down and everyone saw her fanny.

I looked at what Kung Cheng was drawing, he was using lots of green and drew it in pencil before colouring it in. But he was hiding it with his shoulders to stop anyone from seeing. I asked him what he was drawing but he didn't understand what I was saying. I pointed at my picture and then at his so he would know what I meant. He nodded, and let me see, he'd drawn a picture of Touché Turtle – the cartoon from off the telly. It was really good. It looked much better than anyone else's. I told Kung Cheng that it was really good by giving him the thumbs up.

'TOUCHÉ AWAY!' he shouted, and he started laughing.

'Touché away' is what Touché Turtle says when he gets ready to have a sword fight. Everyone in class stopped drawing and stared at me and Kung Cheng.

'You okay Kung Cheng?' asked Mrs Powell.

Kung Cheng didn't say anything and just looked down at the floor.

'It's okay Miss, he was just showing me his picture of Touché Turtle, it's really good Miss,' I said, trying not to get Kung Cheng into trouble.

Mrs Powell asked if she could see his picture, she put her hand on his shoulder cos he didn't want to show her.

'It's okay, let me see,' said Mrs Powell, smiling.

Kung Cheng showed Mrs Powell his picture, but I could tell he didn't want to.

'It's very good Kung Cheng, do you like Touché Turtle?'

Kung nodded but I don't think he knew what Mrs Powell was saying. Mrs Powell patted him on the back to let him know she thought his drawing was good. She looked at mine as well, I told her it was Regan and Carter arresting some robbers. But I still had to draw Regan putting some handcuffs on a baddie. Mrs Powell said it was very good, but wasn't sure I should be watching The Sweeney. She said it was very violent and they use naughty words. They don't use that many naughty words, they never say fuck, not ever. Dad likes The Sweeney cos sometimes there's ladies showing their boobs. Dad likes it when the ladies on the telly show their boobs.

At dinner time, me and Martyn took Kung Cheng to find Martyn Summers and David Pryce. They were standing by the bogs, David was spitting over the wall.

'David's trying get his gob to land on Pickles,' said Martyn, 'He's having a piss.'

'Ace, this is Kung Cheng, he's new in our class,' said Wayne, then gobbing over the bog wall as well.

Some of the kids in the playground were staring at Kung Cheng. They didn't know who he was, Andrea Harris came skipping over with another girl who never talks.

'Boys from other schools aren't allowed in the playground,' said Andrea, her friend nodded.

Wayne told her to piss off and she went and got a dinner lady. Mrs Combes came over to talk to Kung Cheng, she asked him why he was in school. We told her he didn't speak any English and he was new in our class. She didn't believe us and went to find a teacher. But she never came back.

Andrew Prosser from Year Four asked if Kung Cheng wanted to play football. I did an impression of kicking a ball so he knew what Andrew was saying. He nodded and the older boys had a row with each other about who's side he should play on. He went on Andrew Prosser's side, cos Andrew Prosser is the hardest boy in school.

Kung got the ball and started to run with it. He was brilliant – nobody could tackle him. If anyone got close to him he just pushed 'em out of the way. He ran straight to other end of the yard without anybody tackling him. Andrew Drewett was the goalie, Kung Cheng kicked the ball so hard it hit the chimney breast and made a massive noise – SMACK!

'Touché away!' he shouted, and everyone on Kung Cheng's team cheered – some boys on the other team cheered as well.

Mr Evans was watching, he's in charge of the school team. He was only watching for a couple of minutes, and Kung Cheng scored five goals. When he got the ball, he'd just run to the other end of the yard and score. Andrew Drewett said he didn't wanna be in goal anymore, he said it wasn't fair. Mr Evans went back to the staff room, he was laughing and shaking his head. The bell rang and Kung Cheng's team won 17-3. He scored eleven goals, and each time he scored he shouted 'Touché away'.

In class everyone was talking about how good Kung Cheng was at football. Mrs Powell was happy that he played and let him have a little nap on his desk while we did our times tables. I wished I could have a nap instead of doing times tables. I'm not very good at times tables, but some of the boys and girls in my class can't even do any. Dad's really good at doing sums, he can do hard sums in his head without using a pencil and paper or even his fingers. He's not very good at reading or writing though. I can spell better than Dad, he wrote on his pickled onions jar 'Huneons'. Dad left school when he was little to work in the steelworks, so he missed lots of school.

After our tables, Mrs Powell said we could make some masks cos we'd been very good. We had to wake up Kung Cheng cos he'd fallen fast asleep. Mrs Powell told Kung Cheng what to do by pointing at some paper, drawing on it, and then putting it on her face – Kung Cheng nodded and said 'Okay'. Apart from 'Touché away', that was the first thing he'd said all day.

In our classroom there's a big cupboard full of glue pots, drawing paper, card and paint. Mrs Powell said whoever did the best mask would get a gold star. We have a board on the wall with our names on it. If you do something good or get a good score in a test, you get a star stuck next to your name. I only have three stars, one for a sums test and two for drawing pictures. I cheated on the sums test.

Wayne Ashby was making a Spiderman mask, Pickles was

doing the Hulk. The girls were making silly princesses and girly ones, except for Samantha Bond who was making a Bruce Forsyth mask. I decided to do Gary Glitter, I used lots of silver paint and it looked ace. Kung Cheng was using loads of green paint and I guessed he was gonna do Touché Turtle.

'Touché Turtle?' I asked.

'Touché away', he said, and nodded.

'I think he likes Touché Turtle,' whispered Pickles, cos everytime anyone says Touché Turtle, he shouts it really loud.

When we finished our masks, Mrs Powell made us put 'em on. She said everyone did really well, but she only gave a star to Kung Cheng and Samantha Bond. Her Bruce Forsyth mask had bits of brown wool for his hair and moustache. Dad doesn't like Bruce Forsyth – he's on his slipper list.

After school I walked home with Wayne Ashby. Kung Cheng left early, someone came and got him. We didn't have any money for sweets, but we went to the shop to look at the comics. The man behind the counter told us off and said he wasn't running a bloody library. We walked past the Chinky and there was a knock on the window. It was Kung Cheng. He was waving and shouting 'Touché away'. The Chinky was closed, but Kung Cheng had a battered cod and a saveloy. Wayne pointed at Kung Cheng's food and rubbed his belly. Kung Cheng nodded and did an okay sign with this finger and thumb. He went behind the counter and got two saveloys. He poked them through the letterbox, and me and Wayne got one each. We gave Kung Cheng the thumbs-up and walked up the road eating our saveloys. I was so full I didn't eat all my tea, Dad made Birds Eye Potato Waffles, fried egg and beans.

Mam was visiting Gransher down the hospital with Nana Balding. Dad said he was really poorly and it didn't look very good. I wanted to see Gransher as well, but cos he's so ill, I'm not allowed. I could have cheered him up with my Gary Glitter mask, but Dad didn't think Gransher liked Gary Glitter. I went to my bedroom and drew a picture of a boxer instead. When I finished, I showed Dad.

'You love yuh Gransher, don't you son?'

'I dunno, s'pose so, but not a girly way.'

Dad put his hand on my shoulder and said I was a good lad.

'But sometimes things happen to people that aren't very nice, but that's life, son,' said Dad, but I didn't know what he was going on about.

When Mam got home from the hospital, Dad told me to go and play in my room 'til it was time to go to bed. I wanted to watch Selwyn Frogget on the telly, but I thought I'd better do what I was told. I was playing with my Meccano, making a crane, and I could hear Mam crying. I felt funny, like a tingly feeling in my belly. I was a bit scared. Scared that something was gonna happen to Gransher.

Chapter 20.

Closing The Curtains.

Uncle Jack and Aunty Grace live in a place called Hereford. They're not my real aunty and uncle, they're Nana and Gransher's friends from the olden days. Uncle Jack and Aunty Grace are ace and they talk funny – like pirates. Aunty Grace has even gorra funny eye. Dad says she's cock-eyed and I shouldn't keep staring at it.

Gransher's been in hospital for ages. I went to see him when Mam said he was looking a bit better, but I wish I hadn't. He was really skinny and he didn't look like Gransher anymore. It made me sad, it made Mam sad too.

Uncle Jack and Aunty Grace were coming to visit. Mam was gonna pick 'em up from the railway station with Uncle Graham. Mam failed her test again, so she still has to have someone with her when she drives. Mam's gonna take it again soon – it will be the fifth time. Dad said if she keeps failing, she'll be on Record Breakers. I like Record Breakers, I like it when Roy Castle does his tap-dancing and plays the trumpet.

Uncle Graham's home from the Navy. He got me a football shirt and Mam had a bottle of Cinzano. I tasted some when nobody was looking. It was horrible. Mam and Uncle Graham drove Nana down the hospital in Newport, then they were gonna pick up Jack and Grace from the station. I went out on my bike with Martyn Summers and Dad did some digging in the garden. I was looking forward to seeing Uncle Jack and Aunty Grace. Uncle Jack gives me money, sometimes a pound, but only if he's been down the pub with Dad.

Me and Martyn played a game of The Sweeney. I was Regan and Martyn was Carter. We pretended to be on surveillance for some robbers that were gonna nick lots of money from a bank. We were cycling up Springfield Road as fast as we could, making siren noises when Mam's car came up the street. They'd not been very long and I couldn't see Uncle Jack and Aunty Grace, just Mam, Nana and Uncle Graham. I waved but they didn't see me, they drove past and parked outside our house. Uncle Graham helped Nana out of the car and she didn't look very well.

'I'm going home, I'll see yuh later,' I told Martyn.

I went round the back garden and parked my bike. Dad was in the kitchen with Mam and they were having a cuddle – yuck. It's horrible when Mam and Dad are all soppy, it's not very often though. Dad only gives Mam a kiss or smacks her bum if he's been down the pub. I opened the back door and I could see Mam was crying, crying loads and loads.

'Look, Son, can you go back outside for a minute? Mam's a bit upset, I'll be out in a sec,' said Dad.

I locked up my bike and looked at my tadpoles. I got 'em from the canal and put 'em in an old sink that Dad used to grow flowers in. Dad came outside and said he had some bad news. I hoped Uncle Jack and Aunty Grace were still coming, I was hoping I'd get some money from Uncle Jack, I wanna buy the new Scoop football comic. It's got a free football chart to put on your wall.

'Is it about Uncle Jack and Aunty Grace? Are they still coming?'

'Yeah, son, they're still coming, it's Gransher, lad. He's passed away, Son. I'm sorry.'

'Passed away? Like my goldfish?'

'Yes Son, like your goldfish.'

'Does that mean I won't see Gransher anymore?'

'Aye Son, it does. But Gransher was in a lorra pain so now he won't be suffering anymore.'

This was just like my goldfish. Hutch turned a funny colour and was swimming on his side. I got home from school and he was gone from the tank. There was just Starsky, swimming about looking sad. Dad told me Hutch had passed away and had gone to a better place. Wayne Ashby said when goldfish die, they go down the toilet and then the sewer. That doesn't sound like a better place to me. I don't think Gransher will be flushed down the toilet though.

I followed Dad into the kitchen, he put the kettle on and lit a rollie. Uncle Graham came in and his eyes were all bloodshot.

'You wanna hand with the tea, Cliff?' asked Uncle Graham, staring out the window – he could see Mr Morgan next door scratching his arse.

'It's alright, Graham, lad, I'll sort it all out. How's Mary doing?'

'She's not saying anything, she's just sitting there staring at the butter dish.'

'It's shock, it won't hit her 'til later. What about Jack and Grace?'

'I'll take Beryl's car down and pick 'em up. I'll have to tell 'em the bad news I s'pose,' said Graham, scratching his head and looking down at the kitchen floor – I wondered if he noticed the peas from yesterday's dinner against the cooker.

'Uncle Graham, can I come down the station with you?'

Dad said it might be good to get me out the house for a while. I was being very good and not being noisy, but Dad said Mam and Nana needed to be on their own for a bit. Dad finished making the tea and took it into the living room. I stayed in the kitchen and nicked some Ritz biscuits from the cupboard. I like Ritz biscuits, but Dad says I eat too many. He hides 'em behind the Shredded Wheat. I don't like Shredded Wheat.

Uncle Graham looked at his watch and said we'd better get a move on down the station. He got the car keys from Mam, and Dad told me to behave myself. Dad's always telling me to behave myself. We drove down to Newport and Uncle Graham was really quiet. He normally tells me about the different countries he's been to. Exciting places like where James Bond is always killing baddies or escaping with gadgets Q has given him. I like the mini helicopter in You Only Live Twice and the ejector seat in Goldfinger. Uncle Graham's been to loads of ace places.

We parked Mam's car and went into the station. Uncle Graham asked a railway man about the train from Hereford. We walked on the platform and saw Uncle Jack and Aunty Grace. Graham told me not to say anything about Gransher, he said he'd break the bard news.

'Hello Uncle Jack, hello Aunty Grace,' said Graham.

'Hello Graham lad, how's Arthur? Mary coping with it all?' asked Aunty Grace. Her funny eye was looking at a chocolate machine behind. I wanted some chocolate, but I had no money and I didn't want to ask for any. Dad says it's rude.

'Got bad news, I'm afraid. Dad died earlier this morning.'

Uncle Graham looked at the ground, I thought he was gonna cry. His voice went a bit wobbly, but Uncle Graham is in the Navy, and Mam says being in the Navy makes you tough.

'Oh no, oh Graham, I'm sorry, lad,' said Aunty Grace, her wonky eye was filling up with tears.

Aunty Grace looked in her handbag and brought out a hanky, she wiped her eyes and blew her nose.

'I don't know what to say to you, lad, just don't know what to say,' said Uncle Jack, holding his coat and shaking his head.

Uncle Jack and Gransher were best butties, Dad said back in the olden days, they were like two peas in a pod. They were in the army together as well.

We got in the car and drove back home. Aunty Grace was crying and Uncle Jack kept saying 'There, there' to her. I thought about singing a song to cheer her up, but last time I sang a song, Dad hit me round the head and told me to shut up. I sang 'Four and Twenty Virgins' in the Post Office. Dad said it was not a nice song to sing and not to sing it again. But when he told Bernard Cox up The Exchange, Dad was laughing. He wasn't laughing in the Post Office when I sang it for him and Mrs Parry.

When we got home, Dad was in the front garden watering the flowers. Uncle Jack and Aunty Grace said hello and went in the house. Dad said Nana was still not saying anything and was still staring at the butter dish. Dad said he wants to use the butter later, and have some toast.

'How did they take the news, Graham?' asked Dad, watering a flower that had a massive bug on it.

'Just shocked really, Cliff. They knew it was coming but I think they're just upset cos they didn't get to say goodbye.'

'Aye, well, Jack and Arthur go way back. Known each other

most their lives.'

I went inside the house and went into the living room. Mam had closed the curtains and it was really dark. Mam says when someone dies, you have to close the curtains as a mark of respect. Aunty Grace had her arm around Nana Balding, who was still staring at the butter dish. Mam was crying, her eyes were all puffy and there were loads of screwed up tissues sticking out her cardie pocket.

'I can't believe he's gone, Grace!' cried Mam, grabbing another tissue and pushing it up her sleeve.

'I know, Beryl, I know.'

Uncle Jack was sitting in the armchair next to the telly. He was shaking his head and muttering to himself. Dad popped his head round the door and said he was gonna make a fresh pot of tea. I looked through the Radio Times to see what was on telly, but Mam said that I couldn't have it on. Doctor Who was on later, it's about some Chinese blokes in the olden days. I like it better when it's about robots and space monsters.

Nana Balding stopped staring at the butter dish and looked in a carrier bag that was on the settee.

'You okay, Mam?' asked Mam, stuffing another snotty tissue up her sleeve.

Nana Balding didn't say anything. She opened the carrier bag and looked inside. She pulled out a washbag, it looked like it was Gransher's. Nana opened the washbag and pulled stuff out. First a razor, which she put on the coffee table next to the butter dish. Then a piece of soap, some nail clippers, a small mirror and a bottle of Old Spice – Gransher's favourite aftershave. Nana put all the bits and bobs on the coffee table and lined 'em up, all nice and tidy. Nana picked up the Old Spice bottle, pulled the stopper out, and sniffed it. Nana's face went all strange and she started to shake. She cried like I've never heard anyone cry before. It was really loud and it made me wanna run away, I didn't like it.

'Oh Mam, MAM! Come on now, try not to upset yourself,' said Mam, who was crying as well.

Aunty Grace gave Nana a big cwtch. Nana Balding cried and cried, the more she cried the more Mam cried as well, then Aunty Grace joined in. Uncle Jack just sat in the armchair shaking his head. I looked at Gransher's bits and bobs on the coffee table and it made me sad. But I didn't wanna cry, Dad doesn't like it if I cry, he's says he'll give me something to cry about, and not to be such a big girl.

I had a funny feeling in my belly, like being scared, like when I've done something naughty but didn't wanna get caught.

Dad brought in a tray with tea and biscuits. Nana stopped crying and wiped her face in one of Mam's tissues, the box was nearly empty. Aunty Grace took Gransher's bits and bobs off the coffee table so Dad could put the tray down.

'Nice cuppa tea for everyone. Still have five sugars Jack?'

Nana looked back inside the carrier bag, I hoped she wasn't gonna start crying again. She reached in and pulled out Gransher's boxing medallion – the one he used to wear round his neck.

'Yuh Gransher said he wanted you to have this, Gwyn,' said Nana.

Nana Balding's hand was shaking as she held out the medallion. I'd never noticed Nana's hands before, but they were wrinkly and boney. I took the medallion and said thank you. Dad said to look after it and to remember it wasn't a toy. On the back there was some writing;

Arthur 'Kid' Balding
Welterweight
Bedwellty & District Champion 1939

Dad poured the tea and Uncle Graham put a pile of biscuits on a plate. I put a pink wafer in my mouth and went upstairs to my bedroom. I took off my t-shirt and put the medallion round my neck. I did a pose in the mirror, like in the picture of Gransher, Nana Balding has on top of the telly. I wish I had some proper boxing gloves so I could look like a real boxer. Gransher used to have a pair somewhere in the shed. Mam used to say that Gransher's shed was like a bloody Tardis.

I sat on the edge of my bed looking at Gransher's medallion. I was glad Nana Balding gave it to me, but I'd like it better if Gransher still had it, and he wasn't passed away. I thought about Gransher doing pretend boxing, giving me my red football, sliding on the back seat of the Woolsey, and giving me the five pound note from his secret hiding place. I loved my Gransher. He never told me off or shouted at me, and I liked sitting with him in the garden outside his shed. I couldn't help it, and I tried not to, but I was crying.

'It's alright son, come on now. Come downstairs and have a Jaffa Cake,' said Dad, 'That'll cheer you up a bit, lad.'

I didn't notice Dad had come into my bedroom. I didn't like it that he saw me crying.

'I'm sorry Dad, don't tell anyone about me crying, I didn't mean to.'

'Why are you sorry for crying, son? You've just lost yuh Gransher. You loved yuh Gransher, I know that, lad.'

Dad put his arm round me, he smelt like the garden and rollies. Dad never gives me a cuddle or a cwtch, says it's soppy.

And he only gives Mam cuddles and cwtches when he's been down the pub.

'I didn't know we had any Jaffa Cakes?' I said.

'Got a little hiding place, keep 'em out the way from yuh mother,' said Dad ruffling my hair. 'C'mon, put yuh shirt on and come downstairs.'

I took the medallion from around my neck, and hung it round my King Kong toy – his eyes light up in the dark. I put my t-shirt on and went down to the kitchen. I saw Dad reach behind the fridge and pull out a box of Jaffa Cakes. I'd never thought to look behind there. Dad didn't know I saw where he kept 'em.

When Mam had finished crying and Nana said she wanted to go home, Uncle Jack and Dad went up The Exchange to 'Raise a glass to Arthur'. I went with Mam to pick 'em up from the pub after Doctor Who had finished. They'd had so much beer, Uncle Jack pee'd his trousers and Dad was sick in a flower pot.

'Oh, bloody 'ell Cliff!' shouted Mam.

'Think I've had a bad pint, luv,' groaned Dad.

'Aye, bloody lots of 'em by the state of you!'

Aunty Grace told Uncle Jack off for being drunk, and Mam made 'em drink Mellow Birds with no milk in it. Mam and Aunty Grace were in the kitchen, Dad said to keep a look-out. He got a small bottle of whisky from his coat pocket. He poured some in their coffee mugs and they raised 'em in the air.

'To Arthur,' said Dad.

'To Arthur,' said Uncle Jack, 'Free at last.'

Chapter 21.

Don't Steal The Animals.

'If you don't stop pulling Sally-Ann's hair, you'll come down the front and sit with me!' shouted Mr Dandy.

Sally-Ann was sat in the seat in front of me and Wayne. Her hair was in pigtails, Wayne thought it would be piss-funny to tie 'em together. He said he does it to his sister. I don't think Mr Dandy thought it was piss-funny. When Sally-Ann screamed, Mr Dandy shouted and his face went purple. Mr Dandy's face is always going purple.

Every year we go on a school trip to Bristol Zoo. We get on big coaches and don't have to do any lessons – it's ace.

'Before we get on our way, I want to remind everyone to behave themselves,' shouted Mr Dandy, and when he said 'behave themselves', he pointed at Wayne Ashby.

'We are very fortunate that we are allowed back at Bristol Zoo, so no larking about!' he said.

Foghorn was a boy that used to go to our school. I think his real name's Ian. Wayne Ashby said he lives down the drain cos his mam and dad were killed by a mad axeman. Colin Scotch said Wayne was talking shit. Foghorn was at Bristol Zoo on a school trip when he made friends with a penguin. He gave it some salmon paste sandwiches, and when no one was looking, he picked up the penguin and put it in his Gola bag. Nobody knew he had it, even on the coach on the way back. It must have been a quiet penguin or it was very scared. Foghorn put the penguin in the bath when he got home and gave it some fish fingers. When Foghorn's mam came home, she went mental. Someone came and got the penguin, and took it back to the zoo.

Pickles did some actions to show Kung what Foghorn did on the school trip. We laughed our heads off when Pickles walked like a penguin up the aisle of the bus, then pretended to climb in a bag.

'Wanker,' said Kung Cheng, pointing at Pickles.

Kung now knows lots of words, and Wayne's taught him all the best swears. Richard James told us about wanker, he learnt it from his brother. Richard James calls everyone a wanker. He called Mrs Harvey, one of the dinner ladies, a wanker. She didn't tell him off or get a teacher, she just went all quiet and sat down. Kung likes saying wanker as well, Mrs Powell told him off cos he said it after the Lord's prayer in assembly.

Before we went on the trip we had to take a letter home from school. Mam said it was a form to sign, just in case I fell over or got eaten by a lion. Then it wouldn't be the school's fault and they wouldn't have to pay Mam and Dad any money.

Mam gave me some cucumber spread sandwiches, a banana and a Taxi bar for my packed lunch. I ate the banana and Taxi on the way to school. I asked Dad for some money for the zoo. He said I must think he's bloody Rockefeller, whoever he is, and I think money must grow on trees. He gave me five pounds and said not to tell Mam – she might want some too.

The coach was really posh, there were curtains for the windows, light switches and air vents. Mr Dandy told us not to touch anything or we'd be in trouble. Wayne Ashby blew his nose on his curtain, it was horrible. I could see the slimy snot on the orange fabric.

We got to Bristol Zoo and everybody cheered. Before we got off the coach, Mr Dandy made us sit in our seats and listen to him talk about behaving ourselves in the zoo again.

'Keep your hands off anything that you're not supposed to touch. AND DON'T STEAL ANY OF THE ANIMALS!'

The other coach that came from school got to the zoo before we did. They were already inside, we could hear Mr Evans shouting, 'You do not throw peanuts at the monkeys!' I saw Mrs Powell laugh, but Mr Dandy didn't.

We walked into the zoo in a neat line. Mr Dandy said we had to meet back at the same spot at three o'clock, and not to be late. As soon as he said 'Off you go and stay out of trouble,' everyone ran off in different directions. I went with Wayne, Martyn and Kung to look at the tigers.

'AND DON'T RUN!' shouted Mr Dandy.

Some of the girls wanted to see the monkeys. Pickles and Claire Pearson went to see the flamingos. David Pryce called Pickles a bummer, Richard James called him a wanker, and Paul Button wanted to know what a flamingo was.

The tiger was really ace and had big massive paws. It said on the cage there were two tigers. A bloke that worked at the zoo said the other tiger was asleep. Wayne told him to go and wake him up. All the animals were ace, there was a massive snake that flicked his tongue out. The sign next to his glass cage said they smell with their tongues – that's mental. I saw lots of monkeys that showed their bums, one of the monkeys looked like Nana Balding. Kung Cheng did a brilliant impression of a monkey, he did noises as well.

'Let's go and find the polar bear. Andrew Drewett says it's

gone mad and just walks up and down,' said Martyn Summers.

There were loads of people looking at the polar bear, he was in a big concrete pit with his own swimming pool. On the telly, polar bears look really white and fluffy, this one was dirty and didn't look very well. He was doing a mad walk, back and forth, and he had no other polar bear butties to play with. The polar bear made me sad. We were just about to go and find some happy animals to look at, when Richard James and Colin Scotch came running up.

'Pickles has fallen into the duck pond,' laughed Richard, 'We're gonna go and have a look. Coming?'

'Fuckin' 'ell! Ace!' said Martyn, and we legged it over to the pond. When we got there Mr Power, the headmaster, was pulling Pickles out of the water with an umbrella. There were loads of people watching. Pickles got out of the water, and a man from the zoo put a blanket round him and took him away. Mr Power told everyone to get back and enjoy the rest of the zoo. He said everything was okay and Pickles was alright. But he didn't call him Pickles, but Lloyd, cos that's his name.

'Pickles is gonna get the cane when we get back to school, I reckon,' said Wayne.

'Why will he get the cane? He only fell in the water,' said Martyn.

'Yeah, but Mr Dandy told us not to do anything naughty or there would be big trouble!' said Wayne, making his hand into a gun shape and pretending to fire it in the direction that Pickles went with the zoo man.

Martyn said we should go and have a look at the elephant, and if we were lucky we might see him have a shit. He said he saw one shit on a wildlife programme on the telly, he said it was massive. When we got to the elephant bit, a man was washing him with a big hose pipe. Another bloke was scrubbing him with a big brush. I looked on the ground to see if there was any elephant shit, but I couldn't see any. Martyn said they probably clean it up and take it away in a wheelbarrow. Dad would like to have a wheelbarrow full of elephant shit. He's always going up the mountain with carrier bags getting horse poo from the fields up Machen and Ochrwyth. He says it's good for the garden and makes his vegetables grow better. He doesn't like it if a cat shits in the garden though, he runs out shouting and throws stones to make it run away. 'Go and shit in next door's garden!' he shouts.

The elephant was a bit rubbish. It wasn't doing much and it didn't look like it was gonna do a shit. Pamela Ravenstock and Janet Sayle were watching as well. Pamela took her cardie off cos she said she was getting hot. The elephant must have thought it was some food. He reached down with his big trunk and ripped it away.

'That's my new cardie, my nana gave me that!' shouted Pamela Ravenstock.

The zoo keepers tried to get the cardie from the elephant. They grabbed the sleeves and pulled, but the elephant didn't wanna let go. The zoo keepers were pulling really hard, one of the men was shouting and waving a brush. The elephant did a big shit and let go of the cardie – we cheered. Martyn was right, elephant shit is massive.

Pamela's cardie was ripped and all stretched. One arm was longer than the other – just like if Mam had knitted it. Pamela tried it on to see if it would still fit. We were pissing ourselves laughing, even the zoo keepers were laughing. I thought Pamela was gonna start crying but she didn't. She said her nana wouldn't believe that an elephant tried to eat it. One of the zoo keepers took Pamela to find one of our teachers.

Martyn told us it was half-past two, so we went to the zoo shop to spend our pocket money. There were loads of ace stuff to buy and I couldn't make my mind up. Wayne Ashby had a plastic crocodile that filled with water and squirted like a water pistol. He was chasing Sally-Ann with it – Mr Dandy shouted at him. I bought a wobbly snake and a tiger mask. We wanted to ask Pickles about him falling in the pond, but he went on the other coach on the way back home – he still had a blanket round him. Pamela Ravenstock had her cardie in a Bristol Zoo bag, but she got a free t-shirt with a monkey on it. On the bus, Kung did an impression of the elephant eating Pamela's cardie. Mr Dandy told him to sit down and said it wasn't very funny. But it was.

Chapter 22.

Bernie Clifton Stole My Crisps.

The Queen wanted everyone to have a big party. All the boys and girls, mams and dads, were told to have lots of blancmange, crisps, jelly, ice cream, sausage rolls, and fizzy pop. Mr Harris had beer.

The Silver Jubilee is about the Queen being in charge for twenty five years. Dad says that's twenty five years she's been living it up on his bloody taxes. Mam told him not to be so grumpy. Mam's been looking forward to the party for ages. All the street helped sort it out and everyone was going dressed up in a costume. I decided to be Miss World. I got a wig from Aunty Maureen, a pair of tights, and one of Mam's old swimming costumes. It's got red and black stripes on it. Dad said when Mam used to wear it at the seaside, she looked like a giant bee.

At school we did lots of Jubilee stuff and dressed up our bikes for a prize. I put lots of tinsel and a Union Jack on mine. I came third and won a box of Maltesers – Mam ate lots and said they didn't have many calories. We had to push our bikes round the park, some people were filming it on their cine cameras.

For a special treat at school, we had a picnic on the playing field. We had to carry our chairs from our classrooms and we sat in a big circle. Mr Power did a rubbish speech about the Silver Jubilee and we stood up and sang 'God Save The Queen'. We normally sing with Mrs Marsh playing the piano, but cos we were outside, we had to sing without it. Mrs Marsh is rubbish at playing the piano, she's always out of tune, like Les Dawson off the telly. But I think Les Dawson does it on purpose. The dinner ladies gave us a packed lunch in a paper bag. We had a bag of crisps, a ham bap, a slice of cake and some pop. Mr Evans said there might be a special surprise, we wondered what it was. Wayne Ashby reckoned it was a Dalek, Martyn Summers said it would something rubbish, like the Mayor.

When we finished our baps and cake, the dinner ladies came round and took away our rubbish. We kept our pop and crisps and we got some balloons to blow up. A posh car was outside the school gate, and Mr Power went over and talked to a lady who had got out of the car. After a couple of minutes, Mr Power came back with a man who had a hat covering his face. We couldn't see who he was, Mr Power was smiling like a mad loon.

'Right boys and girls, we have a very special guest that I want you to give a big Danygraig School hello to... BERNIE CLIFTON!'

Everyone went berserk. We jumped up and down, danced on our seats and shouted 'Crackerjack!'. That's the name of the programme on the telly that Bernie Clifton is on – Bernie Clifton is ace. On the telly he dresses up like an ostrich. He looks like he's riding it, but he has false legs. When we had a fancy dress competition at Christmas, Russell Silletoe had an ostrich costume, just like Bernie Clifton's. Russell won first prize. I dressed up as a Roman soldier, but I didn't win anything.

Bernie Clifton did a mad walk and pretended to fall over. It was really funny and we shouted 'Crackerjack' again. He went round to everyone saying hello, he told some jokes and messed about with some of the teachers. When he came round to where I was sitting, I asked him if he wanted a crisp.

'Thanks very much,' said Bernie Clifton, he put his hand in the packet and pulled the bag out and ran away.

Everyone laughed but I wanted my crisps back. I'd only just opened 'em, and they were my favourite – Smoky Bacon. He gave 'em back, but he'd eaten loads. I didn't mind that much cos I got to talk to him. I'd never talked to anyone that's been on the telly before. Well, Uncle Ronnie was on the telly once, but only on the Welsh news cos he dressed up like a chicken.

Somebody asked Bernie Clifton if he had his ostrich costume with him. He said it wasn't a costume, but was a real ostrich. Bernie Clifton must think kids are stupid. He did his crisp trick to someone else and everyone laughed again. Mr Power told us to say goodbye to Bernie Clifton cos it was time for him to go. We shouted 'Crackerjack' and he waved goodbye, he got back in the big posh car and it drove away beeping its horn. We shouted Crackerjack again.

I told Mam and Dad about Bernie Clifton coming to school and about him stealing my crisps. Mam said that it was very nice of him to go to the school. Dad said he only did it for the bloody money, and Bernie Clifton was probably a dinner-masher.

The street party was at the church hall at the end of Springfield Road. Dad wasn't going to the party cos he had to go to work, but he said he was bloody glad he was gonna miss it. Everyone was excited being dressed up in costumes. Mam went as an Indian and so did Mrs Wakefield, Mrs Morgan and Mrs Hockey. Mrs Knight went as a mummy, like in the horror films. Julian Wakefield dressed up as a cowboy and Geraldine Wakefield was a cat. I was the only one that went as Miss World – Dad said I would be. Lots of people didn't dress up as anything, Mam says that's cos they're miserable – just like Dad.

Before we could eat any of the food, we had to stand up and sing 'God Save The Queen'. Mrs Morgan played the piano – she played it proper and in tune. There was lots of food and I put as much as I could on my paper plate. Mam said I wasn't to be so greedy and I had to put some back. Everyone in the street brought lots of food for the party. Mam made some jelly and bought Viscount biscuits, she gave the paper plates too. She said there were loads left over from party for Uncle Junichi and Aunty Maria. I stuffed loads of food in my mouth. I had a competition with Julian Wakefield to see who could get the most sausage rolls in our mouths. I got five, Julian got seven. I made him laugh by squeezing my pretend boobs in my swimming costume. He spat his sausage rolls out all over the floor. Mrs Wakefield got really angry. But the more she smacked him the more he laughed. I laughed too, but none of the grown-ups thought it was very funny, except for Mr Harris from number 76. He was really drunk and trying to kiss all the ladies. He had a piece of mistletoe and was waving it about.

'It's not bloody Christmas, Jack, yuh daft bugger,' laughed Mam, as Mr Harris tried to give her a big sloppy kiss.

Mrs Harris didn't care that Mr Harris was acting the goat. She was too busy eating all the food on her paper plate. It was piled really high, she had loads more than I did. Mam didn't tell her off though.

After we finished our food, everything was cleared up and

the tables were put away. A bald man with a ponytail, dressed in a shiny suit, brought in lots of cases and some big speakers. He had a butty with him that set up some flashing lights. Mam got all excited and shouted it was time for the disco. The grown-ups looked drunk, just like Dad when he comes home from the pub. The bald man finished setting up his stuff, a sign at the front of his record player said:

ERIC'S FUNKY DISCO – KING OF THE DISCS

Mr Harris said 'King of the dicks, more like,' and Mrs Harris told him to shut up. The man in the shiny suit had a microphone so he could speak over the music. He talked really funny, like Tony Blackburn and Dave Lee Travis on the radio.

'Okay you funky people, get yuh feet moving to this floor stomper, it's Showaddywaddy and Under The Moon Of Love!'

The grown-ups did old fashioned rock 'n' roll dancing, like on the telly. It was rubbish. Me and Julian Wakefield jumped up and down and waved our arms about. A little boy from down the road did an impression of an aeroplane. Even Mam was dancing – and she's got a bard leg. Mr Harris still had his mistletoe but only Mrs Hale give him a kiss. She lives at number 73 – she's 84. She says she still has most of her own teeth and can remember two World Wars. Mr Harris doesn't have any teeth and Mrs Harris said he can't remember last week.

I was glad Mam was having a good time – she's not been very happy. Dad said she's been missing Gransher. I had to stay with Nana Sugden for a couple of days, Mam and Dad had to go to Gransher's funeral. Dad said loads of people turned up, lots of his old boxing butties and men he used to work with down the mines. Uncle Malcolm got drunk and Uncle Graham had to tell him off. Mam said they nearly had a punch-up.

The disco went on for ages. Most of the records were rubbish, but all the grown-ups liked 'em and danced with each other. When the 'The Monster Mash', came on – that's my favourite song – I did a special monster dance and Mr Parry from number 63, took my picture. Mrs Knight danced to The Monster Mash as well, she looked ace cos she was dressed in her mummy costume.

When the disco was over, Mr Morgan plugged in a portable telly and we watched the Queen in London doing her special speech. It was really boring. At the end, we sang 'God Save The Queen' again and we all stood up, except for Mr Harris who was sleeping and snoring really loud. He still had his mistletoe in his hand.

Everyone tidied up the hall and put the rubbish in black plastic bags. There was lots of food left over and Mam shouted if anyone wanted some sausage rolls. I'd had loads of sausage rolls and lots of jelly and I didn't even want any more crisps.

'JULIAN! STOP THAT AT ONCE, YUH LITTLE BUGGER!' shouted Mrs Wakefield.

Julian was drawing on Mr Harris's face with a marker pen. Mr Harris was so drunk he didn't wake up.

'Ooh, I'm ever so sorry Audrey,' said Mrs Wakefield to Mrs Harris.

'It's alright luv, it serves the drunken old sod right,' she laughed.

Julian ran away before he got a smack. The grown-ups didn't find it funny when Julian spat out all his sausage rolls, but they were all laughing when they saw what he'd written on Mr Harris's face:

DON'T OPEN TIL XMAS

Chapter 23.

May The Force Be With You.

For my birthday, Mam said I could have the day off school and go to the pictures to see Star Wars. Richard Hovis at school has seen it four times. It's his favourite film and he's got all the Star Wars toys. Richard Hovis lives in a posh house cos his dad's got lots of money. Richard Hovis gets all the new toys, and he's got Arsenal, Liverpool, Man United and Derby County football kits – he doesn't even like football.

On my birthday I got up early to open my cards. I opened 'em to see if there was any money inside before I read who they were from. Aunty Maureen gave me two pounds, I got three pounds from Nana Sugden and a present. Nana Balding got me a Doctor Who colouring book. Aunty Joan's card had a badge with 'I AM 9' on it. Mam said I should wear it so everyone could see it was my birthday. Mam and Dad got me an Arsenal football kit – the away one, it's yellow. I don't support Arsenal, Mam said she saw me watching 'em on Match Of The Day. I don't support a team yet. Lots of boys at school support Liverpool. Dad said that's cos they win all the time. Some boys support Manchester United and David Moore supports Doncaster Rovers – David Moore is strange.

For breakfast Dad cooked me a big birthday fry-up. I had sausages, egg, bacon, black pudding and laverbread.

Laverbread is my favourite. Dad says it's made from seaweed, it's salty and I dip my sausages in it. Mam said she wasn't very hungry but she had two bacon sandwiches and some black pudding.

Mam said it would be better to watch Star Wars in the afternoon, cos everyone would be at work or in school. Mam still hasn't passed her test and cos the pictures is down in Newport, we had to catch the bus. Mam said there's too many coppers down Newport, and she might get caught again. She was up Risca buying Dad some bacca and a copper pulled her over, Mam said he was waiting for her.

'I got pulled over by the fuzz!' Mam said when she got back home.

'Sounds painful that, Bullo,' laughed Dad.

Mam reckons that Mrs Parry at number 63, grassed her up to the cops. She says she's in cahoots with 'em cos she's a lollipop lady. The police gave Mam a warning but said next time she'd be in big trouble.

On the bus, Mam asked me to test her on the Highway Code. She takes it everywhere with her but she still doesn't know any of it. I tested her on some road signs – I know lots of the road signs.

'What's this one 'en, Mam?' I said showing her a 'No Waiting' sign.

'Ooh, I know this one, hang on... it's no reversing up the street.'

'No, Mam, it means no waiting.'

'Same thing.'

I asked her five questions and she got 'em all wrong. For the 'National Speed Limit Applies' sign, Mam thought it meant 'Don't use your blinkers'. Blinkers is what Mam calls her indicators – but she doesn't use 'em. She reckons other drivers know when she's gonna turn off by the way she slows down and moves over. Cars are always beeping their horn and other drivers flick V's at her.

Dad gave Mam some money so we could go to Wimpy for a burger – I like Wimpy. I like cheeseburgers and milkshakes the best. So does Mam. The waitress saw my 'I AM 9' badge and wished me happy birthday. She gave me extra chips as a treat and told Mam I had lovely curly hair. I hate my curly hair. Our burgers were ace, I ate everything on my plate and drank all my milkshake. So did Mam.

We walked to the pictures from Wimpy. We went under the road, past the old castle and over Newport Bridge. I like the old castle, it's got a big metal dragon next to it. We got to the pictures a bit early so we had to wait before they let us in. There was a Star Wars poster on the wall. I asked Mam if they sold 'em behind the counter cos I wanted one for my bedroom. She said they didn't, but she didn't ask the man. We were the only ones waiting to see the film. The boys at school who went to see it said there was loads of people queuing when they went.

The man behind the counter said we could buy our tickets and go in. There was a special Star Wars magazine with a free badge. Mam said cos it was my birthday I could have one, but not to tell Dad. Mam bought some chocolate as well. We were the only ones in the pictures but some people came in when the adverts started.

I tried to read my magazine but it was too dark. I wanted to see what the free poster looked like but Mam told me to wait til we got home.

The adverts finished and a short film came on about music

called punk. It was very noisy and the groups didn't sing very well. Mam said they were a load of old rubbish. One group had a singer who looked like Dracula – they were called The Damned. They weren't very good but looked ace. At the end of the film they showed a band that looked scary. The man telling the story over the pictures said that they cause a lot of trouble. Whenever they play a concert, people jump up and down and spit. Mam said they never did that when the Beatles played. The group was called the Sex Pistols and I thought they were much better than all the others.

'Can I have a Sex Pistols record, Mam?'

'Not on yuh bloody life,' she whispered.

The film about punk music finished and the lights came on. A lady stood at the front with a tray of ice cream and drinks. Mam asked if I wanted anything but I was still full of burger and milkshake. Mam bought a tub of ice cream and a bar of Fruit & Nut. When Mam sat down the lights went out and the film started. A boy cheered and bloke told him to shut up.

The nasty man in Star Wars was called Daft Vader. He's really scary and you never see his face. He had a big black cape and a helmet. The best bit of Star Wars was the space fighting – lots of laser guns and spaceships that flew mega fast. The baddies had spaceships that looked like a telly aerial. The good guys are called the rebellion and had a princess in charge, who the baddies had locked up. Luke Skywalker, Han Solo and a big hairy monster, called Chewbacca, had to rescue her. Luke Skywalker wanted to give the princess a kiss, that was the only rubbish bit.

When Star Wars finished, Mam told me get my arse moving cos we had to catch the bus. I took off my 'I AM 9' badge and put my Star Wars badge on. It said 'May The Force Be With

You' – it's ace. Mam said it looked very nice. I asked if she liked Star Wars and she said it was a bit far-fetched. I thought it was brill, but not as good as Goldfinger.

When we left the pictures there were loads of people queuing. Mam said that's why we went to see it in the afternoon. Loads of boys had the Star Wars magazine and were wearing their badges. Mam said we had to get a move on or we'd miss the bus – Mam didn't want to miss Crossroads. There were some people waiting at the bus stop, but I was the only one with a Star Wars badge.

'Hello Beryl,' said a lady on the bus stop.

'Ooh, hiya Pamela, how are you, luv?' said Mam.

The lady was really tall, nearly as tall as Chewbacca. She had big blonde hair that curled up on her head like an ice cream.

'I'm alright Beryl, still plodding away. You still living up Crosskeys?'

'Nor, moved from there nearly two year ago now, we live in Ty-Isaf, down in Risca.'

'Ooh, yuh not far from me, up just up in Channel View.'

The tall lady, called Pamela, and Mam talked for ages. They talked when we got on the bus and kept talking when we sat down. All the way home, Mam told Pamela about all the people they knew, and what they get up to. They talked so much I got a headache, we nearly missed our stop cos Mam was talking so much. Pamela got off the bus the same time as us, and all the way up the road Mam was still talking. She told Pamela about not passing her test, Gransher dying, Dad's bard cold after Christmas, and me dressing up like Miss World. Mam said goodbye and she'd see Pamela again soon so they could have a proper catch-up.

'May the force be with you,' I said, Pamela laughed and walked up the street.

'Gor, that women can talk,' said Mam.

Chapter 24.

Taking Off The L-Plates.

I'VE PASSED, GWYN, I'VE BLOODY PASSED!' shouted Mam, waving her L-plates around in the air.

Mam was waiting for me at the school gates. Richard James said my Mam was mental. I said I know. Some kids were laughing and I felt my face go red. Dad said that they were probably fed up of seeing Mam at the test centre. When the examiner told her she'd passed, she gave him a big kiss. Dad said 'The poor bugger'.

Mam wanted to go up Nana Balding's to tell her the news. She said I could have pie and chips from the chippy cos she was in a good mood. I like pie and chips, especially from Risca Fish Bar. We ate our chips in a lay-by on the bypass, on the way up. Mam had cod, large chips and a fish cake. She was gonna have a pot of curry sauce, but she said she was being weighed soon for Keep Fat Club.

Since Gransher's been passed away, Nana Balding's been really quiet, not like before. She hasn't told me off like she used to, but still gives me horrible Welsh cakes. Uncle Graham came home from the Navy for a bit, but he had to go back. Mam said he had to go to a place called Gibraltar. Only Uncle Malcolm lives with Nana now, Mam says he's always half-cut and Nana would be better off getting a dog.

We got to Nana's house and Mam thought the garden looked like it needed sorting. She said she'd ask Dad to do it. Mam told Nana she'd passed her test. Nana said Gransher would have been proud of her. Mam nearly cried when Nana said that, I think she did, but she said she had something in her eye. Nana made a pot of tea. I watched her go to the kitchen and she held on to the side of the cooker looking all sad. Her head was bent forward and she rubbed her eyes.

'Yep, Beryl. Yuh father would be proud of you, but then again, he always was, he always was,' said Nana when she brought the teapot into the room and put it on the table.

There was a piece of toast on a plate, next to the teapot. It looked like it had been there for ages. There was some jam on it and a bite had been taken. Nana said she tried to eat it for tea, but she wasn't very hungry. Nana poured the tea and her hand was shaking, the tea was watery and tasted horrible. I was glad when we went home.

#

After Mam passed her test she got a job at Asda in Rogerstone. Mrs Wakefield got a job there as well. They go to work together in Mam's car and Mrs Wakefield pays half the petrol money. They wear a blue uniform, the same colour that Coventry City play in. I got a poster on my wall with all the football teams and their football kits.

On Friday, Mam gets her pay packet. She spends it all on shopping from Asda, but Dad still has to give her money as well. She buys lots of ace stuff that we've never had before, Mam buys special diet meals, she eats loads of 'em. Dad says she's only supposed to have one at a time.

I don't read Warlord anymore. I read Plug comic. I've got every issue. Mam gets it on Friday when she does her shopping. I have to help get the shopping out the car and then I read my comic and eat my Space Dust. Space Dust is fizzy and crackles in yuh mouth. Martyn Summers said if you drink Coke with Space Dust, your stomach will explode. I never have Space Dust with Coke.

Plug is the main character in my new comic, he's also in The Beano with the Bash Street Kids. Sometimes I get The Beano but I don't think it's as good as Plug. There's lots of ace stories in Plug. My favourite is Antchester United and Sporting Life. Antchester United is a football team who are insects. There's Gnat Lofthouse, Anty Gray, Stirling Moth and George Beastie. The manager is called Matt Bugsy – he got all the players on a flea transfer. Sporting Life is about football as well. They tell you about the history of different teams and their best players. I like finding out about football teams.

I've decided to support West Bromwich Albion, just like Kevin Walsh. We're the only boys in school who support West Brom. Everyone says they're shit, but they beat Manchester United 4-0 – I saw the goals on The Big Match. My favourite player is Cyrille Regis. He scores lots of goals cos he's brilliant. On Football Focus, Bob Wilson did a special report on Cyrille Regis and other black footballers in the first division. Some people at football grounds shout things at the black players, nasty things. I'd never shout anything nasty at Cyrille Regis – he's ace.

Mam likes her new job at Asda. Dad said it's Mam's perfect job. She can gossip all bloody day and get paid for it. She comes home with lots of stories. There's always people shoplifting and it's not just yobs and druggies. Mam said one day the security man followed an old lady who looked a bit shifty. She was stealing tins of cat food – putting 'em in her coat pocket. She paid for the rest of her shopping but didn't pay for the cat food. They caught her and took her to the manager's office. Mam said she was posh and had over fifty pounds in her purse. Another lady tried nicking stuff by hiding it in a pram. Mam said she didn't even have a baby.

Mam had to go to Asda on her day off to see what days she was working. Me and Wayne Ashby went with her in the car. Mam said we could look round the store as long as we didn't get into trouble. While Mam was finding out what days she had to work, me and Wayne looked at the toys. We were messing about with the Action Man stuff when there was an announcement over the tanoy.

'COULD A MRS ELSIE MORGAN, THAT'S A MRS ELSIE MORGAN, COME TO THE INFORMATION DESK AT THE FRONT OF THE STORE PLEASE, FOR AN URGENT MESSAGE. THANK YOU.'

Me and Wayne wanted to see what Mrs Elsie Morgan looked like and see what the message was. We ran to the information desk. There was a woman behind the counter reading a magazine and chewing gum. We pretended to look through the comics and waited for Mrs Elsie Morgan. It was ages and I thought Mam would turn up before we got chance to see the lady, but then an old granny walked up to the information desk.

'Hello, I'm Elsie Morgan, you have a message for me?'

'Oh, yeah, hang on a minute luv,' said the women behind the desk, looking at note pad. 'It's from yuh husband, he says can you get some black boot polish.'

Mrs Elsie Morgan went red, I'm sure she said 'The cheeky bastard', I didn't think old grannies used swear words. The dinner ladies at school don't swear. We waited for Mam outside in the car park. We sat on some bollards, there was a dead wasp on the ground and Wayne squashed it with his foot.

'So you can just phone up Asda and get 'em to call out a person's name and give 'em a message then?' asked Wayne.

'Dunno, guess so.'

'Have you got two pence?'

'Why?'

'So we can phone the information lady.'

'But we don't need to give anyone a message?'

'We can make one up for yuh Mam, it'll be brilliant!'

I gave Wayne two pence and he said he'd phone the lady. I looked at the information desk to see what the phone number was. It was written on the wall. I ran back out to the car park, I shouted the number to Wayne before I forgot it.

'Yeah, hiya, is that Asda? Can I get a message to my Mam, she's shopping in yuh shop. Huh, her name? It's Mrs Sugden, can you tell her that our dog's been run over and she's to come home as soon as she can. Mrs Sugden... yuh... yeah, it's sad, thanks, bye.'

We ran back into Asda to hear the woman say our message on the tanoy. We got through the door when we saw Mam talking to some Asda lady, then the message started.

'IF THERE'S A MRS SUGDEN... THAT'S A MRS SUGDEN IN THE STORE, COULD SHE PLEASE COME TO THE INFORMATION DESK FOR AN IMPORTANT MESSAGE. THANK YOU.'

Mam was still chopsing to the Asda woman, when she heard her name being called out over the tannoy. She looked all worried and went to the information desk. Me and Wayne walked behind her so we could hear.

'Hello Sandra, it's me luv, I'm Mrs Sugden, what's this about a message?'

'Oh, sorry Beryl, it's not good news really. Yuh dog's been run over. Sorry luv.' said the information desk lady, trying to look sad.

'DOG? I DON'T HAVE A BLOODY DOG!' shouted Mam, her face going all beetroot.

Me and Wayne couldn't stop laughing, Wayne said that he thought he was gonna piss himself. He held his cock to try and hold his wee in. Mam saw us laughing and realised that it must have been us that gave the message.

'You bloody little buggers!'

Mam said sorry to Sandra, the information lady, for wasting her time. Sandra just shrugged her shoulders and went back to reading her magazine.

We ran out of Asda before Mam could tell us off in front of everyone. We waited by the car for her to come out, she took ages. We could see her inside the main doors talking to some ladies in Asda uniforms. When she came out, Mam's face was still all beetroot. She told us to get in the car before she banged our heads together.

'I've never been so bloody embarrassed, what's the bloody matter with the pair of you?' shouted Mam.

'We thought it would be good fun, sorry Mam,' I said, trying not to laugh.

'Wait till I tell yuh father!'

I knew Dad would think it was funny. He's always playing

189

tricks on Mam. He sent her up to Terry Howells, the builders, to buy some sky hooks once. And he told her to ask in the post office how much a fifty pence postal order was, cos he heard they'd gone up.

'We don't even have a bloody dog! I thought something serious had happened, frightened the bloody life out of me when my name was called out!'

I looked at Wayne and we both burst out laughing, we couldn't help it. I laughed so much I couldn't breathe. Then Mam started laughing as well, she laughed so much she had to stop the car in the bus stop. There was an old lady waiting, the windows were down in the car so she could hear us laughing.

'You can't stop 'ere, there's a bus due in a minute!' said the old lady.

'Sorry luv, our dog's died,' laughed Mam.

Chapter 25.

Volcanos Go Boom!

'GWYN SUGDEN, TURN AROUND AND PAY ATTENTION TO THE BLACKBOARD!' shouted Miss O'Connell.

A piece of chalk flew past my head into the back of the classroom. I was looking at Colin Scotch's volcano drawing. It was really good. Colin sits behind me, Miss O'Connell turned round and saw me looking at his picture. Miss O'Connell's very strict. Everyone's scared of her, even some of the teachers.

Martyn Summers and Kevin Walsh are in my new class as well. Wayne Ashby's in Mr Parker's class – Mr Parker is six foot four inches tall. His class is in the green hut in the middle of the playground. We use the chimney breast as a goal at playtime. Kung Cheng's not in school anymore, he had to go back to Hong Kong – that's where he's from. We don't get free chips anymore.

I like volcanos. We've been learning about them in class. They explode and lots of stuff called lava comes out. Lava is really hot and can burn yuh face off. In the olden days, when the Romans were about, a big massive volcano called Mount Vesuvius erupted and killed everyone in a place called Pompeii. Miss O'Connell said nobody stood a chance and everyone died a horrible painful nasty death. They found loads of dead bodies in the ash – even some dogs. Kevin Walsh asked if there was any volcanos in Wales – there's not. But millions of years ago there were loads, exploding and shooting out lava. That must have been ace.

I went to the library with Mam to find out about volcanos. I asked the library lady how many books they had, she said there were lots. I was only allowed to take three books out, but there were loads more about volcanos. Mam joined the library so she could take some books out from the grown-up section. Mam said I could choose a book from the grown-up section, but only one. She didn't want the library lady thinking we were a bunch of nutters just having books on volcanos. Mam had some books about knitting and DIY. She wants Dad to put a sliding door in the living room, Mam reckons they're all the rage and really posh. Mrs Wakefield at number 79 has got one. Mam says in the future everyone will have sliding doors, but they'll be automatic – like on the Space 1999.

Miss O'Connell didn't tell us to go and find out about volcanos – I just think they're ace. I'd like to go and see a volcano for real. I asked Dad if we could go and see one next year on holiday instead of going to Butlins. He said not to be so bloody daft and he wasn't gonna spend his week off looking at a bloody old mountain – especially if it could blow up. Mam and Dad love Butlins. Dad likes to drink beer in the Butlins bar and Mam likes to play bingo – just like they do at home.

Miss O'Connell finished doing the register and stood in front of the classroom. She started talking about the lessons we've been doing and how pleased she was at how much we've learnt. Miss O'Connell stood with her arms behind her back and marched up and down in front of the classroom. Just like

Captain Mainwaring on Dad's Army.

'Somebody from class went to the library and asked for some books on volcanos.'

My face went red, I wondered how Miss O'Connell knew I'd been to the library. Perhaps the library woman phoned the school to tell her?

'Stand up, Gwyn Sugden.'

I stood up from my desk. My face was all red and everyone was looking at me. Colin Scotch was kicking the back of my legs, trying to make me laugh.

'Gwyn Sugden went to Risca library to find out more about volcanos. Didn't you, Gwyn?' asked Miss O'Connell, pointing a bit of chalk at me.

'Yes Miss,' I said, but I wished I hadn't bothered.

'Now, Gwyn took it upon himself to find out more about what we study in class. And if you want to do well in your lessons and get ready for the comprehensive school, this is exactly what you should be doing.'

I knew I was gonna get the piss taken out of me at playtime for this. I wanted Miss O'Connell to leave me alone.

'Sit down please, Gwyn.'

Colin Scotch gave me a piece of paper that he got from Richard James. It had 'Bamber' written on it in big red letters. If anyone's brainy or does well in a test, you get called a Bamber. I'm norra Bamber. Bambers are good at spelling and know how to do sums and stuff. Martyn Summers told me my face went as red as a baboon's arse. We learnt about baboons in class, their arses are red. Miss O'Connell showed us a picture of one and we all laughed. She told us off and shouted at us. We also saw some pictures of some seabirds – one was called a shag. Richard James had to stand in the corner of the classroom after she showed us.

Miss O'Connell said that Mrs Tamplin heard me ask for the volcano books in the library. I hadn't seen her, she must have been hiding. I was glad that it wasn't the library lady that had grassed me up.

At playtime only a couple of boys took the piss cos I got books from the library. Martyn Summers said he thought it was a good idea, but Martyn's a bit of a Bamber. He gets high scores in all the spelling tests – one time he got 19 out of 20. But he never gets called a Bamber, I reckon it's cos he's good at football.

Colin Scotch was telling Tony Keane about what happened in class. Tony Keane's a new boy in school, he's from Liverpool. He's got a funny accent and can run very fast. Tony Keane said in Liverpool he had to run fast to get away from the coppers. He's always pissing about and likes fighting. He climbed on the roof of school and Mr Parker had to get a ladder to get him down – that was in his first week.

'What d'yuh go to the library for? You soft 'ed!' laughed Tony Keane.

'I'm norra soft 'ed! Volcanos are ace!' I shouted, feeling my face going red.

'Yeah you are, you fuckin' soft 'ed!'

Tony pushed me in the face with the palm of his hand, laughing. I told him to fuck off but he did it again and called me a wanker. I told him to fuck off again and he was just about to push his hand in my face, when I hit him in the side of the head. Some boys ran over to watch.

One of the boys shouted 'FIGHT! FIGHT!' and everyone in the playground came running over. Tony Keane tried to hit my face, but he missed. I hit him again and it made my hand hurt. I kept punching his face, as hard as I could. Everyone was shouting, 'FIGHT! FIGHT! FIGHT! FIGHT!' Then, Tony Keane swung his arm round and caught me on the nose. Blood spurted out everywhere and everyone went 'OOOH!'. Then, someone grabbed me from behind and picked me up from the ground – it was Mr Parker – the biggest teacher in the world. Tony Keane tried to hit me again, even though Mr Parker was there, holding me in the air.

Mr Dandy pushed his way through the crowd and grabbed Tony Keane by his t-shirt. He marched him off to the headmaster's office. I heard Tony Keane call Mr Dandy a bastard. My nose was bleeding and Mr Parker stuck a hanky on it to try and make it stop. He took me to the staff room and Miss O'Connell cleaned me up. She checked my nose to see if it was broken, she said it was okay.

'So, what was the fight about then?' asked Mr Parker.

'Tony Keane called me names cos I got a book from the library, sir. Then he kept pushing his hand in my face.'

'He's a trouble maker, that boy,' said Miss O'Connell, cleaning some dried blood off my face with a wet tissue.

I thought I was gonna be marched off to the Headmaster's office like Tony Keane, but when the bell rang for lessons, Miss O'Connell told me to go back to class.

'I reckon you gave Tony Keane a black eye,' said Martyn Summers when I sat down at my desk.

'I just saw him come out of the Headmaster's office with Mr Dandy,' said Kevin Walsh, picking his nose and looking to see how big his bogies were.

'He's gonna wanna fight you after school in the park,' whispered Colin Scotch. 'He'll wanna smash your face in!'

I didn't wanna fight Tony Keane in the park after school.

And I didn't wanna get my face smashed in. My nose bleeds really easy. The only other fight I've had, I got a really bard nose bleed and it went on my Action Man t-shirt – Mam couldn't get the blood out. The fight was with Julian Wakefield in Sunday School. He punched me in the arm when we were singing 'Oh Jesus I Have Promised', so I punched him back. Julian hit me in the face with a Bible. Julian Wakefield doesn't go to Sunday School anymore – he's not allowed.

At afternoon break Tony Keane came over to talk to me. I thought he was gonna start a fight again, I was shitting myself.

'Alright Gwyn?'

'Yeah, my nose hurts a bit, thought you'd broken it.'

'Yeah, sorry. Good fight, wasn't it? You got a good whack at my head. Doesn't hurt though.'

Tony Keane spat on the floor and rubbed it across the concrete with his daps. He said 'See yuh later' and ran off to pull Tanya Burns' hair.

'Fuckin' 'ell, he didn't wanna fight in the park after school!' said Martyn Summers, 'Yuh jammy bastard!'

I was glad Tony Keane didn't wanna fight after school. He would've kicked my 'ed in. I saw him fight Karl Stone. Karl Stone was knocked to the floor when Tony kicked him in the bollocks. Karl Stone was the hardest in school – well, that's what he used to tell everyone. Colin Scotch says Karl Stone is full of shit. Colin reckons Tony Keane is the hardest in school, so I was even more glad he didn't wanna fight me.

That's the last time I'm getting a book from the library.

Chapter 26.

Aim, Fire.

'I don't care if it's about space and monsters, yuh not having the bloody telly on,' shouted Mam.

Everyone at school was talking about Blake's Seven. Martyn said it was ace. Lots of monsters and laser guns, but Mam was doing one of her tea leaf things. Now and again fat ladies come to the house and Mam tells 'em their fortune – just by looking at their tea leaves. Dad calls it Mam's PG bullshit.

'When Mrs Trundle gets here, I want you to go to yuh room. I don't want you in the living room, laughing.'

I only laughed once. A lady with big massive boobs and a jumper that smelt like cat food, came to have her tea leaves read. Mam said she could see her wearing white. 'Of course I'll be wearing white, I work in the chemists,' said the lady with the massive boobs. I thought it was funny and Mam told me off.

There was a knock on the door.

'Ooh, that'll be Mrs Trundle, right get to yuh room.'

Mam opened the door and a tall lady with funny hair came in.

'Is this Gwyn? Goodness me, he's grown,' said the lady.

'Yeah, and a bloody handful as well, he's a boy un half.'

I went upstairs to my bedroom, it was really cold. Mam

wants Dad to buy something called central heating, but Dad says it's too expensive. I've got a Calor Gas heater in my bedroom. Dad only let's me have it on if it's really cold. But it's always really cold in my bedroom – Dad says it's never cold enough.

I could hear Mam talking to the lady downstairs. Mam talks really loud, Dad says she's like a bloody foghorn. I played with my plastic soldiers, pretending to beat up the Germans. I want more toy soldiers, I want more Germans. I was bored of playing soldiers, I looked at my football books for a bit, but then I got my new gun from under my bed. It's ace, I got it for Christmas. It looks like a real one, Mr Sheppard from across the road says it's a Lee-Enfield bolt-action replica. He said he killed some Germans with one when he was in the war.

My new gun had some caps that were really loud. I used 'em all up firing at the cat from down the road. He's called Ginger, cos he's ginger. He was really scared and didn't like it when I fired my gun at him. He ran away and hid under the scout hut, he was under there for ages. I tried to get him to come out by showing him some of my crisps, but he didn't come out. He mustn't like crisps very much, I do. I like Monster Munch the best.

Mam was still telling PG bullshit to Mrs Trundle. I crept downstairs for a glass of squash, on my way back upstairs I heard Mam tell the lady she'd come into some money.

'You said that last time Beryl, all I've had is bloody bills.'

I went back to my bedroom and put my green jumper on cos I was cold. I got out my gun and pretended to be a marksman. A marksman is a soldier that hides and shoots people from far away. My new gun has got a telescope, but it's not very good. I opened my bedroom window and turned off the light. I pretended to be looking for Germans – sniping from a secret army den. Like I saw on the telly in a film about the war.

A bloke was walking up the street with his dog. I followed him with my gun, I could see it was Mr Parry. His dog's called Brownie and he's really old. He's got a gammy eye and it's always watery with stuff leaking out. Mr Parry stopped so Brownie could do a shit. Brownie does a lot of shitting. They walked up the street and I followed them through the telescope on my gun until they disappeared.

Nobody came down the street for ages, I was gonna put my gun away when an old lady walked past our house. She was walking really slow and she had a walking stick. I pretended she was a wounded German trying to get back to a bunker. I made a radio noise and said 'I have the enemy in sights'. She turned around and looked at my window. I ducked my head down and waited for a bit. I looked again and she was walking up the street. I followed with my gun and the lady kept looking back. She was trying to walk faster, I could hear her walking stick hitting the ground. When she was gone I put down my gun and looked up in the sky to see if I can could see any planes. Sometimes they fly over, you can see the lights flashing on the wings. I couldn't see any planes, but coming down the street was a policeman. Just behind, at the end of the road, I could see the old lady with the walking stick. The policeman turned around and was talking to her. She pointed down the street and the policeman started walking towards our house. I closed my window and climbed into bed. I was shitting myself. I heard the gate open and his footsteps up the path.

Knock, knock, knock.

I heard Mam say, 'Who could that be this time of night?' I pulled my blankets over my head, I thought about hiding in the wardrobe. Mam opened the front door.

'Hello there, sorry to bother you, but I've had complaint that someone in your upstairs window was brandishing what appeared to be a gun ,' said the policeman.

'GWYN! Get yuh arse down 'ere, NOW!'

From the top of the stairs I could just see the policeman outside the front door. Mam's face was red and she was telling the copper she was very sorry.

'Here he is, the little bugger, what have you been playing at?' shouted Mam, 'Get down here and explain to the policeman.'

I'd seen the copper before, up Risca, walking about, checking shop doors and telling boys off for riding their bikes on the pavement. He's never caught me riding my bike on the pavement.

'Right then, young man, what's all this about a gun?'

I looked at the carpet, Mam had her new slippers on.

'Sorry, I was just playing sniper.'

'I'll sniper you in a minute, yuh little bugger,' shouted Mam.

'It's very dangerous to point guns at people, young man, even if it's not a real weapon. Can you go and get your gun and show me please?' asked the policeman.

I went upstairs and grabbed my gun. I hoped the copper wasn't gonna take it away – I love my gun. I went back downstairs, Mam was telling the copper that I was a boy un half. I gave my gun to the copper and he held it up in the air, having a really good look at it. I wondered if he was checking to make sure it wasn't real.

'It's a Lee-Enfield bolt-action replica,' I said, just so he knew it wasn't a proper one, and I wasn't really gonna shoot old ladies.

'Wow, it's a beauty, looks like the real thing,' he said.

I told the copper that I got it for Christmas. I also told him about my new football kit and that Dad only got pants and socks. The copper gave me my gun back and told me not to be so silly with it in the future.

'Right then young man, don't let me catch you sniping out of your bedroom window again,' said the policeman – I told him he wouldn't.

Mam said to go back to bed and Dad would not be happy when he got home. I said goodnight to the copper and ran up the stairs, Mam shouted to be careful.

I could still hear Mam saying sorry to the copper as he walked up the path.

'Is that your car in the driveway, madam?'

'Yes it is, I'm a disabled driver, it's got special controls,' said Mam.

'Well, that may be the case, but that doesn't excuse you from having an out of date tax disc.'

Mam had to go up the police station and say sorry. Dad had to pay a fine and said Mam needed shooting.

Chapter 27.

Eye, Eye, Captain.

Uncle Graham was home from the Navy. He didn't bring back as many presents as he normally does. Mam said he'd been very quiet and not his normal chirpy self. Dad said that he's probably just tired and Mam should leave him alone.

I learnt about the Navy in school. Miss O'Connell told us about a man called Admiral Lord Nelson and how he won the Battle of Trafalgar. He sank lots of the enemy's ships and he didn't lose one of his own. But Lord Nelson got injured during the fight and kicked the bucket. Miss O'Connell said he was one of Britain's most important war heroes. I like James Bond better.

I asked Dad if Uncle Graham had ever been in any battles. Dad said that Uncle Graham was only a chef in the Navy, but he might have poisoned a few people.

We were doing sums, I hate sums, when Mrs Woolly, the headmaster's secretary, came into the classroom to talk to Miss O'Connell.

'Gwyn Sugden, get your things together and go with Mrs Woolly please,' said Miss O'Connell, not looking very happy cos I was getting out of doing sums.

I grabbed my bag, pulled a face at Martyn Summers and went with Mrs Woolly. I got my coat from the cloakroom and

Mrs Woolly said Mam was waiting outside. I wondered what was wrong, perhaps Dad had hurt himself at work again, or my goldfish, Starsky was dead. Mam had a big stupid grin on her face, like when she came home from bingo when she won five pounds.

'We're gonna go on a big ship!' said Mam, all excited.

'Wha', like on holiday?'

'Don't be so bloody daft mun, nor, down Cardiff docks.'

'Cardiff docks? Eh?'

Uncle Graham was waiting in Mam's car, parked by the school gates. He was in the front so I had to get in the back. I don't like being in the back, it makes me feel sick. Uncle Graham said hello, but he was really quiet. Just like Mam said he was.

'So why are we going to Cardiff to go on a ship?'

'Graham's gorra go and pick something up, haven't you, Graham?' said Mam, Uncle Graham nodded.

'So, can we go on the ship as well 'en?'

'Yeah, Graham spoke to 'em, but no mucking about and wandering off getting into mischief.'

It took ages to get to Cardiff. Mam took the wrong turn off the motorway and we had to ask a bloke for directions. He looked like a villain that Regan and Carter have fights with in The Sweeney. When we got to the docks Mam parked the car next to a big ship. It was called HMS Lancaster. A sailor looked at Uncle Graham's I.D. and said we could go aboard. The sailor had a gun, I asked Mam if she saw it. She told me to keep my eyes to myself or we might get thrown off.

We had to go and see a man called a Petty Officer. We got to a big metal door and Uncle Graham knocked on it. I heard a man's voice say to come in. A big fat man was sat at a desk, he had a big beard like Captain Birdseye. Uncle Graham told the man who we were and he shook ours hands. Mam tried to do a little curtsy.

'I'm not a member of the royal family, madam,' said the man with the beard.

Uncle Graham talked to the man about Navy stuff. I didn't understand what they were talking about, neither did Mam. Mam hates it when she doesn't know what people are talking about. The man with the beard gave Uncle Graham an envelope. Mam tried to look to see what it said, but Uncle Graham put it in his pocket.

'Did you fight with Lord Nelson?' I asked the man.

The man laughed, he was really loud. Like Father Christmas. Mam laughed too, but I don't think she knows who Lord Nelson is.

'Well young man, if I'd been with Nelson at Trafalgar, that would make me a very old man indeed,' he said, but he did look old, nearly as old as Dad.

We said goodbye to the man and went off the ship. I wanted to look around, but Mam said we had to get back.

'Who the bloody hell is Lord Nelson?' asked Mam, when we got in the car.

I told Mam all about Lord Nelson and all the ships he sank, but I don't think Mam was listening. She said he sounded very nice, and hoped he was living in an old peoples home somewhere. I told her he was dead, Mam said that wasn't very good.

Uncle Graham opened his envelope and read his letter. He didn't say what it said and when Mam asked him, he said it was just Navy stuff. Mam said she wanted to pop home to tell Dad we were going to drop Uncle Graham back up Nana's.

When we got to Risca, it was dark and raining. The windows were steamed up in the car so I couldn't see out proper.

'Right, I won't be a minute, just gonna tell Cliff we're going to drop you off, Graham,' said Mam.

'How's things at school, Gwyn?' asked Uncle Graham, after Mam got out of the car.

'It's okay, Mam says I should make the most of it, she says it's the best time of my life. But Mam doesn't have to do sums with Miss O'Connell.'

Uncle Graham did a little laugh. It was the first time I heard him laugh since he'd been back home. I could see his reflection in the windscreen. He looked sad.

'Did you like school, Uncle Graham?'

'Not much, was glad to leave really, I never fitted in much.'

'Is that why you joined the Navy?'

'Yeah, think so. I just remember looking at a book in school. There were lots of pictures of all these wonderful places. Places that looked a million miles away from here. I just wanted to go and see them.'

Uncle Graham went quiet again. I knew what he was talking about though. Me and Martyn Summers went up the mountain once to look for conkers. We didn't see anyone else all day. I thought it would be ace to live up the mountain in a hut or something.

'Gor, all yuh bloody father cares about his going up the pub and drinking beer,' moaned Mam, as she got back in the car.

She said Dad didn't give a monkey's about us going up Nana's, and said he'd get his own supper when he got home from the pub. All the way up to Nana Balding's, Mam talked to Uncle Graham, but he just nodded. I started to feel a bit sick, cos Mam kept driving over bumps in the road. We got to

Nana's and Mam said we'd stay for a bit and have a cuppa tea. Nana was smoking a Woodbine in the kitchen, stirring some baked beans on the stove. She moaned we'd been ages and didn't know what to do for Graham's tea.

'Well, looks like beans again then,' said Uncle Graham.

'Don't be so bloody cheeky,' shouted Nana, 'It's Malcolm that gives me the lip, it's not normally you, Graham.'

I was tired, and Nana shouting gave me a headache. I wanted to go home and read my comics. I can see why Uncle Graham ran away with the Navy. Mam shouts and moans all the time, but not as much as Nana. Dad says the Balding women suffer from verbal diarrhoea. I had diarrhoea once, Mam said it made the bog smell like Bristol Zoo. I couldn't help it, Mam give me out of date curry flavour Findus Crispy Pancakes – it made my poo go all runny.

Uncle Graham was in the living room. He read the newspaper for a bit, then switched the telly on.

'Yuh tea'll be ready in a minute, Graham!' shouted Nana.

'He's been bloody quiet all day,' whispered Mam.

'I dunno what's up with him, Beryl, he's been like it since he got home last week. Can't get a civil word outta him.'

While Nana was chopsing, some fag ash fell from her Woodbine into the beans. Nana didn't notice and carried on stirring. Nana smokes loads of Woodbines, Dad says that why she is so small, cos it stunts her growth. But Dad smokes loads as well, he's not small. Mam said something about it stunting growth somewhere else. She must mean Dad's hair.

Nana poured the beans over some cold, burnt toast, and took it to living room on a plate with a big chip out of it.

'Ere yuh go, boy,' said Nana, 'All I do is bloody cook.'

Uncle Graham went to the table and started to eat his tea.

He didn't look like he wanted to eat it, but Nana tells him off if he doesn't. She shouted at him once for leaving half a biscuit – even though it was stale.

'So, did you find out where yuh going then, boy?' asked Nana, lighting up another Woodbine.

Uncle Graham nodded while he ate his fag-ash beans and toast.

'Well, where to 'en? Cat gotcha tongue?'

'Not allowed to say, confidential,' said Graham

'You can't tell yuh own bloody mother! I only goes up the Bingo and up the Co-op, who the bloody hell am I gonna tell?'

'Well, there's everyone at the Bingo and everyone at the Co-op,' mumbled Uncle Graham, with his mouth full of fag-ash beans.

'Don't be so bloody cheeky! C'mon, where yuh going lad?'

'Narnia, but don't tell anyone.'

'See, you could tell me. Sounds foreign. Wait till I tell everyone at Bingo, they'll be impressed.'

Nana told Mam all about the man at the butchers who cut his finger off. She reckoned they couldn't find it and it might have ended up in the sausages. The living room was getting smoky and it made my eyes sore. I wanted to go outside, but it was raining. Sometimes I go to the front room and listen to the record player, but Uncle Malcolm was sleeping in there cos he came home drunk. Uncle Malcolm's got lots of records, he lets me play 'em. Groups with funny names, The Doobie Brothers and The Bonzo Dog Doo-Dah Band. I like Bob Seger and the Silver Bullet Band.

My eyes were getting sore from all the smoke from Nana's Woodbines. I rubbed my eyes and Mam told me off. I always get sore eyes, I get lots of nose bleeds as well. I had one in C&A once, I wiped my nose on a skirt in the shop. Mam went mental.

When Mam finished her tea and talking about all the family and neighbours, she said it was time to go home. I could still smell Nana's fags on my coat when I got in the car. Smoking is smelly and horrible. My eyes were still sore and, when Mam wasn't looking, I gave 'em a rub.

When we got home, Mam made spaghetti hoops and potato waffles. Mam had a fried egg with hers. Mam said eggs are good diet food. Dad was up the pub. He does his own supper when he gets home. If he's had too much beer he goes in the chippy. Dad doesn't like spaghetti hoops.

Mam let me stay up to watch some telly but the programmes were rubbish. Mam was watching a soppy film with people kissing and saying 'I love you' all the time. My eyes still hurt and Mam said they were all bloodshot. I went to the bathroom to have a look in the mirror. I washed my face with soap and water, but the soap got in my eyes and made 'em worse.

'Just go to bed and try to get to sleep. You've got school in the bloody morning!'

My bedroom was really cold, and my eyes were still itchy and sore. I put my pillow over my head to rest it over my eyes. It was a bit better but I couldn't breathe proper.

'MAM!'

'What the bloody 'ell d'yuh want, yuh noisy bugger!'

'Can I have a damp flannel to put over my eyes? They still hurt, they do Mam!'

Mam muttered to herself, she didn't sound very happy. I heard her go to the bathroom and run the tap. She brought up a flannel, moaning all the way up the stairs.

'Ere, yuh bloody bugger,' said Mam, handing me the damp flannel, 'Have you been rubbing yuh eyes?'

'I can't help it, they're sore Mam, honest.'

I put the flannel over my eyes, it was nice and warm. Mam stopped being moody and asked if the flannel made it better. I said it did. It made me feel a bit dozy. Mam closed the bedroom door and went back downstairs. I thought about the big ship we went on in Cardiff docks and wondered what it would be like to fall asleep, and when you woke up, you were somewhere else. Uncle Graham says in really bard weather, you don't sleep at all.

I woke up and the flannel wasn't nice and warm, but cold and wet. Mam was downstairs turning off the telly and putting her false teeth in a jar. It's not a proper false teeth jar, it's one of Dad's old Vasoline tubs. Dad just puts his false teeth on the mantelpiece. It's horrible. They have bits of food stuck to 'em. In the morning, Dad wipes 'em on his vest, and puts 'em back in his mouth.

My eyes were still sore and I couldn't get back to sleep. Mam came into my bedroom to see if I was alright. I told her the flannel was cold and my eyes still hurt.

'I know what you can stick on yuh eyes,' she said, and went into her bedroom. Mam came back with white cotton thing. It had a piece of tape stuck to it and Mam peeled it off.

'Ere,' she said. 'Put this over yuh eyes.'

Mam stuck it on my face, pressing down over my sore eyes. It felt much better.

'Where did you get this from, Mam?'

'Oh, it's from my drawer. It's a special towel for ladies.'

'Do ladies get sore eyes 'en?'

'Uh, yeah, now get to sleep before yuh father gets back

from the pub.'

Mam went to bed and I started to doze off. I was nearly asleep when Dad woke me up coming through the front door. He was talking to himself and making a noise like a steam engine. When Dad's really drunk he always makes mad noises. He'd bought some chips from the Chinky. I could smell 'em and I could hear him unwrap the paper in the kitchen. The smell of the chips from downstairs made me hungry. Dad only buys chips from the Chinky when he's had beer.

'BULLO! DO YUH WANNA CHIP SANDWICH?' shouted Dad, from downstairs.

Mam must have been asleep, cos she didn't answer back. Mam loves chip sandwiches. Dad came upstairs and went into their bedroom.

'You asleep, Beryl?'

Mam woke up and Dad asked her again about the chip sandwich.

'Ooh! That'll be nice Cliff, I've only had a small tea,' said Mam. 'But be quiet Cliff, Gwyn's got sore eyes and he hasn't long got to sleep.'

Dad opened my bedroom door, I pretended to be asleep. Even though I wanted a chip sarnie and a glass of squash.

'What the fuckin' 'ell has he got on his 'ed!' laughed Dad.

'Cliff! Stop yuh bloody swearing and be quiet!'

'He's gorra sanitary towel on his face!'

'I told you, he's got sore eyes! He thinks that's what they're for, Cliff!'

'Well, I've bloody seen it all now,' laughed Dad.

'Be quiet before you wake up the whole cowing street. Let's have that chip sandwich – I'm starving.'

Chapter 28.

Talybont vs The European Cup.

I didn't think Dad would pay, Mam's always saying he's really tight. But Dad said he'd gladly pay sixteen pounds to get rid of me for three days, he'd even pay a bit more if they took me for a week.

Cos I'd been good in school and learnt lots about volcanos and stuff, Mrs O'Connell said I could go on the trip. It's only for boys in year four, but a few of us in year three are going. Martyn Summers could go, cos he's good at sums. Richard James, David Pryce and a boy called Stewart Flowers are going as well. I don't know Stewart Flowers very well, he looks like a hamster.

I looked at Mam's RAC road map to see where Talybont was. It's near somewhere called Brecon. Dad said that's where they teach the army blokes to kill people – special army men called Gurkhas.

Mam gave me sixteen pounds to take to school, she put it in an envelope and stuck it inside my jacket with lots of safety pins. Miss O'Connell took ages getting it out. I think she said bugger when she pricked her finger on one of the pins.

Karl Stone said the trip was for bummers, but only cos he couldn't go. Richard James told him to fuck off and said if he called him a bummer again, he'd kick his head in. Richard

James is the second hardest in Year Three, Tony Keane is the hardest, he beat up Karl Stone. I was glad, I don't like Karl Stone, he's a twat.

David Pryce's brother went to Talybont. He said it was ace cos you sleep in a bunk bed and have farting competitions. David Pryce's brother also said Mr Evans snogged Mrs Tamplin when they went to the pub.

'How did yuh brother know, did he see 'em at it, then?' asked Richard James.

'I dunno, s'pose so,' said David Pryce, but we didn't believe him.

Mrs Tamplin wasn't coming on our trip, Mr Dandy was in charge, but Mr Evans was coming. I don't reckon Mr Evans would want to kiss Mr Dandy. But Richard James said Mr Dandy might like it, cos he's a bummer.

Mam packed my bag and told me to make sure I changed my pants and socks everyday. Mr Evans drove the mini-bus and Mr Dandy made sure we didn't flick Vs at the cars. I sat next to Richard James and we played I Spy. I had F for field, L for lorry and S for seats. Richard did a C, I said lots of things begining with C: car, cow, coat, clouds...

'I give up,' I said, 'What is it?'

'Cunt,' whispered Richard.

'Huh? What's a cunt?'

'Dandy's a cunt.'

Richard James said cunt was a bard word – the bardest word in the world. Up the big school they say it all the time. If someone's a twat, like Mr Dandy, they call 'em a cunt. Mr Dandy was definitely a cunt. He's always shouting at us, getting angry and throwing stuff. He smacked Pickles on the back of his head cos he said he had a funny look on his face.

Martyn was sat in front of us, he was reading a book about planes. Martyn likes planes.

'Oi, Martyn, Dandy's a cunt, pass it on,' I whispered.

Martyn told David Pryce, and David Pryce nodded his head. Mr Dandy shouted at one of the boys from Year Four. I could see Mr Evans' face in the rear view mirror, driving the bus, he shook his head. I reckon Mr Evans thinks Dandy's a cunt as well.

We were driving for ages, so when we saw the sign for Talybont-on-Usk, we all cheered. Dandy told us to shut up. We drove up to a big building, Mr Evans said it was an old railway station. A man with a dog was waiting for us. Dandy got out of the mini-bus and talked to him. Dandy then made us get off the mini-bus and line up. He shouted to keep quiet and marched us into the building. Inside, the walls were covered with wildlife posters, pictures of birds of prey, trees and nature stuff.

'This is Mr Sidebottom, he's in charge of Talybont Outdoor Centre,' shouted Mr Dandy, 'Are there any questions?'

Nobody said anything, then David Pryce said 'Yes sir'.

'Well, what is it lad?'

'What's the dog called?'

Everyone laughed, except Mr Dandy.

'He's called Pike,' said Mr Sidebottom, 'And he's very friendly.'

'Now, does anyone have any proper questions,' shouted Dandy.

I thought David's question was a proper question. Nobody asked anything else and Mr Sidebottom told us about the Centre and what we'd be doing. He said after we've settled in and been shown to our rooms, we'd have some hot soup. Mr

Evans said the boys from Year Three would be kept together. Mr Sidebottom took us to a small room with bunk beds. He flipped a coin to see who would get top bunk, to stop any arguments. I got a top bunk and Martyn Summers was on the bottom. After we put our clothes away, Mr Evans said said it was time for our soup – it was horrible and runny.

'Right then, we'll be leaving in fifteen minutes,' shouted Mr Dandy, after everyone had finished their soup.

Mr Dandy said we were going on a nature walk and doing some drawing. Mr Sidebottom gave everyone a drawing pad, a clipboard and a pencil. We went outside and had to put on big orange plastic coats and walking boots, even though it was really warm and sunny – my boots felt all squidgy.

Mr Sidebottom drove the mini-bus, it didn't take very long, and soon we got to a car park next to the canal. Mr Dandy said we'd be walking back to the centre, and he didn't want to hear anybody moaning. Mr Sidebottom drove off, and we walked up a path to the canal.

'Look boys, this is a full working lock,' said Mr Dandy.

A lock is a big wooden thing with big gates that lets all the water in and out so boats can go up and down hills.

'If we are lucky, we might see a boat go through the lock,' said Mr Dandy, 'Right, get your pads out because I want you to start drawing.'

Locks are easy to draw. But I'd much rather draw a plane or a tank. Martyn is good at drawing planes, he can draw a Spitfire without having a picture to copy. Mr Dandy made sure we were drawing properly and not doing cartoons. Mr Evans didn't look to see what we were drawing, he was sat on a bench, smoking his pipe. Simon Hawkins, one of the older boys, was messing with his clipboard. The clip holding his pad flew off and landed in the lock – plop! Dandy went crackers.

'WHAT THE HELL HAVE YOU DONE BOY? THAT'S THE PROPERTY OF TALYBONT OUTDOOR CENTRE!' screamed Dandy, his face all purple.

'Sorry, sir,' said Simon Hawkins.

'When we get back to the Centre, you can tell Mr Sidebottom that you're sorry. But Mr Sidebottom might not be as nice as me.'

We finished our drawing and carried on walking along the canal. Me and Richard James walked with Mr Evans. We talked about Nottingham Forest winning the league, Mr Evans said Brian Clough should be the England Manager. A manager tells the players what to do when they are playing football. Like how many goals to score, or who to kick.

'Do you think Liverpool will win the European Cup tomorrow night?' asked Mr Evans.

'I thought it was on Saturday, sir,' said Richard, looking worried – Richard James supports Liverpool, lots of boys at school support Liverpool.

'Tomorrow night, lad, against Brugge of Belgium.'

'Can we watch it at the Centre, sir?' asked Richard, 'There's a telly, sir, it's next to the poster about drowning.'

'We'll see, we'll see.'

Some other boys talked about the final and tried to guess what the score would be. 3-0, said Martyn Summers, David Rees reckoned 7-0, with Kenny Dalglish getting four goals. Mr Evans laughed, he said Brugge were a good team and he'd be surprised if there was more than a couple of goals. One boy, Ian Morgan, supports Manchester United and said Liverpool were rubbish.

'Then why don't Manchester United win the League and

the European Cup 'en?' one of the boys said, I think it was Kevin Poole.

'That's enough talk about football. We're here to learn about nature, not the exploits of overpaid sportsmen,' shouted Mr Dandy, as he was telling someone the difference between an oak and a birch tree.

We walked for ages, my feet were wet from my damp boots. We got to a bridge, Mr Dandy said it was a special electric one. It went across the canal so cars could drive over. When a boat needed to go through, cars have to stop and the bridge lifts up. We had to do drawing of it, it was a better than drawing a lock. Mr Dandy said we might get to see a boat go through, but he said that about the lock. Richard James was drawing a cartoon of Dandy with a big purple face. I said if he caught him, he'd go mental. When Dandy walked past, Richard pretended to be drawing the bridge. Holding up his pencil, pretending to be getting the angles right.

A boat turned up, we all cheered. A man got off and tied it to the canal bank. He had a key that opened a metal box on the bridge, and he pressed a big red button. The bridge made a mad beeping noise and some barriers came down to stop the cars. The bridge lifted up and the man got back in his boat and drove it under the bridge. We all cheered, and the man waved. Mr Dandy told us to be quiet.

We walked back to the Centre but before we went inside, we had to take off our coats and clean our boots. I could smell our tea cooking, I cleaned my boots really fast cos I was hungry. I hoped our tea was better than our runny soup. But it wasn't. We had fish and mashed potato – it was cold.

After tea we watched a film about nature. It was really rubbish and boring. David Pryce fell asleep. When the man on the film said to listen for the sound of a hawk calling, David Pryce did a loud snore. Everyone laughed, except for Mr Dandy. He told us off and said to go to our rooms and get ready for bed. We put on our pajamas and were allowed the light on for half an hour.

'Do you reckon they'll let us watch the final tomorrow?' said Martyn Summers.

'Mr Evans will wanna watch it,' I said.

'Yeah, but Dandy hates football. He might not let us,' said Stewart Flowers, putting on his Spiderman pajamas.

Mr Evans came into our room, he told us to settle down and then turned off the lights. Richard James did a big fart, it stunk. I was glad I wasn't sleeping under his bunk bed.

#

Mr Evans woke us up really early and made us make our beds. I'd never made a bed before, Mam makes my bed. Martyn Summers helped me. We had to have a shower and clean our teeth. Stewart Flowers did a massive wet fart. He cupped his hand over his arse to make it louder.

For breakfast we had sausages, egg and toast. It was nice, Richard James opened his mouth to show us how much food he could stuff in. He got two sausages and most of his egg. When we finished our breakfast I had to help collect the plates and take them to the kitchen. Some of the older boys were doing the washing up. They were moaning cos their pink rubber gloves made 'em look like Jimmies. A Jimmy is a bummer. We don't get told off for saying Jimmy, cos the teachers don't know what it means. Dandy goes mental when anyone says bummer. Richard James says that's cos he is one.

'Right boys, could you all listen please!' shouted Mr Dandy. 'Today we are going to the museum in Brecon. Remember you are representing the school, so no messing about!'

It was raining, so I was glad we weren't going on another nature walk. We didn't even see any proper nature, just Mr Sidebottom's dog and a dead bird. The mini-bus was cold and someone did an eggy fart. Mr Evans made us open all the windows to let some fresh air in. I reckon it was Stewart Flowers, cos it smelt the same as the one he did in the showers.

It wasn't very far to Brecon. Mr Evans said we could look around the town for an hour before we went into the museum.

'Eleven o'clock, on the dot,' said Mr Dandy as everyone ran off from the the mini-bus.

I had some money from Dad and I wanted buy something ace. I walked around with Richard James and Martyn Summers, we found a really cool shop that sold toys and stuff. Martyn got a Liverpool scarf, I bought a World Cup '78 Top Trumps pack. Richard James didn't buy anything. Martyn said we only had five minutes left. We ran down the road really fast, we didn't want to be late and get told off. Mr Evans was waiting in front of the museum, looking at his watch. Dandy was shouting at someone for bringing back a beef burger.

'Only just made it lads, right, line up, so we can get inside,' said Mr Evans.

Mr Dandy reminded us not to mess about, and counted everyone to make sure we were all there. The museum had lots of cool stuff, things from the olden days. There was a dummy of a caveman, he was all hairy and he looked like Mr Evans. There was a nature bit, with lots of stuffed animals. We had to do drawings of the things we liked the best. I drew a picture of a stuffed fox. Someone did another eggy fart.

'That fuckin' reeks!' said Richard James, pulling his jumper up over his nose.

'Who smelt it, dealt it!' laughed a boy who wasn't even from our school.

When we came out of the museum, it was still raining. Mr Evans said he didn't want to smell any foul odours on the way back to the Centre in the mini-bus. Stewart Flowers looked worried.

'Mr Dandy, can we watch Liverpool play tonight, sir? It's the European Cup Final,' asked Richard James.

'It's on when you lot are in bed. So I don't see how you can,' said Mr Dandy.

Everyone groaned. One lad, who had his Parka zipped-up, said 'Oh, sir!' Like when Mam won't let me stay up to much a horror film.

'We are not here to watch football. We are here to see and learn about nature!' shouted Mr Dandy, 'Now, that's the last I want to hear of it.'

Everyone went quiet and Stewart Flowers farted. It stunk.

#

After we had our dinner, we put on our orange coats and damp boots. It was still raining, but Dandy said we had to go on a walk, cos it would be fun. Nobody believed him, not even Mr Evans.

'I hate Dandy,' said Richard James, as we walked up the road, freezing our bollocks off, 'He's a cunt.'

We walked for ages, my feet were wet and I could smell Stewart Flowers' stinking arse. Dandy shouted things out for us look at – an old canal sign, broken bits from a boat or a rubbish tree. Mr Evans was walking behind us, smoking his pipe, humming. One of the boys asked him about the football, and if he could get Mr Dandy to change his mind. Mr Evans said it wasn't up to him, and if Mr Dandy had made his mind up, then that was that.

We got to another lock on the canal. A boat was waiting to go through and Dandy got excited.

'Look boys, we're in luck, we'll get to see a boat go through an actual working lock.'

'Stupid cunt,' whispered Richard James.

Dandy talked to the bloke with the boat and asked him if it was okay for us to watch him go through the lock. The man nodded and shrugged his shoulders, 'Whatever turns you on, mate,' said the man. I heard Mr Evans laugh.

The boat went into the lock and two big gates closed behind it. The man had a lever and turned something on the other gate. There was a big noise, Dandy said it was water rushing in. The boat slowly floated to the top. Two front gates opened and the boat went through. Dandy was still excited and told us about a bloke called Brunel from the olden days. Nobody was listening.

'Look, Dandy's got a stiffy, he's so excited,' laughed Richard James.

'The twat,' said David Pryce, gobbing on the ground.

Dandy heard us laughing and shouted at us to pay attention. We couldn't hear what Dandy was saying, cos it was raining so much. Even the ducks were hiding under the trees. Our coats were supposed to be waterproof, but I was soaking. We walked for a bit more, Dandy pointing things out along the path. Nobody cared about the stupid trees and the olden days. Then, we saw our mini-bus parked up on the side of the road. Mr Sidebottom was in the driver's seat. Everybody cheered, even Mr Evans.

'My goodness, been swimming, lads?' laughed Mr Sidebottom when we got in the mini-bus.

When we got back to the Centre, our tea was ready. We had burgers and chips, it was ace. Simon Hawkins got told off for putting too much red sauce over his chips. Dandy said it would spoil the flavour.

'If we can't watch the football on the telly, perhaps Dandy will let us listen on the radio,' said Richard James, chomping on his burger.

'You ask him, I'm not gonna ask him, he'll go mental,' I said.

Richard James finished his burger and made a sandwich from the last of his chips. Dandy was walking towards us, he was making sure nobody was messing about, or using too much red sauce. I don't like red sauce, I like brown sauce better.

'Sir, can we listen to the football on the radio, if we can't watch it on the telly?' asked Richard James.

'I'M SICK TO DEATH OF HAVING TO TELL EVERYONE! YOU WILL NOT BE WATCHING OR LISTENING TO THE FOOTBALL! NOW THAT IS THE END OF IT!' screamed Dandy.

Everyone went quiet. We wanted to watch the football, even the boys who didn't like Liverpool wanted to watch it. We ate our pudding and nobody talked. The plates got collected, I had to help scrape the waste into a big bin in the kitchen. Mr Evans came in to help, he grabbed a tea towel and started to wipe some plates.

'It's a shame we can't watch the footie, sir,' said Andrew

Thomas, who was washing up.

'I know lad, but it's not up to me. Mr Dandy's in charge of this trip, I'm just here to help supervise.'

'Mr Dandy's a nutter, sir, sorry if he's yuh butty or anything, but that lad only asked if he could listen to the match on the radio,' said Andrew Thomas, 'Mr Dandy went mental, sir.'

Mr Evans chuckled. I don't think Mr Evans is butties with Dandy. I reckon he thinks he's a twat, like everyone else does.

After all the kitchen stuff was cleared away, we had to do some more drawing. We had to draw something from the day's walk or from the museum. I drew the canal boat going under the bridge. Richard James drew a picture of Dandy going mental with a speech bubble, saying 'I'M A BIG TWAT'. He drew his face all purple and really massive. If Dandy had seen it, he would have gone mental. Richard James drew another picture of a tree and some ducks – just in case.

Mr Evans made us get ready for bed and made sure we got into our bunks. He came back and turned the lights off, and said sorry cos we couldn't watch the football. I like Mr Evans. We heard Mr Sidebottom leave the Centre and go home – he lives in the house next door.

'I bet Dandy and Mr Evans are watching the football in the telly room, the bastards,' said Richard James.

'They're very quiet if they are,' I said.

We listened to see if Dandy and Mr Evans were watching the football. We couldn't hear anything, then one of the boys from the next bedroom came into our room.

'Dandy and Evans have gone out,' said the older boy.

'What! Where?' asked Richard James.

'We reckon they've gone up the pub.'

'So is there anyone here 'en?'

'Don't think so, Andrew Thomas is looking around the Centre.'

'Fuck, if they've gone down the pub, we can watch the football!' said Richard, all excited.

We all got out of our bunks and piled into the telly room. Andrew Thomas came back from looking around the Centre, he said there was nobody there. Someone turned the telly on and the volume was on full – it made us jump. The bloke on the telly said it was nil-nil. A couple of the boys who didn't like football said they'd go on watch – just in case Dandy and Mr Evans came back from the pub.

The match was a bit rubbish, none of the players looked like they wanted to score a goal. Kenny Dalglish had a couple of shots, so did David Fairclough for Liverpool. At half-time it was still nil-nil. Some of the older boys got a glass of squash from the kitchen. I shared a glass with Martyn, we washed and wiped the glasses and put them back in the cupboard.

The second half was a bit better. The managers must have told them off for not scoring any goals. Then, Graeme Souness passed the ball to Kenny Dalglish, he hit it and scored. We went mental, we were all jumping up an down, cheering. On the telly the crowd were going mental as well. Loads of Liverpool fans waving their red scarves, going crackers. Brugge nearly scored. Richard James shouted at the telly cos he thought it was gonna be a goal. The game seemed to go on for ages, but Liverpool won and they ran around the stadium with the big European Cup. Someone turned off the telly and we all went back to our bunks. Richard James was singing 'We Are The Champions' and 'There's Only One Kenny Dalglish'. We told him to be quiet, just in case the teachers came back.

I was nearly asleep when I heard Dandy and Mr Evans come

back to the Centre. Mr Dandy came into our room to make sure we were asleep. Stewart Flowers pretended to snore.

In the morning, after we had our showers, Mr Dandy told us we were gonna have a special treat. We ate our breakfast and then we had to pack our bags, ready to go home. Mr Evans said he wasn't feeling very well and had a glass of water with a special fizzy tablet in it.

'Surprised none of you boys have asked what the score was last night?' said Mr Evans, his eyes were a bit red.

Nobody said anything, then Richard James asked if Liverpool had won.

'One-nil, Kenny Dalglish scored,' said Mr Evans, drinking his fizzy water.

'Cracking pass from Souness sir, wasn't it?' said Andrew Thomas.

'WHAT!' shouted Dandy. 'HOW THE HELL DID YOU KNOW GRAEME SOUNESS PASSED THE BALL TO KENNY DALGLISH?'

'Dunno sir, sorry sir,' said Andrew Thomas, his face was bright red.

Andrew Thomas was so scared he told Dandy about everyone watching the match on the telly. He even told him about the two boys keeping a look-out and that we had a glass of squash from the kitchen. Dandy went berserk. He was shouting and screaming so much we couldn't understand what he was saying – like Captain Caveman.

We weren't allowed our special treat – Dandy said we didn't deserve it. So we didn't go to Tredegar to see the owl sanctuary.

On the way home in the mini-bus I played I spy with Richard James. C is for...

Chapter 29.

Argentina '78.

I rode my bike as fast as I could. I was playing footie with Richard James, we played the World Cup final. I was Holland, Richard was Argentina, he won, 43-37. I didn't wanna miss the start of the proper match. I wanted Holland to win, but everyone at school liked Argentina.

Martyn Summers was coming over to my house to watch the match. Neil Gerald was as well. Neil's new at school and lives across the road, they moved in, just before the World Cup started. Mam said I had to be friends with him. Mam's friends with Neil's mam already, she smokes more fags than Nana and Dad put together. Dad calls her fag-ash Lil. I have to call her Mrs Gerald. Mam calls her Betty.

Mam said she'd be glad when the World Cup was finished. She said she was fed up of football, football, football, everyday. I think it's ace. Scotland got knocked out early and Willie Johnston, who also plays for my favourite team, West Brom, got sent home for taking drugs. Mam says Uncle Malcolm takes drugs, but Uncle Malcolm isn't very good at football. Jimmy Hill on the telly, said Scotland were unlucky. Dad said they were just shit.

For my birthday, I got a portable telly for my bedroom. Dad let me have it early cos the World Cup started before my birthday. Mam didn't want me watching football on our new coloured telly in the living room. But Dad let me watch it anyway. On my birthday I was ten. There were supposed to be ten candles on my cake, but Mam only used eight. She said that's all there was left in the box.

When I was with Mam, up Asda, I saw a World Cup game. Mam bought it, but said not to tell Dad cos he'd go bananas. Dad doesn't let Mam buy bananas unless someone's not very well. Mam's bought me lots of Golden Wonder crisps cos they had free World Cup Soccer All Stars cards. I like KP or Smith's crisps better, but they didn't have any free football cards. There's thirty six to collect, I've got twenty seven. I've eaten loads of crisps, but Mam's ate loads as well.

I played my World Cup game with Neil Gerald. We don't know the rules, so we made up our own – Scotland won the World Cup six times. Andrew Drewett at school has got Subbuteo. I wish I had Subbuteo. Mam says Andrew Drewett's dad makes lots of money. He goes to work in a posh car and wears a shirt and tie. Dad only wears a shirt and tie if someone's died, or when he goes to see Doctor Davies. That's when Dad has a bath as well – Dad says only dirty people wash. I asked Mam if I could only have a bath when I go and see Doctor Davies. Mam said no.

Neil Gerald and Martyn Summers were already at my house when I got home. They both wanted Argentina to win cos they liked their blue and white striped shirts. I like Holland cos they play in the same colour as Newport County. Dad was in his armchair, Mam and Mrs Gerald were on the settee. We had to sit on the floor. Mrs Gerald was telling Mam about Mrs Hodge from down the road who was having it off with the gas man. I don't know what she was having off him, perhaps free gas.

'Come on Argentina!' shouted Neil.

'Come on Holland!' I said, and punched Neil Gerald in the arm.

Mam slapped me on the head and said it was rude to hit people if they're a guest. When Mam wasn't looking, Neil punched me in the bollocks. I thought I was gonna be sick.

'Stop rolling round on the floor like a fool,' said Mam, but she didn't know how much my bollocks were hurting.

The stadium on the telly looked brilliant. The pitch was covered in paper and stuff from the crowd. Everything was blue and white with lots of smoke and firecrackers. There was a nappy on the football pitch over the park once.

Holland came out on the pitch first, but when Argentina came out, the crowd went mental. It wasn't like anything I'd seen on Match Of The Day, it was amazing Even Mam thought it was brilliant, and she doesn't like football very much.

'They do go berserk these foreigners,' said Mrs Gerald, blowing smoke into the back of Mam's head. Mam didn't notice cos she was too busy getting a Rich Tea biccie out of the packet.

'Well, they do eat all that spicy food don' they, Gwyn's the same when he's had curried beans.'

'Ooh, I saw them new curried beans up the Co-op, awful dear though, but they do have sultanas in 'em, I suppose.'

'Well, that's why I do give 'em to Gwyn, see Betty. Gorra have their fruit un' veg somehow, haven't they?'

'I give Neil faggots and peas, he'd do cover 'em in red sauce though, don't yuh, boy?' asked Mrs Gerald.

Neil didn't say anything, he was watching Holland sing their national anthem. When it was Argentina's turn, the crowd went mental again, some of the players were crying as well.

'They're just like the Ities those Argies, always crying and waving their arms about,' said Dad.

'I told you, it's that spicy food, Cliff,' said Mam. Mrs Gerald nodded her head, agreeing.

'Whatcha bloody mean, spicy food? You're thinking of bloody Mexico, yuh daft bugger.'

'Oh, it's the same thing, Cliff.'

Dad shook his head and muttered something under his breath. Dad knows loads of stuff about different countries, he watches loads of programmes on the telly. Mam says he only watches 'em cos sometimes ladies have their boobs out.

The game started and Holland were playing really good. They looked like they were gonna score, I shouted 'Come on Holland'. But just before half-time, Argentina scored a goal, Martyn and Neil jumped up and down, Martyn dropped his Wagon Wheel.

'Ooh, I'll have to buy Neil an Argentina football shirt now. Is that your new favourite team, Neil?' asked Mrs Gerald.

'Nor, Mam, Liverpool are my team, they are the best!' he said, doing a dance, like the ladies on the telly that the camera was showing. Dad said they had a cracking pair of Bristols. Mam told him off for being rude on a Sunday.

At half-time I helped Mam bring in some french bread pizzas, crisps and pop. Dad said Mam was wasting money on rubbish.

'I didn't waste any money, got it from the out-of-date bin from the back of Asda,' said Mam, as she put some crisps in her mouth.

In the second half, Holland tried really hard to score a goal. I shouted at the telly and Mam kept telling me off. Martyn and Neil said there was no way Holland would score, and Argentina were gonna win the World Cup. The man on the telly said there was only ten minutes to go, then the ball crossed into the Argentina box and a Holland player did a brilliant header and scored – GOAL! I danced round the living room and called Martyn and Neil, Jimmies.

'Stop yuh bloody performing or you'll get a nose bleed,' said Mam, eating the last Rich Tea.

'See, I told you Holland would score, come on Holland!' I shouted.

The referee blew his whistle for the end of the game. Dad said they would have to play for another thirty minutes.

'So they're gonna play more bloody football then?' asked Mam, 'I wanted to watch Songs Of Praise, Harry Secombe is singing tonight.'

'You'll be lucky. Anyway, if there's still no winner, they'll have to have penalties,' said Dad, making some more rollies.

'We could be 'ere all bloody night!' moaned Mam, stuffing a piece of french bread pizza in her gob.

They started the extra time and Argentina were playing really well. Then, one of the Argies ran past loads of Holland players. Holland's goalie came out to try and get the ball off him, but the ball hit his legs and the Argie scored. Neil and Martyn danced round the living room, Dad shouted at 'em to get out the way. The crowd on the telly went mental and threw loads of toilet paper on the pitch.

'Ooh, what a waste, I paid nearly sixty pence for four rolls of toilet paper the other day up Asda,' said Mam.

'I know, Beryl, it only ends up down the bloody toilet, I sometimes just rip up the Argus. Let 'em use that to wipe their arse on instead,' said Mrs Gerald.

'Aye, but the problem using the Argus is more shit comes

off it!' laughed Dad.

'Cliff!' snapped Mam.

'Mrs Hales puts the Argus in the bottom of her budgie cage. She used to use the Daily Mirror, but she said the stories made the bird depressed,' said Mrs Gerald, nodding to herself.

Dad chuckled as he smoked his rollie.

Just before the end of the game Argentina scored another goal. Martyn and Neil didn't go mental like before, they just waved their arms in the air and went 'Yeah!'. Mam and Betty weren't watching, they were chopsing about Mrs Hodge and the gas man. The ref blew the final whistle and Dad did a big fart. The Argies ran around the pitch, jumping up and down and hugging each other, like Jimmies.

'Silly buggers,' laughed Mam, as one of the players took his shirt off and started crying. The Argies lifted the World Cup on a special stage that was quickly built on the pitch. Dad said the World Cup was made of solid gold and was worth a lot of money. So much money that even if you won the pools it wouldn't be enough to buy it. Mam brought in some chocolate biscuits and Dad made a pot of tea.

'Well, I'm glad that's over with. Can get back to watching proper telly again,' said Mam.

I didn't want proper telly back on, I liked the World Cup. I liked watching all the different teams from all the different countries. Mam said I could go over and watch Risca United play if I wanted to watch more football. Risca United are rubbish and Dad said the season didn't start for ages. I asked Dad if we could go down to see Newport County – he told me to bugger off.

Martyn, Neil and Mrs Gerald went home, and the living room was all smelly from Mrs Gerald's fags. Mam asked Dad what he thought about Mrs Hodge having it away with the gas man. Dad said he didn't give a monkeys – it was up to her who she had fiddling with her meter.

Chapter 30.

Crushing Bobby Crush.

Dad doesn't like going on holiday. He says it's a waste of good money and it's cheaper to stay at home and sit in the garden. Mam calls him old Scrooge. Mam was nagging Dad to go on holiday for ages. Every time a holiday programme was on the telly, Mam would say everywhere looked nice and wished she could go there. Dad got fed up of her moaning and sent her up the travel shop to get some holiday brochures. I came home from school and Mam and Mrs Gerald had 'em all out on the coffee table.

'Ooh, Jersey looks nice, Beryl,' said Mrs Gerald.

'Nor, Cliff won't go on a ferry, went to Ireland to watch the rugby once, he kept sicking up his beer.'

'You can go on a plane.'

'He won't fly, Betty, says it costs too much.'

Betty is always over our house. Mr Gerald died in an accident at work. Neil Gerald didn't come back to school for ages. It must be rubbish having a dead dad, I felt sorry for Neil. He looked really sad in the playground when he came back to school. I didn't talk to him for ages, I was worried he'd start crying. But he didn't. He was just really quiet. I'm glad my Dad's not dead. I'd get no pocket money, and he makes the best sausage sandwiches in the world.

Mam said Nana Balding had to come on holiday with us. I didn't want her to come with us, neither did Dad cos he has to pay for her. Mam said Nana needed a break cos she hadn't had a holiday since Gransher died. I hate going anywhere in the car with Nana Balding, she gives me a headache. Dad says she's got two volumes, loud and not there. Dad likes it when she's not there.

Mam said she wanted to go to Pontin's in a place called Christchurch. I looked to see where it was in the RAC map. It was a long way from Risca, Dad said it would cost a bloody fortune in petrol. On the day we left to go on holiday, Dad put two big suitcases on the roof rack. I had to sit in the back with Nana. As soon as we drove off, Nana and Dad started smoking. Mam had her window down to let in some fresh air.

'Ooh, Beryl, close that window, it's blowing smoke back in my face!' said Nana.

'Well, I don't want it in my face when I'm driving!'

Nana didn't stop moaning, first she was too cold, then she was too hot. Then she said Mam was driving too fast, then too slow, and we wouldn't get there 'til it was dark. Nana had a small bottle of whisky and she kept taking little sips. She fell asleep when we went past a place called Dorchester. She started snoring and Dad said we should put her on the roof rack – even Mam laughed.

When we got to Pontin's, Nana woke up. We had to get the keys to our chalet. Mam likes the word chalet, she was saying it to everyone before we went on holiday – 'And we can just relax in the chalet if we don't want to go out in the evening,' she said to Mr Watkins, the insurance man. Dad said Mam thinks chalet sounds posh, and she says it in a funny voice. Like Mrs Walker from Coronation Street. She's the posh lady in The Rovers Return. Dad says he wouldn't wanna pint in the Rovers, they pour too much head.

A lady showed us the way to our chalet. She was really pretty and had a blue uniform and a short skirt. Dad whispered she was a nice bit of stuff. Nana said she looked like a tart. Nana thinks lots of ladies look like tarts, even Mrs Wiltshire, and she's in a wheelchair. I asked Dad what a tart was, he said it was a lady who likes to give out crumpet. I like crumpets.

Dad had to make two trips to bring in the suitcases, cos they were heavy. I tried lifting one, but I couldn't get it off the ground.

'What the bloody 'ell you got in those cases, Beryl? We're only 'ere for a bloody week!'

'Stop yuh swearing, Cliff, everyone's looking' said Mam, but nobody was.

The chalet was rubbish, it was just like our old flat, but smaller. I asked Dad what the difference was between a chalet and a flat, he said they could charge more money to idiots like my Mam, cos they thought it sounded French. I had to sleep in a tiny bedroom with no windows. Nana was gonna sleep on a settee that turned into a bed. She said she didn't want to cause a fuss, but she didn't stop going on about it.

After Mam unpacked the suitcases, we went for a walk around the holiday camp. There was a swimming pool, a play area with lots of swings, and an entertainment building where they had lots of shows and singing. Mam loves shows. We went inside the entertainment place cos Mam wanted to see what shows were on. Dad said he wanted a pint. There was a big poster on the wall, with all the different shows and stuff. Nana Balding said her feet were killing her, and went to the bar to buy a Guinness.

'Ooh, look Gwyn, they've got wrestling!' said Mam, all excited. There was a poster with a picture of a big fat man who looked like Big Daddy – but he wasn't Big Daddy. He was a pretend Big Daddy.

SEE WORLD OF SPORT WRESTLING, JUST LIKE ITV. STARRING FAT LARRY AND THE STARS OF THE RING!

It said there was an exhibition tag fight. They'd choose some lucky boys from the audience to get in the ring and have a go, just like the pros.

'Do yuh fancy that, Gwyn? Sounds fun,' said Mam.

I didn't fancy having my face smashed in. But I did wanna see the fat men in tights prance about. Mam was looking at the big poster on the wall, then, all of a sudden she got really excited.

'Look Cliff! They've got Bobby Crush!'

'What, the poofter on the telly who plays the joanna?'

'He's not a poofter, you think everyone's a poofter, you do Cliff. Anyway, he's playing 'ere on Tuesday night. And we're goin'!'

Dad wasn't very happy about having to go and see Bobby Crush. It cost extra to see Bobby Crush. Not all the shows were free. But Mam likes Bobby Crush, she likes watching him on the telly. All he does is smile and play the piano. When Mrs Morgan's son, next door, plays the piano, Mam bangs her slipper on the wall and shouts for him to shut up.

'Ooh, look Gwyn. And it's says 'ere you can have yuh picture taken with him, only three pound.'

'Only three pound! No wonder he's always bloody smiling,' shouted Dad, 'He should be in hysterics!'

Mam said we should go and sit with Nana in the bar. Dad said it was a good idea, but only cos he wanted a pint of beer. We walked down a corridor and I could hear mad beeping noises and boys laughing. Just before the bar, there were some fruit machines, a pinball machine and an electronic game called Boot Hill. It was ace, like something from the future on Tomorrow's World.

'Dad, can I have a go on the games?'

'No, yuh bloody well can't, it's a waste of good money.'

'Go on Cliff, give him a few bob for the diddlers, we're on holiday, you old Scrooge,' said Mam, looking to see where Nana was sitting.

Dad said I could have a go on the machines later. He was dying for beer and had a throat like an Arab's dap.

'Anyway, I don't have any change,' said Dad, but I could hear loads of coins rattling in his pockets.

Nana was in the corner of the bar. She had a Guinness and was smoking a Woodbine. There was a big telly in the corner, the biggest telly I'd ever seen. Grandstand was on, Frank Bough said Nottingham Forest had beaten Ipswich Town 5-0 in the Charity Shield at Wembley.

'Another Guinness, Mary?' shouted Dad, as he went to the bar.

'Go on 'en, and get me a whisky as well, it'll settle my nerves.'

Dad shook his head and asked Mam if she wanted a bitter lemon. Mam always has a bitter lemon. Mam told Nana about Bobby Crush and the wrestling. Nana said she didn't like Bobby Crush, thought he was a bit odd-looking, like he kept bodies in the cellar.

'They got ballroom dancing, you like ballroom dancing,' said Mam.

'Who am I gonna dance with?'

'I expect there'll be other people on their own.'

Dad came back from the bar with our drinks on a tray. Nana sipped her whisky and drank some of her Guinness. Dad did a burp and Mam told him off.

'Better out than in.'

'Can't take you bloody anywhere, Cliff.'

#

After breakfast, me and Dad went to the entertainment hall to watch the wrestling. Dad didn't mind cos it didn't cost anything. Dad likes it when things are free. There were lots of people queueing, boys with their dads and some grannies.

'Like big bloody kids,' said Dad.

A man in a funny suit and a big dickie-bow said we could go in. The doors opened and in the middle of the dance floor was a big wrestling ring. Just like on World Of Sport on the telly. We sat at the front, I wanted to see the wrestlers close-up when they were being hit.

'LADIES AND GENTLEMEN, BOYS AND GIRLS!' announced the man into a microphone. 'PREPARE FOR TODAY'S WRESTLING EXTRAVAGANZA, LET'S HAVE A BIG WARM PONTIN'S WELCOME FOR FAT LARRY AND THE STARS OF THE RING!'

The wrestlers came running out from behind a curtain. Fat Larry was massive, bigger than Dad's butty, Tiny. Tiny's dead now though, he kicked the bucket cos he drank and smoked too much. They put him in a special coffin, Dad said it took ten blokes to carry it.

Fat Larry got into the ring and hit his chest with his fists, like King Kong. The man in the dickie-bow gave him the microphone and Fat Larry told us to make some noise. I shouted as loud as I could, so did all the other boys and the grannies. Dad smoked his rollie and shook his head.

The first fight was a tag match. Fat Larry's partner was Harry The Viking, he had a hat with horns and big furry boots. They were fighting The Grim Reaper and Charlie Chopsticks. Charlie Chopsticks was dressed up like a Chinese man, but he wasn't really Chinese. He was just some bloke that didn't have any hair, like Dad.

The tag fight was rubbish. Fat Larry bounced The Grim Reaper and Charlie Chopsticks with his big belly. But they were running into him on purpose. Everyone loved it, boys were shouting 'Easy, easy' and one of the grannies flicked Vs. Dad said she was old enough and ugly enough to know better. There were some more fights and Fat Larry won them all. Dad said he'd never seen so much rubbish. The man with the dickie-bow got back into the ring, he said if any boys wanted to have a go, they should queue up.

'You wanna have a go, son?' asked Dad, checking his watch, and looking at the bar.

'I'd rather watch the other boys get their heads smashed in.'

'A wise choice, son.'

The boys that wanted to fight, queued up. The man in the dickie-bow said they would have boxing matches, smaller boys fighting first.

'Let's have our first bout,' said the man.

Two small boys got in the ring, they looked funny cos the boxing gloves looked massive on them. They ran at each other, lashing out like nutters. It was really funny, Fat Larry was laughing, but then one of the boys got punched on the nose and he started to cry. The man said it was a draw and two older boys got into the ring and put on some boxing gloves. They were better than the younger boys.

Dad kept looking at the bar, waiting for the shutters to come up. At eleven o'clock, a bloke in a blue jacket shouted the bar was open. Dad was first in the queue, the grannies were just behind him. After the boys finished boxing, Fat Larry and the other wrestlers went back into the ring and took a bow. There were only a few boys cheering, all the grown-ups were at the bar like Dad and the grannies. The man with the dickie-bow thanked everyone for coming and said the show was over.

After a few minutes, the wrestlers came in the bar, they were wearing jeans and t-shirts. Fat Larry drank a pint of beer in one massive gulp, and then bought another one. Dad said he was very impressed, so was I. I tried drinking my Coke in one gulp, but it went down my shirt and made me burp. Dad told me off and said to stop acting the goat. Fat Larry drank seven pints of beer. Dad said Fat Larry has to keep his strength up cos he's a professional sportsman.

Mam made Dad go and see Bobby Crush play the piano at the entertainment hall. I stayed with Nana in the chalet, she wasn't feeling very well. She fell over doing ballroom dancing. Nana said it was Mam's fault for making her go, Dad said it was all the Guinness and whisky she drank.

In the morning Mam told me all about the Bobby Crush show. She said he was really good. Dad thought it was a pile of shit. Mam told him off for swearing at the breakfast table.

'Eat up yuh egg and soldiers, then we can go and get our picture taken with Bobby Crush,' said Mam.

Dad wasn't coming to have his picture taken with Bobby Crush, he thinks he's a dinner-masher. Dad had a sore head, he reckoned it was something he ate, but Mam said it was all the beer.

When I finished my breakfast we walked to the entertainment hall. It was really sunny and I wanted to go in the pool. Mam said I'd have to wait til after we'd had our picture taken with Bobby Crush. Mam had her new red trouser suit on that she bought from C&A. I had to wear my new shirt and purple tank-top. I hate my purple tank-top. I have to wear it whenever we go somewhere posh or the doctors. Mam said there'd be lots of people queuing, but there was only two old ladies and a bloke in a purple jacket. Dad would say he was a dinner-masher. There was a sign on the door:

MEET BOBBY CRUSH!
BE THE ENVY OF YOUR FRIENDS AND FAMILY,
AND HAVE YOUR PICTURE TAKEN WITH ONE OF
BRITAIN'S BIGGEST RISING STARS!

The man who wore the dickie-bow at the wrestling show, was in charge. He wore a blue suit that had some stains. Mam paid him some money and we queued up behind the old ladies. They told Mam they never missed Bobby Crush when he's on the telly.

Right, ladies, yuh can go in now,' said the dickie-bow man, to the old ladies – they went 'ooh!'.

I wondered if Bobby Crush would notice they smelt like old biscuits and they had whiskers like Dad. When it was our

241

turn, Mam got all excited. She rushed in, grabbing me by my tank-top. Bobby Crush was sitting on the edge of the stage. He had a pair of massive flares on and looked taller than on the telly. But he's sat down on the telly, playing the piano.

'Hello there, and what's your names?' asked Bobby Crush, smiling like someone on a toothpaste advert.

'I'm Beryl and this is my son, Gwyn. We're both really big fans, aren't we Gwyn?'

Mam was lying, she didn't have any of his records. Mrs Gerald has one though, called Piano Party, I saw it when I was playing with Neil. It was the only record they had apart from Remember You're A Womble.

'Well, it's always lovely to meet my fans,' said Mr Crush.

'Yeah, we've got all your records at home,' lied Mam.

'Oh yes, what's your favourite?'

I wondered what she was gonna say to Bobby Crush. Mam had only ever seen him on the telly. Her face went red cos she didn't know the names of any of his records.

'You like Piano Party, Mam.'

'Ooh, that's right, Piano Party. That's the one I like.'

Cos I'd stopped Mam looking stupid, I thought Mam might give me some money for the pinball. A man with a camera told us to sit on the stage with Bobby Crush. Bobby Crush put his arm around us and Mam gave him a big hug.

'Ooh! Bobby Crush is being crushed!' he laughed.

The man with the camera told us to say 'Cheese' and his big flash went off as he took a picture. Bobby Crush signed a piece of paper for Mam, then we had to go.

'How was Bobby Poof then?' asked Dad when we got back to the chalet.

'He's norra poof Cliff, he's a very nice man, wasn't he Gwyn?'

I said he was nice and wasn't a poof, but only cos Mam gave me a pound for the pinball. I thought Bobby Crush was okay, I wasn't going to listen to any of his records though. But when we got back from holiday, Mam bought one from the bargain bin at Woolworths. It was ten pence, but she still hasn't played it.

Chapter 31.

Mr Dandy Loves Canals.

When I went to back to school, after the summer holidays, I was in a new class. Miss O'Connell isn't my teacher anymore, it's Mr Dandy. Dandy's mental. I wanted to be in Mr Evans' class, like Martyn Summers. Dandy's always shouting, when we went to Talybont, he shouted all the time. Dandy loves the olden days, he even makes us use old-fashioned pens. You have to fill them with ink from an ink pot. My pen keeps blocking, I have to flick it really hard to get it to work again. Loads of ink sprays out over the floor. Dandy goes mental when he sees ink on the floor. He shouts like a loon, screaming and saying stuff like 'I don't have any respect'.

On Monday morning Dandy gives us a spelling test. We have a list of words on Friday, before we go home. We're supposed to learn them on the weekend. I never learn my words, I play footie with Martyn and Wayne instead. On Sunday we go to Nana Sugden's, then we go home and Mam makes me have a bath – even if I'm not dirty. After my bath I watch The Professionals. I love The Professionals. It's even better than The Sweeney. Bodie and Doyle run around catching villians, smashing their faces in. It's ace. When The Professionals finishes, I have to go to bed so I don't learn my words for Monday's test. I have to cheat, but I only cheat on a few, so

Dandy doesn't think I'm brainy or I don't come bottom of the class. Judith Broome comes bottom. Sometimes she doesn't get any right at all. Judith Broome's rubbish at lessons. Dandy's always telling her off and making her cry.

Dandy makes us learn about a bloke called Brunel from the olden days. He made canals, trains and stuff and wore a big hat. Dandy loves Brunel, he thinks he was brilliant. Richard James said Dandy would like to get a time machine so he could go and bum him. Dandy says Brunel was a genius. A genius is a very brainy person. A massive Bamber. If Mr Brunel wasn't dead, he'd get 20/20 in the spelling test.

Mr Dandy has been teaching us about Risca in the olden days. There used to be a big viaduct, that's a big bridge for trains. The viaduct in Risca went to an iron works, but when the iron works closed down, they smashed the viaduct and built lots of houses from the bricks. I like some of the stuff Dandy tells us, but I don't tell Richard James, cos he'd call me a bummer.

Dandy told us about a new museum with loads of stuff about Risca from the olden days. He said if we were good and didn't muck about, we would go and have a look around and learn stuff. Mam had to sign a piece of paper to let me go. Judith Broome said she didn't want to go, Dandy went mental. He shouted so much that he made Judith Broome cry. She was still crying at dinner time.

The museum was up the road from school, in the old big school. The new big school is in Ty-Sign, up on the hill. The Queen opened it when it was her Jubilee. It's got a swimming pool. I went with Dad to see the Queen open the school, he made me wear a brown tank-top and I had to comb my hair. I hate combing my hair. The Queen was in a big shiny black car and waved. Loads of people were there, cheering and waving flags with the Union Jack on. Dad didn't cheer, but I don't think the Queen noticed.

'Right everyone, I want you all to walk in pairs and keep together,' shouted Mr Dandy when we were lined up in the playground.

Russell Silletoe showed me a trick with a paper bag, it was ace. He pretended to flick a ball in the air, then catch it in the bag. He said he saw it on the Morecombe & Wise Show. Russell was in Miss O'Connell's class, but I don't know him very well. He doesn't play football or throw stones at the trains after school. He's got long hair and likes loud rock music. Russell's got two older brothers with even longer hair than him. Mam says blokes with long hair and beards have something to hide.

We walked up the road to the museum. We went past the chip shop and we could smell chips cooking. It made me hungry. I didn't eat my Ready Brek for breakfast, it was all lumpy and made me feel sick. Dad says Mam's Ready Brek is thick enough to stick tiles up in the bathroom. A van drove past and beeped its horn. Wayne Ashby's dad was driving and a bloke in the front flicked Vs at Mr Dandy. Dandy told us off cos we all laughed.

The museum was in a big hut at the back of the old school. The playground was massive, much bigger than ours. A man came out of the museum, he had a big beard. He had a massive jumper that had holes in it and one arm was longer than the other – like the jumpers Mam knits. He was called Mr Donalds, Richard James said he looked like a Jimmy. We went into the museum and Mr Donalds told us about Risca in the olden days. He told us about the canals and how the railways were better for taking away the coal and stuff. So the canals stopped being used and people lost their jobs. There were loads of old pictures on the walls, all in black and white. There were pictures of boys and girls, the girls had big crazy skirts and the boys had short trousers. Dad said he didn't have long trousers 'til he was fourteen. He must have been cold.

Mr Donalds was very good at telling stories, like someone on Jackanory. He didn't even mind when Judith Broome asked him if he had any photos of dinosaurs, he just laughed. Dandy would have gone mental and told her she was stupid.

When Mr Donalds finished his stories, Mr Dandy told us to thank him for his time. Then we lined up outside and walked back to school. When we went past the chip shop, there were people queuing up for dinner. I wished I was getting chips from the chip shop, school dinner is rubbish. Once, Richard James said to one of the dinner ladies his meat was cold and horrible. She told him not to complain and there were people in Africa that would be glad of it. He nicked an envelope from class and put his meat in it. He wrote 'To Afrika' on it, and he put it in a post box on the way home.

'So, did we all learn something today?' asked Dandy, when we got back to school.

We said yes and Mr Dandy said after dinner we'd be writing an essay about the canals and Brunel. Somebody said 'Oh, sir!', and Dandy went mental. At dinner time I told Wayne Ashby about our trip to the museum.

'Sounds like a pile of shit,' said Wayne, stuffing his face with mashed potatoes.

'Wasn't shit, it was ace.'

'Bollocks, that Mr Donald Duck bloke sounds like a twat.'

'He's wasn't a twat, he just had a crap jumper and a big beard.'

'He sounds like Captain Birdseye,' laughed Wayne.

When we went back to class, Mr Dandy made us write our

essays on canals and Brunel. I liked doing my essay. I wrote about how the railways made it better for the factories to get their stuff around, but the canals stopped being used. Dandy collected up all the essays.

'Right, while I read your essays, get on with some sums from your maths book,' said Dandy.

I was doing a sum that was really hard. Then, all of a sudden, Dandy jumped up from his desk and started shouting. His face was the reddest I'd ever seen, and Dandy's face is always red. Especially after dinner time when he smells like the pub.

'JUDITH BROOME! DID YOU ACTUALLY LISTEN TO ANYTHING THAT MR DONALDS SAID TO YOU THIS MORNING?' he shouted.

'Yes sir,' said Judith, I thought she was gonna start crying.

'Really? Well, lets see what the rest of the class thinks about it.'

'Mr Brunel came for tea and said we could go and have a ride on his boat. It was a big boat and was on the canal. First we went to France and did some shopping. Then we went to America to see my Aunty Janet. Aunty Janet is a nurse and is very good at dancing. Then we came home just in time for supper, but Mr Brunel didn't want any and had to catch the last bus home.'

Dandy told us off for laughing and said it wasn't funny. I thought it was funny, so did Richard James. Richard James couldn't stop laughing.

'IT'S NOT FUNNY, LAD!' shouted Dandy.

Dandy made Richard stand outside the classroom. Judith Broome wasn't laughing though, she was crying into the sleeve of her cardie. I'd never seen Dandy so angry, even more angry than when we watched the football at Talybont. Dandy kept shouting at Judith, saying she should pay attention, and he was wasting his time. I felt sorry for Judith Broome, she can't help being thick. She's very good at skipping. I can't skip, my legs get tangled in the rope.

'I don't know why I bother, I really don't!' shouted Dandy.

Judith Broome jumped up from her seat and screamed. It was the loudest scream – ever!

'LEAVE ME ALONE!'

She ran out of the class, through the hall, and out of school. We could hear her shoes outside as she ran away. Dandy just stood there, staring at the door.

Richard James, who was still outside, poked his head around the door.

'Sir, if Judith Broome can go to the toilet, can I go too?'

Chapter 32.

Bump In The Night.

'When do you go back?' asked Mam, searching through the Quality Street tin.

'Sometime in January. But I don't know if want to go back, I'm fed up of being at sea. I fancy working on the land, something with animals,' said Uncle Graham.

'Something with animals, what, like in a pet shop?' asked Mam, with her mouth full of toffee.

'Working on a farm or something, away from the sea.'

When Uncle Graham went back to Nana's, Mam said she thought he was going doolally. She didn't know why he wanted to give up the Navy, perhaps he'd been taking some of Uncle Malcolm's drugs.

Cos it was Boxing Day, we had to go to Aunty Nita's house, she's Dad's baby sister, but I reckon Aunty Nita is really old. We always go to Aunty Nita's on Boxing Day. I wanted to take some of my Christmas presents, but Mam said I had to leave them at home. I got a new Brazil football shirt from Uncle Graham. All my aunties and uncles from Dad's family go to Aunty Nita's too, and my cousins. Only Uncle Ernie doesn't go cos he lives in Australia. I've only ever seen pictures of Uncle Ernie. Dad says he hasn't seen him for over twenty years – and he owes him five quid.

Mam made Dad put on his new jumper, it's got a moose on it.

'Ooh, you look all nice and Christmassy, Cliff,' said Mam.

'I look like a burk,' said Dad, pulling down his jumper and looking at the picture of the moose.

I wanted to wear my new Brazil football shirt, but Mam said it wasn't very Christmassy, even though it was yellow. She made me wear my purple shirt and brown tank-top. Dad said we looked like a pair of nincompoops. Mam said we looked lovely.

Aunty Nita's house is very posh. It's on big stilts with a big garage underneath. Like a house on the telly on Charlie's Angels. We have to take our shoes off before we can go in. Mam made me and Dad wear clean socks and made sure there were no holes in 'em. Sometimes Dad wears his socks all week. Then his feet smell like cheese.

Aunty Nita's living room is massive with a big fluffy white carpet – a shag-pile. Mam said saying shag wasn't funny. My cousins, Melanie and Michaela, got told off for rolling around on the shag-pile. I wanted to roll around on the shag-pile, but I didn't wanna get told off again.

Aunty Nita makes us eat our Boxing Day dinner at the table in the dining room. Aunty Nita is the only person we know who has a dining room. We just have a table in the kitchen, Aunty Nita's kitchen is five times bigger than ours. She has a breakfast bar and stools as well, Mam thinks it's really posh. On the dining table, everyone's names were written on a piece of card. I asked Dad why we had our names on the table, he said cos Aunty Nita thinks she's a member of the royal family. We had something called a starter, that was just a small bit of food. Starters are stupid.

'It's like foreplay,' said Dad, 'You have pretend you like the bit before yuh main meal, to keep yuh missus happy.'

I didn't know what Dad was talking about, but he said I'd understand when I'm older. Nana Sugden told Dad off and she wouldn't tell me what foreplay was, it sounded like a game. I like games, except Twister.

Aunty Nita told us off for talking at the table. Dad's not even allowed to have any bread to make a sandwich. Dad loves making sandwiches with his dinner. When we finished, Aunty Nita said we had a choice of afters, but she didn't call it afters, she said dessert. We don't have afters at home, but sometimes Mam makes an Angel Delight.

It took ages for everyone to finish their dinners, and Nana Sugden said I had to ask permission to leave the table. After we had our dinner, and were allowed to leave the table, we went back in the living room. Me, Melanie and Michaela rolled around on the shag-pile before any of the grown-ups came in. Dad, Uncle Ron, and Uncle Denis were allowed to have beer, as long as they promised not to spill any. Last Boxing Day, Nana Sugden spilt her Warnicks, Aunty Nita said accidents do happen, and cleaned it up. When Uncle Ron spilt a tiny bit of beer, she went bananas and called him an silly oaf.

We always have the telly on in our house, even on Sunday. But sometimes Mam watches Songs of Praise if Harry Secombe is singing. Aunty Nita doesn't like having the telly on, but we always watch the Bond film on Boxing Day. Everyone likes the Bond film, except Nana Sugden. Sean Connery is the best James Bond, better than Roger Moore. Mam thinks Sean Connery is dishy, but thinks Roger Moore is a bit slimy. Dad doesn't care as long as there's some ladies with big tits.

'Nice pair of Bristols on that one, Cliff!' said Uncle Ron,

when James Bond was snogging a pretty lady with big massive boobs.

'Aye, she could have someone's eye out with 'em.'

'Gor, all you ever think about is sex, you two,' laughed Mam.

'Yeah, all I can do is think about it these days,' said Dad.

'Clifford! Please, not in front of the young 'uns,' said Nana Sugden, waving her finger at Dad.

James Bond killed loads of baddies and snogged loads more ladies with big boobs. The film finished and Nana Sugden said she was glad it was over. Dad, Uncle Ron and Uncle Denis had some more beer, Nana, Aunty Ann and Aunty Nita had some wine. Dad let me have a sip of his beer when no one was looking. It tasted yucky. I told Dad I wasn't gonna drink beer when I grow up. Uncle Ron laughed. Dad whispered to Mam, but I could hear him – 'I'm a bit pissed, luv,' said Dad.

Mam said it was time to say goodbye to everyone. We got in the car and Dad was singing 'Daisy' and 'When I'm Cleaning Windows'. Mam told him to shut up cos she couldn't concentrate on driving, she didn't see a man walking his dog, trying to cross the road. She nearly ran him over. Dad farted and we had to open the windows, it was freezing, but it was better than smelling Dad's arse. Dad's arse smells horrible, he said it wasn't his fault, it was the beer.

When we got home, Dad made some turkey sandwiches and we watched some more telly. Dad had a sherry and Mam had a Snowball. Mam told me to go to bed, and Dad did another big fart.

I fell asleep really quick. I was dreaming about playing football with Uncle Graham. I had my Brazil football shirt on and Uncle Graham was riding a horse. I woke up, I could hear a noise. All the lights were out and I couldn't hear the telly downstairs. I looked at my alarm clock and it said one o'clock. The noise was a banging sound. I thought it was in the attic, maybe a bird or mouse moving about. Then I heard Dad. He was groaning, like when he does a fart. I got out of bed and quietly crept onto the landing. I was outside Mam and Dad's room, Dad was grunting like a caveman. Something was banging – Bang! Bang! Bang!

'Be quiet Cliff, you'll wake Gwyn up,' whispered Mam.

It sounded like Dad was fixing something, like he was doing some work. Like when he puts some shelves up, and he has to put nails in the wall.

'Come on Cliff, hurry up, I want to go to sleep!' said Mam, giggling.

I wondered what they were doing and what the banging was. There was a little gap in the door, I pushed it open a bit and peeked in. I could see a big lump in the bed, Dad was on top of Mam. The headboard was hitting the wall, and that was what the banging was. I remembered the boy up the Pentlynn, doing press-ups on his girlfriend. Dad was doing press-ups on Mam. I felt sick. I crept back to bed and covered my ears with my hands. Soon, Dad stopped groaning and Mam went downstairs to the toilet. I heard Dad do another big fart. When Mam went back to bed, Dad was fast asleep, snoring.

Chapter 33.

There's Only One Trevor Brooking.

I tucked my scarf into my jumper so you could only see the colours. Mam bought it for from Risca Sports shop, but it's got Wolves written on it. Wolves play in the same colours as Newport County, Mam said they didn't have a Newport County scarf and I was to stop moaning.

Mam dropped me and Dad off near the football ground.

'I'm gonna miss the beginning of Coronation Street, and I don't want to be hanging around later when I pick you two buggers up,' shouted Mam, as Dad shut the car door.

There were loads of Newport County supporters, all with amber and black hats and scarves. Dad said he was freezing and bought a cup of tea from a burger van to warm his hands up. The match was supposed to have been on Saturday, but cos of the snow it got postponed. The pools panel on the telly have to make up the results if lots of games get postponed – 'Newport County and West Ham United, away win,' said the man on the telly, reading the results on Grandstand.

I was really excited. I'd never been to a proper football match before. I'd seen Risca United play loads of times over the park, but Newport County have a proper ground with terraces, floodlights, advertising boards and supporters. As we got near the ground I could see the floodlights shining and hear the crowd singing, 'COUNTY! COUNTY!'. Dad said there'd be over ten thousand people watching the game – and it would be on the telly as well.

A couple of West Ham fans were walking in front of us. I knew they were West Ham fans cos they had big rosettes. They had funny London voices and were talking about Trevor Brooking. Trevor Brooking plays for England and he's West Ham's best player. He's been injured so hasn't played in ages. Dad reckoned he was gonna run rings around Newport County.

There was a man selling programmes, I asked Dad if he would buy me one, he moaned cos they were 15p. Dad pulled a load of change from his pocket, fifteen one pence pieces.

'Raid yuh piggy bank?' said the programme bloke.

'Piss off,' said Dad, then told me not to tell Mam he said a rude word.

We had to queue up to get in. Dad asked for an adult and one child, then moaned at the price. We pushed through the turnstile and then we were in the ground. It was ace. Dad said he wanted a cup of tea and he'd get me a squash. I waited behind a big advertising board that said 'South Wales Argus'. I read my programme and recognised some of the West Ham players from my football stickers. I had Billy Bonds and Mervyn Day, I swapped my Trevor Brooking to Richard James for three West Brom players. When Dad came back he said his tea was too milky.

Loads more supporters came into the ground and we were pressed against the advertising boards. I looked behind and everyone around us were West Ham fans. All the Newport County supporters were in the other bits of the ground. We were in the away end. I buttoned my coat up so you couldn't see my scarf. A man behind us started shouting, 'C'MON ON YOU 'AMMERS!'. I felt a bit scared and didn't want the West Ham fans to beat us up. On 'News At Ten' some football supporters smashed up a train. Mam saw it too and didn't want to drive us down to the football.

The teams ran out onto the pitch and everyone cheered. The West Ham fans started singing 'I'm Forever Blowing Bubbles'. They were really loud. When they stopped, Dad shouted, 'C'MON ON THE COUNTY!'. I thought we were gonna get our 'eds kicked in. A bloke next to Dad told him we were in the wrong end, and laughed. He was really nice and even gave Dad a fag.

The game kicked off and Newport County kept smacking the ball in the air. Dad said you'd think they were playing bloody rugby. The West Ham fans started singing 'I'm Forever Blowing Bubbles' again. I could hear the Newport fans shouting 'COUNTY! COUNTY!' at the other end of the ground. The ball came out of play and rolled over by where we were. A West Ham player ran over to get it – it was Trevor Brooking. One of the West Ham supporters behind us started singing, 'There's only one Trevor Brooking' – I sang as well. Trevor Brooking did a wave and everyone cheered.

I was really cold. There was still loads of snow around the edges of the pitch. The game was a bit boring and there'd only been a few shots. Then, County got the ball and ran towards the West Ham goal. A County player crossed it, and our number nine put it in the back of the net – 1-nil! I forgot we were with the West Ham fans and jumped up and down and went mental. Dad said it was a very good goal. A man on a loudspeaker said the goal was scored by Howard Goddard. The West Ham fans didn't cheer, but started singing 'I'm

Forever Blowing Bubbles'.

From the kick-off, West Ham tried really hard to score. Trevor Brooking came close, and another player, Alan Curbishley did as well. Newport County couldn't get the ball off the West Ham players. West Ham were passing it to each other really well. Then, the ball was hit from way outside the County box and West Ham scored – 1-1. It was an amazing goal. The West Ham fans went crackers and starting singing 'There's only one Pop Robson' – he was the bloke who scored. Dad said they'd show it on Grandstand on Saturday – cos it was so good.

The ref blew his whistle for half-time and Dad went through the crowd to get some hot tea. Some of the West Ham fans said in the second half they were gonna bury the game. I thought County played really good. I hoped they'd play as well when they kicked off again. Dad came back with his tea and got me a hot Bovril. I love hot Bovril. Mam thinks it's horrible, she says it's like drinking gravy.

The second half kicked off and West Ham almost scored straight away. Trevor Brooking did some good passes and they came really close again. The match got a bit boring – just like the first half. Nothing much happened and the ball kept going out for throw-ins. The players were getting really muddy and the pitch looked slippy.

'Bloody 'ell, County are hanging on for their bloody life 'ere!' said Dad, sipping his tea.

But County got the ball in midfield and passed it down the wing. A Newport County player crossed it into the box and a West Ham defender couldn't reach it. County's number ten got the ball and smacked it into the West Ham net. BANG! – 2-1! The County fans went crazy – so did I. The man on the loudspeaker said it was scored by Eddie Woods. The West Ham fans tried to sing 'I'm Forever Blowing Bubbles', but the County fans were really loud, so they gave up.

'There's only one Eddie Woods,' sang the County fans, but me and Dad didn't – we didn't want the West Ham fans smashing our faces in.

The game seemed to go on forever. Dad kept looking at his watch and I kept asking how long there was to go. Dad didn't care if West Ham got a goal back. He just wanted to get home and have some beer in the pub. The West Ham fans started shouting at their players to get a move on. But it was no good. The ref blew the whistle for full time. Trevor Brooking shook hands with some of the County players and everyone clapped – even the West Ham fans. Some blokes behind us said County were too good to stay in the Fourth Division. One West Ham bloke, who was really fat and had no teeth, asked if I enjoyed the game. I said I did and I told him I was sorry West Ham lost. I wasn't though, I was really glad.

'C'mon lad, let's find yuh mother,' said Dad, grabbing me by my arm and pushing us through the crowd.

Mam was gonna pick us up in Lysaghts Working Men's Club car park. That's Dad's work pub. I met Father Christmas there once – he smelt of booze. I don't think he was the real Father Christmas. We walked down the road and some County fans were singing. There were loads of coppers making sure everyone was being good and not fighting. They didn't look very happy, Dad said that's cos coppers don't have a sense of humour.

'Dad, do you reckon County will win the FA Cup?'

'Don't be so bloody daft, lad.'

'But they've beaten West Ham, and they've got Trevor Brooking!'

'They were just bloody lucky, that's all. They'll get knocked out in the next round, I'll bet.'

Mam was waiting in the car. She had her dressing gown on and didn't look very happy. She said we were late and she was gonna catch pneumonia. We drove the long way around Newport to avoid the football traffic. Dad said he was bloody frozen and sat on his hands to warm 'em up.

'You can drop me off at the pub, luv,' said Dad.

'You what! You're gonna drink cold beer after you've been moaning about being frozen?' shouted Mam, 'Yuh bloody mad, Cliff!'

Mam dropped Dad off at the pub and he said he'd catch the bus back. On the way home, Mam gave me some money to go in the chippy to get our supper. A man was waiting for his chips and he saw my scarf.

'You been down the County 'en butty?' he asked – I think he was a bit drunk.

'Yeah, we played West Ham in the FA Cup.'

'Get stuffed, did they?'

'Nor, County won, 2-1'

'Yuh bloody kidding me? Well I never, pigs do fly after all.'

Chapter 34.

Uncle Graham Goes Doolally.

Dandy told me off for flicking ink at Genevieve Daniels' canal painting. It was on the wall next to my desk. Dandy thought it was brilliant. Dandy likes Genevieve Daniels, she's brainy and always does well in class. I hate Genevieve Daniels. My ink pen gets clogged and the only way to unblock it is to flick it really hard. I flicked it so hard, loads of ink went all over her stupid painting. Blue ink covered her frogs and tadpoles. She cried when she saw it. But when Dandy wasn't looking, she poked her tongue out at me. When I go to the big school, I hope I'm not in the same class as her.

I walked home with Colin Scotch and Richard James. We sang 'Hit Me With Your Rhythm Stick' and went in the sweet shop. I bought some Panini stickers, I'm trying to fill my book but I'm missing loads. I've got hardly any stickers on my Liverpool page. I keep getting Derby County players and nobody wants to swap.

When I got home, Nana Balding was sat on the settee. Uncle Graham was home from the Navy, and Nana was telling Mam he'd been acting really strange. She said he kept laughing, and when Nana asks him what he's laughing at, he just shrugs his shoulders. Nana cooked him a breakfast and he made a face out of the sausages, eggs and bacon. She said he made the face sad by using bacon for a mouth. And he didn't eat it.

'What a waste,' said Mam.

'I'm bloody worried about him, Beryl, he's not right. I expect some palaver from our Malcolm, but not our Graham.'

Dad was in the garden, talking to Mr Morgan from next door. I made a brown sauce sandwich and a class of squash. We hardly ever have any fizzy pop, but when we do, Mam drinks it all and I get the blame. Dad came into the kitchen to wash his hands.

'You want some tea, or you gonna go with yuh Mam to take Nana back?'

'I've had a brown sauce sarnie, I made it myself. When's Mam taking Nana back 'en?'

'Well, now in a minute,' said Dad, drying his hands on a Windsor Castle tea-towel.

Mam shouted from the living room she was taking Nana home. I drank my squash and put my coat on.

'C'mon, Nana wants to get back to watch Winner Takes All,' said Mam.

We got in the car but I had to get in the back. All the way up, Nana Balding kept talking, she talked so much I got a headache. Nana moaned and gossipped about everyone, even about Mam, and she was driving her home.

As we turned into Nana's street, all the neighbours were out in the road. Like the time when Mr Lovsey had a big row in the street with Mr Harris. I wondered if there was a fight, like on the telly.

'What's going on 'ere?' asked Nana.

'Dunno, I can't see an ambulance or anything,' said Mam.

As we got closer, there was a man standing on top of a car. He only had a pair of jeans on and was covered in blood. He was waving his arms in the air, shouting – it was Uncle Graham.

'What the bloody hell's he doing?' shouted Nana.

We got out of the car and one of the neighbours ran over. Uncle Graham was jumping up and down on the car. He was shouting 'I'M A FAIRY, I'M A FAIRY' and laughing like a nutter. Blood was dripping off his hands onto the car. He was covered in blood and he had loads of cuts on his arms and chest.

'GRAHAM! GET DOWN FROM THERE, WHAT THE HELL YOU PLAYING AT!' shouted Nana, shaking her fist.

'I'm a fairy, Mam, a big fairy!' sang Uncle Graham.

Mr Williams, one of the neighbours, said he'd smashed all of Nana's windows. Then, he'd ran out into the street and jumped on everyone's cars, singing and shouting. They were waiting for the police and an ambulance to turn up.

Uncle Graham jumped down from the car and tried to hug Nana Balding. She shouted and pushed him away, but then he tried to hug her again. Mr Janus, from down the road, tried to grab him. Uncle Graham hit him in the stomach and Mr Janus fell to the ground.

'GRAHAM!' screamed Nana. 'STOP THIS BLOODY NONSENSE RIGHT NOW, YUH BUGGER!'

Nana was crying and Mam put her arm round her. A couple of the neighbours managed to hold on to Uncle Graham and pin him on the ground. Mr Janus got up and sat back down against a wall, he said he was alright and was just winded.

'Why is our Graham doing this, what's wrong with him, Beryl?'

There were some sirens and a police car came up the road. Two coppers got out of the police car, some of the neighbours told 'em about Uncle Graham. One of the coppers went back to the police car and talked into a radio, just like on The Sweeney. The other copper tried to talk to Uncle Graham, but he just kept shouting he was a fairy and he wanted to dance. The neighbours that were holding him had Uncle Graham's blood on 'em.

An ambulance arrived and another police car. Uncle Graham went crackers. He got really angry and managed to break free. Some coppers ran after him, it took three of 'em to hold him down. His face was in the gravel of the road and he was shouting.

'YOU FUCKING BASTARDS! I'LL KILL THE FUCKIN' LOT OF YOU!' shouted Uncle Graham.

I'd never heard Uncle Graham swear before, or even shout, or even be angry. Uncle Graham must be very strong cos the three coppers were struggling to hold him. They put handcuffs on his wrists and tried to get him in the back of the ambulance. Nana was telling the coppers to be careful and she was crying again. Uncle Graham was struggling and the coppers were finding it hard to keep hold of him.

'I'M NOT GOING BACK YOU KNOW, NEVER GOING BACK!' shouted Uncle Graham.

One of the coppers got too close and Uncle Graham headbutted him. He fell straight to the ground, blood spurting out from his nose. The copper held his face and I could hear his muffled voice groaning, 'You bastard!'.

They got Uncle Graham into the ambulance and closed the door. Nana was still crying – more than when Gransher died. Mam took her into a neighbour's house. All the windows at Nana's were smashed in. Mam said she'd go and get Uncle Ronnie, he lives up the road. I had to stay with Nana at her neighbour's house.

'I won't be long, Mam, I'm gonna get Ronnie,' said Mam.

Mrs Lomez gave Nana a cup of tea. Nana Balding put some sugar in and kept stirring it. She stirred it for ages and ages. She did the same when she came back from the hospital when Gransher died.

'I don't know what to make of it all,' she kept saying, over and over again, as she stirred her tea.

A police woman came to talk to Nana. She was really nice and looked like one of the lady coppers Regan would get off with from The Sweeney. She told Nana, Uncle Graham had been given an injection to calm him down.

'He did assault a police officer, but I don't think there will be any charges,' said the police lady.

'Why's he gone doolally?' asked Nana.

'You'll have to ask the doctor, after he's seen him, luv. It's only our job to contain him.'

Mam came back with Uncle Ronnie. He went and talked to a copper to find out where they'd taken Uncle Graham. Mam told Nana she would have to come back and stay with us. Uncle Ronnie was going to sort out the windows, and make sure no one nicked anything. There's not much to nick from Nana's house. She's got a rubbish telly, and all of Uncle Malcolm's records are really old and have hippies singing on 'em.

'Do yuh think it's something to do with the Navy, Beryl?' asked Nana.

'I dunno Mam, we'll have to wait and see what the doctor says.'

'He's been acting all weird though, I'd better tell 'em.'

'We'll tell 'em Mam, but not tonight.'

Mam packed a bag for Nana and said we'd go to the chippy on the way home for some tea. Said she was to upset to cook.

Uncle Ronnie said he'd go up the police station in the morning to see what was gonna happen.

'Will they lock Uncle Graham up in prison?' I asked Mam.

'No luv, yuh Uncle Graham isn't very well. They think he's had a breakdown.'

'A breakdown? Like yuh car?'

'A bit, but we can't call out the RAC, he'll need a special doctor.'

'Can I tell the boys in school?'

'Nobody's gonna wanna know about your Uncle Graham at school, luv.'

'Yeah they will! He nutted a copper, that's cool!'

Mam told me it wasn't cool to nut a copper, but Mam's wrong. On The Sweeney, it's ace and I couldn't wait to tell Martyn and Wayne. I'd never seen a fight with grown-ups before. Only fights at school with Tony Keane and Richard James. Everyone at school was gonna be jealous, I'd seen a proper headbutt and Uncle Graham being handcuffed.

Mam got Nana ready and made me carry her bag. Nana was still shaking and muttering to herself about Uncle Graham. She reckoned it was the Navy's fault. Nana said that she wanted a whisky and we'd have to stop in a shop on the way home. I asked if I could have a can of Top Deck, Mam said I could if I was good and ran into the chippy to get the supper. Nana said she didn't want anything.

On the way home, Nana kept muttering to herself, saying she didn't know what to make of it all. We stopped off at an off licence to get Nana a bottle of whisky. I turned the radio on, while Mam was in the shop, cos Nana's muttering was getting on my nerves. A man on the radio said the next record was a dedication for someone's birthday.

'I don't know what the neighbours must think, seeing our Graham going berserk like that,' said Nana.

The song on the radio was called 'Crazy' by Patsy Kline. Mam got back in the car with some whisky and a can of Top Deck. We drove up to Risca and Mam gave me some money to go in the chippy. Mrs Phillips was putting in a fresh batch of chips.

'Hello Gwyn, luv, where's yuh Mam, 'en?'

'In the car with Nana Balding. Nana's been crying.'

'Crying? Why's that 'en?' asked Mrs Phillips, as she wiped her hands on her apron.

'Our Uncle Graham's gone doolally.'

'Yuh what! Doolally? Eh?'

I told Mrs Phillips about Uncle Graham smashing all the windows, dancing on the car, and nutting the copper. She was very impressed. She kept going 'Ooh' and saying 'Well I never'. Mrs Phillips wrapped up the chips and gave me a free curry sauce.

'Well, give my best to yuh Mam for me,' said Mrs Phillips, as I ran outside to the car.

'You took yuh time,' said Mam.

'I was telling Mrs Phillips about Uncle Graham going doolally.'

Mam wasn't very happy I told Mrs Phillips about Uncle Graham going doolally. She liked the free curry sauce though.

Chapter 35.

Margaret Thatcher And The Nudie Books.

Martyn and Wayne didn't believe me. But Mam told Mrs Summers when she saw her up the shops.

'Did they hit him with a truncheon?' asked Martyn.

'No, but they handcuffed him, like on The Sweeney.'

'Fuckin' ace,' said Wayne, 'I wonder if he'll go mental again? Cool.'

Uncle Graham had to go to a special mental hospital. Mam said he'll have to leave the Navy and would be in the nuthouse for ages. She said he'd been depressed, that's why he went doolally and smashed Nana's house up.

Mam stayed up all night watching the general election. I stayed up til eleven o'clock, but I started to fall asleep, so I went to bed.

'Looks likes Maggie's gonna get in, there'll be trouble if she does,' said Mam, as I went upstairs.

Dad hates Maggie Thatcher. He reckons she'll ruin the country and loads of people would be on the dole. Dad hasn't thrown his slipper at the telly for ages, but when Maggie was on, 'Wallop!'. He threw it so hard, when it hit the screen, it made a big slapping noise. Mam told him off, but then he just threw the other one.

When I got up in the morning, Mam said Maggie and the

Tories had won the election. Dad went to work early, Mam said he was in a bard mood and looked worried. I don't like Maggie Thatcher either, she looks like a teacher. The sort of teacher who would give you the cane. I hope people don't lose their jobs – I hope Dad doesn't lose his. Uncle Eric doesn't have a job, he's fat and lazy. I don't want Dad to be fat and lazy.

I walked to school with Neil Gerald and Martyn. We talked about the general election and Maggie Thatcher. Nobody at school likes Maggie Thatcher, except Linda Oliver, cos she says she looks like her Nan.

'Can you keep a secret?' asked Martyn, by the school gates.

'Yeah, why?'

'I found some of my Dad's nudie books.'

'Nudie books? What, with naked ladies in?'

'Yeah, you can see everything! Even their hairy fannies!'

I told Martyn about the nudie mags Uncle Malcolm used to have under his bed. He doesn't have 'em anymore, Nana found 'em, she went bananas. Martyn said he found his dad's in the shed. There were loads of 'em, and one is really rude. It's got pictures of two ladies kissing and touching each others fannies. I said we should tell Wayne. He likes rude pictures, he's always going on about fannies and tits.

'Okay, but I'm not telling anyone else,' said Martyn.

In class I thought we were gonna do more stuff about canals. But Dandy said we had to do a special test, he said it was important. There were hard sums, some spelling, and questions about how long it a took a train to get to a station if it stopped for five minutes at other stations. I couldn't work it out, so I made up the answer. I thought the test was hard, Genevieve Daniels thought it was easy. I hate Genevieve Daniels.

At dinner time, we told Wayne about the mucky books.

'Let's go and look after school,' said Wayne, 'It'll be ace.'

Martyn said he wasn't sure, he said his dad might be there, and didn't wanna get caught.

'Don't be a bummer,' said Wayne.

'I'm norra bummer, I just don't wanna get my arse kicked.'

I've never found any mucky magazines in our house. Dad likes to watch the ladies on the telly instead. I found some Christmas presents Mam had hidden once. I had to pretend to be surprised on Christmas morning. I found a game of Jaws and Battleships at the back of the airing cupboard. I wanted Subbuteo and a Bionic Action Man. Wayne's got one, you can look through his bionic eye. Wayne's got all the best toys. Mam says it's cos his dad's a crook.

After school, Martyn and Wayne were waiting for me by the school gates. Wayne was excited about seeing the mucky books.

'If my Dad's there, we can't see 'em mind,' said Martyn.

'Yeah, I know, aye, imagine Maggie Thatcher with no clothes on,' laughed Wayne.

'Urgh, that's horrible, it would be like seeing yuh Nan!' I said, pulling a face and pretending to be sick.

'David Pryce reckons Nanas have big hairy grey fannies that stink of piss,' said Wayne, pointing at his dick.

We went past the sweet shop, but we didn't have any money. Wayne used to nick gobstoppers or Chewits. But Wayne doesn't nick sweets much anymore, he got caught in Jackie Jones'. His dad went mental and he couldn't come out for a week. We were by Risca Sports shop, the Maggie Thatcher car was parked outside. It had been going round Risca telling everyone to vote for the Tories. One old lady threw an egg at it. Her name's Dolly, she's crackers. Wayne reckons she's a man dressed up.

'If you look, you can see her cock under her skirt,' said Wayne.

I think he's talking bollocks, Mam knows Dolly, she's just big and ugly. I asked Mam if Dolly was a fella, she just laughed.

There was man and lady in the Maggie Thatcher car, they were talking and looking at a clipboard. We snuck down and crept up to the car. Wayne put his finger to his mouth so we'd be quiet. The driver's window was open, Wayne jumped up and shouted, 'MAGGIE THATCHER'S A FUCKING WANKER!'

We ran up the road as fast as we could. We didn't stop running 'til we got to the bogs by the garage. I was all puffed out and thought I was gonna be sick.

'I don't think they're coming after us,' said Martyn, all out of breath with his hands on his sides. 'Fuckin' 'ell, I've got a stitch!'

'Hey, do yuh wanna see a mucky drawing?' said Wayne. 'There's one on the back of the bog door.'

We went into the toilets, it was empty. Wayne took us to the end cubicle and opened the wooden bog door.

'Look!'

'FUCKIN' 'ELL!' shouted Martyn.

There was a drawing, in black marker pen, of a big stiff cock with some stuff spurting out. Next to the cock was a lady with her mouth open. There was a speech bubble with the words – Drink my spunk.

'What's spunk?' I asked. Martyn looked like he was gonna be sick.

'It's special fuck piss,' said Wayne.

We were looking at the mucky drawing, when an old man

came into the toilets.

'What you lads doing in 'ere?' said the old bloke, he was one of Dad's butties from the pub.

'Nothing, just looking at the rude drawing,' laughed Wayne.

'You better not be doing any graffiti, I'll box yuh ear drums!' said the old bloke – he smelt like the pub.

'We didn't do it, we were just havin' a look, that's all,' said Martyn, not wanting to get into trouble.

The old man did a loud fart and started to have a piss. We squeezed passed him, but Wayne pushed him on the way out.

'QUICK, RUN!' shouted Wayne.

I heard the old bloke shout, 'YUH LITTLE BASTARDS!'. We ran across the main road, a van beeped its horn as we got to the pavement on the other side.

'Fuckin' 'ell Ashby, you're gonna get us into fuckin' trouble one day!' shouted Martyn, but Wayne was running up Springfield Road, way ahead of us.

When we got to my house, Wayne stopped running and waited for us. Dad was in the garden watering the plants.

'Having a race are you, boys?' said Dad.

'Sort of, Mr Sugden. I'm the fastest though,' said Wayne, he was hardly out of breath. Not like me and Martyn, we were knackered.

'Wha' yuh want for tea, son? Yuh Mam's taken Nana Balding up the nuthouse to see Graham.'

I asked for sausage and chips. Dad said it would be about an hour, so I could stay out and play with Martyn and Wayne. We went over to Martyn's and went round the back of his house. His sister, Louise, was in the kitchen making toast. She saw us through the window and opened the door.

'Mam and Dad are up Granny's, they'll be back later to

do tea,' she said, biting into a big piece of toast.

She had her school uniform on. She's older than us and goes up the big school. I don't wanna wear a uniform, but Mam said everyone up the Comp has to wear one.

Louise went back inside and said she was going upstairs to play her Bee Gees record. The Bee Gees are shit.

'Fuckin' ace, yuh Dad's out, let's have a look at the mags 'en,' said Wayne, really excited.

'All right, but be quiet. We'll have to be quick in case Dad comes back.'

Martyn opened the shed, it smelt of paint but everything was really neat and tidy. Not like Dad's shed, everything is piled up in old tins and full of crap – Mam keeps telling him to sort it out. Martyn reached behind a metal cabinet and pulled out a pile of magazines. One was called Fiesta and had a picture of a lady with big boobs on the front.

'That's nothing,' whispered Martyn, pointing at the Fiesta mag. 'It's this one that's got all the rude stuff in.'

Martyn pulled out a small magazine called 'Spuzz'. It was all in black and white. Martyn was right, it was nothing like Fiesta. There were pictures of ladies putting their fingers in each other's fannies. Big hairy ones that looked like they'd smell funny.

'Fuckin' 'ell, she could get her hand stuck up there!' laughed Wayne.

'Be quiet, Louise might hear you, yuh twat!'

'She's listening to the Bee Gees, don't worry,' said Wayne, trying to turn the pages in Martyn's hand.

'Careful, you'll rip it!'

'Well, c'mon 'en, let's see some more pictures.'

There was a bloke with a massive cock, as big as the horse

in the field up by the canal. One of the ladies had it in her mouth. It was horrible. No wonder Mr Summers keeps the mag hidden in the shed. They were putting me off my sausage and chips for tea. Wayne thought Spuzz magazine was ace. He asked if he could take it home, and promised to bring it back the next day. Martyn told him to fuck off.

We heard a noise from the kitchen. Martyn's sister was making a glass of squash and she'd dropped the bottle. Martyn quickly put the mags back behind the cabinet and told us to get out of the shed. Louise saw us and opened the kitchen door.

'What are you three fools doing?'

'Nothin', just looking for my cricket bat,' said Martyn, his face was red.

'Well, Dad told yuh not to go in there, says he's got special tools he doesn't want you to break.'

Me and Wayne laughed – we couldn't help it. Louise wanted to know what was so funny, Martyn said we were just mucking about. She called us stupid boys and went back in the kitchen. I took my jacket off cos I was hot from all the running. Then, Mr and Mrs Summers came back from Martyn's Gran's.

'Okay, lads?' said Mr Summers.

'Tea in five minutes, Martyn, go and wash yuh hands,' said Mrs Summers, carrying a big bag of shopping.

We pretended we'd been playing catch. Wayne picked up a ball, tossed it in the air, and caught it. We could hear the Bee Gees coming from Louise's bedroom, Mrs Summers shouted to Louise to turn it down.

'Aye, Martyn, you ever seen yuh Mam's big hairy fanny?' laughed Wayne.

'Fuck off, Ashby, I'm going in for my tea.'

Martyn went inside, and me and Wayne went to go home.

'Shit, I've forgot my jacket,' I said, 'I'll see you in school tomorrow.'

Wayne shouted 'See yuh', and ran off down the road. I went back into Martyn's back garden. Mr Summers came out of the house, he went into the shed and closed the door behind him. He didn't see me, I grabbed my jacket and ran home.

Chapter 36.

Sunday In The Mental Hospital.

We all got a piece of paper. It said what class we'd be in up the big school, after the summer holidays. Jason Barrett, Pickles, and David Pritchard are gonna be in my new class. I didn't know any of the other boys, they're from Ty-Sign Junior and Risca Town. Helen Gardner and Alison Edmunds are in my class. But I don't talk to any girls from Danygraig.

At playtime, I found Pickles, Jason Barrett and David Pritchard.

'Do you know any of the other kids in our class?' I said.

'Nah, they're all from Ty-Sign. Fuckin' nutters up there,' said Jason. Pickles looked worried.

Sometimes the Ty-Sign kids come down to Risca to nick stuff and pick fights. Ty-Sign is a big council estate, some of the houses don't have windows and are boarded up. Mam said we almost moved there once, I'm glad we didn't.

'So, you lot are in our class, 'en?' said Helen Gardner, who'd walked over with Alison Edmunds.

'Yeah, looks like it,' said Jason.

'Well, just cos you lot are from Danygraig, don't expect us to talk to you,' said Helen. Alison nodded.

We looked at each other and shrugged our shoulders. Helen and Alison walked off holding hands. David Pritchard said they were stupid. I agreed.

'You got yuh uniform yet?' asked Pickles. 'Mam bought mine last week, said it was pricy.'

'Yeah, got mine too, not tried it on yet, don't want to either,' I said.

'You can't wear daps up the big school, gorra wear shoes,' said David Pritchard, looking pissed off.

We went round the playground to see what classes the other boys were in. Tony Keane said he knew some of the boys in our class, he said they were nutters.

'Philip Howells is mental, Christopher Hateley is as well,' said Tony Keane.

I wasn't looking forward to the big school. And I wasn't looking forward to wearing a uniform and being in a class with nutters.

Last week was my birthday, I was eleven. Mam said I'm growing up too quick. For my birthday I got a cassette player, it's got a radio in it as well. I got loads of blank cassettes from Uncle Malcolm, I can record songs off the radio. I like John Peel and Annie Nightingale the best. They play ace songs that Mam and Dad think are rubbish, like Ian Dury, The Boomtown Rats and Dr. Feelgood. I've got four cassettes full of music. When I'm in the car with Mam, she lets me play them, as long as I don't have it too loud.

Colin Scotch at school knows loads about music. He's got loads of records, he did a tape for me with lots of cool new bands on. He drew a special cover as well with his magic markers. He put The Tubeway Army song 'Are 'Friends' Electric' on there – they're number one in the charts. Colin Scotch gets the latest records before anyone else. He had 'Hit Me With Your Rhythm Stick' ages before it was number one and on Top Of The Pops.

Colin says when he grows up, he's gonna be a record producer. That's someone who bosses all the bands about and makes lots of money. He said me and Wayne can work for him. We're gonna be roadies, that's someone who carries guitars and gets beer, drugs and girls for the bands. I told Mam I didn't need to do well at the big school, cos Colin was gonna give me a job with lots of money. She told me not to be so bloody stupid.

Even though it was really hot, Nana Balding had her coat on in the car. The man on the telly said it was gonna be a scorcher – 'The hottest day of the year'.

'Why don't you take yuh coat off, it's boiling,' said Mam, when she could get a word in.

'I might get a chill, and I don't like the look of that sky,' said Nana, even though it was a million degrees and there wasn't a even a cloud in the sky.

Uncle Graham is on special medicine so he doesn't smash people's faces in. As a treat, we're allowed to take him out, but he's not allowed any beer. The doctor said if he has any beer, he'll go crackers. Mam said she saw a nice duck pond with a cafe next to it. She said we should take Uncle Graham and sit in the sun. I hoped he wouldn't go mental and scare the ducks.

We got to the nuthouse and Mam parked the car in a space that had 'Medical Staff Only' written in white paint. There was a sign that said 'NO SHOUTING PLEASE' and there were some patients in dressing gowns, walking really slowly with nurses. They looked scary. One bloke started barking like a dog and a nurse told him off. Uncle Graham was in a special ward. Mam says it's for the nutters who are not so doolally anymore. Last time I came to visit, Uncle Graham was rocking back and forth and dribbling like a baby. Mam said it was the tablets. The hospital was really big, Dad said it showed how many nutters there are these days. Dad's not allowed to say nutters in front of Nana Balding – it makes her upset.

Uncle Graham was in a building away from the big hospital. It was like the outward bounds place I stayed in Talybont. Before we went in, Mam said not to stare at the sick people. But it's really hard not to stare, some are really crackers. One old lady tried to get her tits out while I was watching Superstars in the TV room. A nurse took her away and gave her some medicine.

'Ain't you warm with that big coat on, Mam?' asked Mam. Nana shook her head.

Uncle Graham was sat in a chair. He was dressed all smart and tidy, waiting for us to take him out. He looked different, like he was someone else. He looked tired, he looked old.

'Hiya Graham, luv, ready to go out 'en?' asked Mam, all chirpy, like it was Christmas.

'Oh, hello Beryl, how you keepin'?' said Graham, his voice all slow like my cassette player when the batteries are flat.

'Mam's 'ere Graham, look,' said Mam, pointing at Nana, who looked like a roast chicken in her big coat.

Uncle Graham looked confused, then it was like someone switched on a button and he knew who Nana was.

'Ooh, hiya Mam. Dad not with you?'

'Graham luv, Dad passed away two year ago,' said Mam

Nana looked down at the blue carpet. Dad said they're not allowed red in the nuthouse, it makes 'em angry.

'Why wasn't I told?' asked Uncle Graham, looking confused again, but sad at the same time – like Mrs Young's baby down the road when it shits itself.

'You were luv, you were a bearer. Remember?'

Uncle Graham rubbed his chin. He shook his head, then started to nod. 'Oh yeah, of course,' he said.

'C'mon now, lets get out in the warm sunshine,' said Mam.

'Sunshine? Why's Mam got a big coat on?'

Mam had to sign a form to say we were looking after Uncle Graham. The nurse said it was a lovely day, she didn't see the bloke pissing in the plant pot, he was laughing and some wee went on the carpet.

'C'mon trouble,' said Mam, as she grabbed my t-shirt.

The man finished pissing and went to the TV room. There wasn't gonna be anything on though, it was Sunday. Sunday's shit for telly, except for The Big Match, then later, The Professionals.

I sat in the back of the car with Nana. Uncle Graham was in the front cos he's got long legs. He kept saying it was a lovely hot day, over and over. Nana kept saying she could feel rain.

The cafe was in a wooden hut by a big pond. There were only a few other people there, so we could sit anywhere we wanted. Nana said she wanted to be under the tree in case in started to rain, she sat down while we went to get some drinks. In the corner of the cafe was a big jukebox, it was massive like on Happy Days. Mam asked me what I wanted to drink, I asked for a bottle of Coke. I looked at the jukebox to see what records they had. There were loads. Really old ones I'd never heard of and some new ones as well. They even had Ian Dury. I asked Mam for some money for the jukebox, but she said we were gonna sit outside with Nana.

'I'd like to listen to some records, Beryl,' said Uncle Graham, and he came over to see what they had.

Mam looked in her purse and gave me some money. I heard her tell the lady from the cafe Uncle Graham was out from the hospital for a treat. Mam was trying to whisper, but when she tries to be quiet she's really loud. I don't think Uncle Graham heard though.

The lady came over and opened the jukebox with some keys. She pressed a button inside and said we could have the records on for nothing. I thanked the lady and Mam said she was very kind. The cafe lady said she would bring the drinks outside to Mam and Nana. Nana wanted a pot of tea to warm herself up. She was still wearing her coat, I could see her from the cafe window.

'What yuh want on, Uncle Graham?' I asked.

'There's lots of good 'uns on 'ere, you choose.'

I picked Ian Dury, Blondie, The Police, Gary Numan, Elvis Costello, and a bloke called Wreckless Eric. I'd heard Wreckless Eric on Annie Nightingale's show – he's good. The cafe lady brought our drinks over and we sat by the window. We could see Mam and Nana, Mam waved, so we waved back. I felt like a twat cos there was a boy fishing with his dad and he saw us. I think he thought we were waving at him.

We listened to the records and I drank my Coke. Uncle Graham had a can of Fanta and hummed along to the songs. After each one finished, he said he liked it and asked who it was. During Elvis Costello, he said he saw him in concert. I asked if he was good, Uncle Graham said he couldn't remember. He looked sad and had a sip of Fanta. Mam waved again, so we waved back. The boy fishing didn't see. Nana was still wrapped up in her coat and was now wearing her scarf.

Wreckless Eric came on, my last record. The song was called 'Whole Wide World', it's ace. The song is slow, but it's not soppy or girly. Uncle Graham stared out the window and his eyes glazed over. I wondered if he was thinking about the Navy and being at sea. Or the amazing places he'd been to, like Brazil, America and Scotland. I was feeling sad, cos my Uncle Graham looked scared. I wanted him to come home with us. Not back to the nuthouse, where the man pisses in the plant pot and the old lady gets her tits out. I wanted him to come back to our house, he could have Findus Crispy Pancakes, Angel Delight and watch The Professionals. He would get better and be happy, I just know he would.

The Wreckless Eric record finished and it was quiet. Uncle Graham didn't notice the song had stopped, and was staring out the window. The cafe lady was in the back, washing up, and the light was flicking on the Coca Cola sign.

'The thing is Gwyn, I can't remember what it used to be like,' said Uncle Graham, looking down at his can of Fanta.

'Whatcha mean Uncle Graham, what was what like?'

'What I was like. I can remember bits, but that's it really. I hope I get better so I can remember again'

I didn't know what to say. I didn't understand what he was talking about. But I knew he was scared, I would be too – scared shitless.

'I don't wanna go to the big school, but Dad says it will be okay,' I said, cos that was all I could think of saying.

'I wish I could be going to the big school again. Then I wouldn't have to hear them screaming at night.'

I wanted to give Uncle Graham a big hug. I reckon it would help him not be sad. I'm not a bummer, but sometimes a hug makes things better. But I didn't, I just drank my Coke and looked out the window.

Mam waved at us again. Nana was looking at the sky and

pulling her collar up. I told Graham we'd better go outside, we said thank you to the lady and she smiled. I liked the cafe lady, she was nice.

'It's a lovely warm day, Gwyn, lovely and warm.'

'Yeah, but not everyone thinks so,' I said, nudging Uncle Graham and nodding at Nana.

'She's the one that belongs in the looney bin, not me,' he laughed, so did I.

It was the first time Uncle Graham had laughed since he went bonkers. It made me happy, it was like Uncle Graham before he went doolally, even if it was just for a little bit.

Mam saw us laughing, later she asked what we were laughing at. I lied and said it was about the ducks. I didn't wanna share it with Mam. I thought if I didn't tell anyone, then no one could take it away. Not Ever.

#

In the last week at school, Mr Dandy said we were one of his best ever classes. He said he thought my essays about the canals were very good, but I was to work harder on my maths and spelling. I didn't used to like Mr Dandy, I didn't like it when he shouted at me and made me stand outside the classroom. But I liked all the stuff I learnt, I even got some library books about railways and Mr Brunel, I didn't tell anyone though. We all did a 'hip-hip hooray' and I thought Mr Dandy was gonna cry. The bummer.

Me, Wayne, and Martyn played one last game of footie on the school grass. Some other boys came over and we had the best game ever. No one had a fight or went home bleeding.

'They've got loads of football pitches up Risca Comp,' said

David Pryce, after he scored a goal.

'Yeah, and a swimming pool and basketball court!' shouted Martyn Summers – but there'd be lots of older kids, and we'd be the youngest.

When I got home, Mam made me put my school uniform on. She wanted to take a picture to send to Aunty Maria in Japan. I didn't want to, but she said I could have pie and chips from the chippy and a can of Top Deck. I put on my new uniform and Dad did the tie for me. Mr Morgan from next door took the picture in the back garden. Dad doesn't have a camera, he says they're a waste of good money.

Mam went up the chippy to get our supper. I went upstairs to see what I looked like in the mirror with my uniform on. I wondered what Uncle Graham saw when he looked in the mirror cos he said he couldn't remember who he used to be. I felt sad. I didn't wanna go to Risca Comprehensive, I wanted to stay in Danygraig with my mates. I'd rather stay in Dandy's class and learn about canals and the railways. Going to the big school made me feel scared. I've seen the big kids smoking and fighting in the park. I don't like 'em, they look like they might beat me up.

'You look all grown up, son,' said Dad, from the bedroom door. I didn't hear him come up the stairs.

'I don't like it, Dad. I look stupid.'

'Don't talk daft, lad. Me and yuh Mam are really proud of you.'

'But what if I'm no good at the big school? What if the teachers think I'm stupid?'

'Just do yuh best, son, and whatever that is, that's enough for me.'

I wanted to give Dad a big hug, like when I was really little and banged my knee or hit my head. But I just said 'Cheers, Dad'.

'Gor, it only seems like yesterday you nearly burnt down yuh bedroom and shat in a bucket in the wool shop,' laughed Dad.

He went downstairs and I saw him in the garden. Dad went into the greenhouse and I could tell he was doing a fart – he was wafting the smell away with his hand.

Wayne Ashby said it would be ace if his dad was famous and on the telly, like a footballer or something. I said I'd like George Best, Brian Clough or Noel Edmonds. But I was lying. I'm glad my Dad is my Dad, and Mam is my Mam. And I wouldn't change it for anything in the whole world.

The End

Acknowledgments

Thanks to Mam (she didn't know I was researching and writing a book) for answering all my questions about Pam's wool shop, Gransher's illness and how many times she failed her driving test. Cheers to Mr Shingler for the information about Newport County vs West Ham United, 1979. A suitably large wine, beer or Top Deck for Ian and Christelle for early reading and error spotting. And a big Muppet Show applause for Sarah and Sam for the detailed final edit.